HIGHWAY 61

Also by David Housewright

HIGHWAY 61

David Housewright

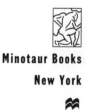

Minotaur Books

New York

HIGHWAY 61. Copyright © 2011 by David Housewright. All rights reserved. Printed in the United States of America. For information, address St. Martin's Press, 175 Fifth Avenue, New York, N.Y. 10010.

www.minotaurbooks.com

Library of Congress Cataloging-in-Publication Data

Housewright, David, 1955–
   Highway 61 : a McKenzie novel / David Housewright.—1st ed.
      p. cm.
   ISBN 978-0-312-64230-3
   1. McKenzie, Mac (Fictitious character)—Fiction.   2. Private investigators—Minnesota—Fiction.   3. Millionaires—Fiction.   4. Extortion—Fiction.
I. Title.   II. Title: Highway sixty-one.
   PS3558.O8668H54 2011
   813'.54—dc22   2011005106

First Edition: June 2011

10   9   8   7   6   5   4   3   2   1

FOR RENEÉ,

AGAIN AND FOREVER

I wish to acknowledge my debt to
India Cooper, Keith Kahla, Alison J. Picard,
and Renée Valois.

HIGHWAY 61

ONE

I watched Erica through my kitchen window while she tossed bread crumbs to the ducks that lived beside the pond in my backyard, and I wondered—when did she become so damn pretty? She was cute when I first met her, but that was when she was nearly fifteen. Now she was twelve days past her eighteenth birthday and nearly as beautiful as her mother. Certainly she was taller—by at least two inches. Erica confided to me once that when she was sure her mother was going to scold her over some offense, she would put on high heels so she would tower over her.

"I keep hoping it'll intimidate her," she said, "only it never does."

The man sitting at the table behind me sighed dramatically. I ignored him. He pulled a pack of Marlboros from his jacket pocket, shook one out, and placed it between his lips. I waited until he lit it with a silver lighter.

"No smoking," I said.

Jason Truhler sighed again, putting more effort into it this time. He moved to the sink, drowned the cigarette with the faucet, and dropped the remains into the garbage disposal.

I continued to watch his daughter while he slipped silently back into the chair. Erica knelt on the grass and scattered bread crumbs so close to her that the ducks came near enough to pet. I almost opened the window and shouted, "They bite, you know." I didn't because I knew she wouldn't like it.

The ducks had moved in soon after my father and I had built the pond a few years back. Dad liked the ducks; one of the things he told me just before he died was to take care of them. So I did, feeding them corn and grain and whatever they put in those bags of wild birdseed I buy at Petco. Ever since, they would leave in the fall and return in the spring, often more than a dozen birds at a time. I used to name them until it became impossible for me to tell them apart.

I glanced at my watch. It told me the day, month, and date— Sunday, November 8. Duck hunting season had been open for nearly a month, and while the ducks were safe within the Twin Cities metropolitan area, I was always worried about how they would fare once they started south. I expected them to take wing at any moment; was surprised that they hadn't left long ago. A pal at the DNR said they might have lingered past their traditional departure date because I fed them, because I domesticated them. I hoped not.

Truhler sighed again.

"What exactly do you want from me?" I asked. I continued to look out the window.

"Rickie says you help people."

"Favors," I said. Since quitting the St. Paul cops to take a three-million-dollar reward for capturing a particularly resourceful embezzler, I have, on occasion, assisted people with their more pressing issues. "I sometimes do favors for friends, people I like. I don't like you."

"You don't know me."

"I know your ex-wife."

"Not everything Nina says about me is true."

"Of course it is."

"You haven't heard my side."

I turned my head just enough to look him in the eye. "I don't want to hear your side."

"But—"

"But what? There's nothing to debate here. I love your ex-wife. I love her enough to say so to complete strangers. Which means I'm more than happy to dislike her ex-husband with as much vehemence as she desires for whatever reasons she deigns to offer. Any questions?"

"I knew it was a mistake coming here," Truhler said.

I returned to the window. Marvelous Margot, the woman with whom I shared the pond, emerged from her house and walked across her lawn. Erica saw her. They screamed each other's name the way teenagers do that have been apart for a while and hugged, although Margot was hardly a teenager. She was pushing forty-five. She had been pushing forty-five for as long as I'd known her.

Margot was a life-loving babe—I could think of no better way to describe her. She was a babe not only in her wolf-whistle appearance but also in her take-no-prisoners attitude, one of those free spirits who lived exactly as she wished, as her three ex-husbands could attest. As far as I knew she and Erica had spoken less than a half dozen times, yet Erica seemed to like her enormously. I wasn't sure if that was a good thing or not.

"I wouldn't have come here at all," Truhler said, "except Rickie said you could help me. She said you could be trusted. I'd hate to see her disappointed."

Meaning *I* would be the one who disappointed her, not him.

"Does Erica know what trouble you're in?" I asked.

"She knows—she only knows I'm having difficulty and that it has something to do with a trip I took in July. I admitted that much to her when she came to visit this weekend. I get her every third weekend. Now that she's eighteen, she doesn't have to obey the court order, but she does. She's a good girl."

"I know."

"She told me if I was in trouble I should talk to you. 'Tell McKenzie,' she said. 'He can fix anything.' "

"You believed her?"

"She told me about some of the things you've done for people. Helping the FBI corral some gunrunners, catching the guy who kidnapped that cop's kid, solving that murder down in Victoria, Minnesota—Rickie thinks you're quite a guy."

I was glad to hear it. Still . . .

"You like her," Truhler said. "I know you do."

"That'll only get you so far."

"I'm not asking for much."

"Yes, you are."

It was my turn to sigh like a bad actor. I pivoted toward Jason Truhler. There was an expectant gleam in his eyes as if he were waiting for an MC to pull a name from a hat and announce the winner of a door prize.

"To put it bluntly, I'm your ex-wife's lover," I said. "I'm the last person you should be talking to. You're the last person I should try to help. Nothing good will come of it."

"Then why did you agree to see me?"

I looked out the window again. Erica and Margot were sitting next to each other on the grass on Margot's side of the pond. God knew what Margot was telling her. Whatever it was, it made Erica laugh.

I was in love with Nina Truhler, so it was important that her daughter like me. To gain Erica's favor I made a point of not calling her Rickie, although everyone else did, until she gave her permission. I never hung around her house, never raided her refrigerator, never watched her TV, never commented on her clothes; never stayed the night while she was there. I always spoke to her like an adult, declined to offer advice unless it was requested, vowed not to reveal her secrets even to her mother, scrupulously avoided phrases like "When I was your age," and refused to take sides when she and Nina quarreled. Most important, I promised to be there whenever she needed me.

Saturday night she called. She said she needed me.

"I can give you the name of a good private investigator," I said.

"I'm afraid to hire an ordinary PI," Truhler told me. "If they come across a crime, they have to report it. If the cops ask them questions, they have to answer or risk losing their licenses, right? They don't have privilege like an attorney or a doctor. They can't guarantee confidentiality."

"What makes you think I can?"

He gestured with his chin at the window.

"She's a pretty girl, isn't she," he said. "Smart, too. We raised her right, divorce and all. No matter what Nina tells you about me or what I could tell you about her if you cared to listen, we managed to keep the gloves on when it came to Rickie. She turned out all right. She loves both of her parents."

It's my dad, she told me. *Will you help him? For me?*

"All right," I said. "Tell me about your difficulty."

Truhler covered his mouth with his hand, turned his head, and coughed. "Excuse me," he said.

Yeah, you had better not let me see you smile, my inner voice said. *You haven't won anything yet.*

"Well," I said aloud.

"First, you have to promise not to tell Rickie, or Nina, for that matter."

"I already promised not to lie to either of them."

"I'm not saying lie. I'm saying—just don't tell them about me."

"As long as it doesn't hurt them."

Truhler thought about it for a few beats. "It won't," he said.

"Okay."

"We have a deal?"

I shrugged in reply.

Truhler stared as if he were trying to see inside my head.

Good luck with that, my inner voice said. *Half the time, I don't even know what's going on in there.*

"How do I know I can trust you?" Truhler asked.

"Because Erica said so."

Truhler thought about it for a moment. He said, "I suppose I have to tell someone."

Don't tell me. Please don't tell me. If you tell me, then I'll become involved, and I don't want to be involved.

"I'm being blackmailed," Truhler said.

Ahh, geez . . .

I moved away from the window and sat at the kitchen table across from Truhler.

"By whom?"

"I don't know. It started four months ago. They've been demanding nine thousand nine hundred and eighty dollars in twenties each month. It's an odd amount. I don't know why they picked such an odd amount."

"Banks are required to report cash transactions of ten thousand or more to the U.S. Treasury Department," I said. "The law was passed in the early seventies to help catch criminals attempting to launder drug money. Now Homeland Security uses it to keep watch over the rest of us. The blackmailers set the amount so you wouldn't attract attention."

"You know about these things. That's good."

"What do they have on you?"

"What do you mean?"

"What secret is worth ninety-nine eighty a month?"

"They say, they claim . . . this is hard to say."

I didn't give him any help.

He stood abruptly and began to pace the kitchen floor. He was nearly as tall as I was and straight. He had fine brown eyes that you could see in his daughter and auburn hair that had been cut short and meticulously scrubbed of all gray, a gesture toward vanity that I found distasteful in a man. Plus, his face was far too pretty for someone his age. He looked like a guy whose problems had always been solved with a smile or by someone else. He stopped pacing, stared at the miniature guillotine I used to halve bagels as if it were the first time he had ever seen one, then turned toward me.

"They say I murdered a girl."

Dammit!

"What girl?" I asked.

"I don't know."

"Of course you do."

"I don't."

"The blackmailers—I presume they have hard evidence that connects you to the girl."

"They have photographs."

"Yet you claim you don't know the girl."

"It's true."

"That requires explanation," I said.

"I went to the Thunder Bay Blues Festival."

"In Ontario?"

"It was held during the Fourth of July weekend, but that was just a coincidence. The Fourth doesn't mean anything up in Canada."

"Who did you go with?"

"No one," Truhler said. "When I go to these things, I just want to be alone with the music. I don't want to bother with other people. I don't want to worry if they can see the stage, if it's too cold or too hot for them, if they're hungry or thirsty, if they want to leave early or stay late, if they can find me in the crowd or if I can find them. Haven't you ever done anything like that?"

I once went to the Lowertown Music Festival in St. Paul to catch Moore By Four by myself and to Peavey Plaza in Minneapolis to hear bluesmen Tinsley Ellis and Big Daddy Cade, and there have been plenty of Minnesota Twins baseball games, but those events took place in the afternoon and I only went alone because most of my friends were at work—such is the lot of the idle rich. But drive alone 350 miles from the Twin Cities to Thunder Bay just to hear some tunes?

"No," I said.

He seemed surprised by my answer.

"I heard you were a music guy, like me," he said. "I guess all this is because I love music. I love it even more than Nina does. That's what attracted us to each other in the first place, you know, our mutual love of music."

Truhler paused as if he expected me to comment. I refused. If I admitted that I also harbored a deep affection for music, then we'd have something to bond over, and I didn't want to bond with him.

"Get to the point," I said.

According to Jason Truhler, it had been one of those summer days that Minnesotans dream about when it's January and the snow is blowing and the wind is howling—seventy-eight degrees with a light breeze wafting off of Lake Superior and not a cloud in the sky. Truhler entered Marina Park where the blues festival was being held from the pedestrian bridge spanning North Water Street, a blue canvas camping chair folded into a blue canvas bag slung over his shoulder.

He had checked in at the Prince Arthur Hotel the evening before. The hotel was a hundred years old and reeked of old-world charm—that was the word he used, reeked. He did not care about the hand-carved woodwork, the vaulted ceilings, or the early twentieth-century appointments. Nor did Truhler care that he had a spectacular view of the Sleeping Giant, one of Thunder Bay's most popular tourist attractions, a natural rock peninsula jutting into Lake Superior that resembled a giant lying on his back when viewed from the city. He stayed there solely because of the convenient pedestrian bridge that abutted the hotel's parking lot. Truhler was all about convenience.

He ignored the daredevils riding skateboards in the retro-California-style swimming pool bowl at the bottom of the bridge and the nearly 250 boats moored in slips at the marina to his right. His destination was the new, improved band shelter several hundred yards to his left where the bluesmen were holding forth. To reach it he crossed yet another bridge; this one arched above a small inlet that separated the marina from the rest of the park.

That's where he met the girl.

Her hair was the color of red roses and wheat, her eyes were big and brown, and her skin was pale and unblemished. She was wearing a light blue sleeveless blouse over khaki shorts that had a flap of fabric in front to make them look like a skirt. Her legs were long and slender.

The girl was leaning against the railing at the center of the bridge and looking out toward Lake Superior. When Truhler reached her, she turned her head and smiled as if she had been expecting him. Her eyes twinkled.

"What kind of ducks are those, do you think?" she asked.

Truhler stopped and glanced over the railing. Beneath him was a large duck with a pale brown head and body, a dark brown back, a dark bill, and a subtle cinnamon neck ring. A squadron of ducklings surrounded it. While he watched, the large duck dove headfirst into the lake. The ducklings followed.

They stayed under water for nearly ten seconds before popping up like bubbles. The girl giggled when they dove and giggled even more when they reemerged.

Truhler said he didn't know from waterfowl.

The girl said, "I think they're ring-necked diving ducks."

"If you already knew, why did you ask," Truhler said.

"Do you mind that I asked?"

No, Truhler didn't mind. Nor did he mind when she asked other questions—where was he from, where was he staying, was he alone? The more he answered, the more the girl smiled, and the more she smiled, the more Truhler felt compelled to be polite—that's what he said, he was being polite.

"Are you here for the blues festival?" she asked.

"I am."

"So am I."

Perhaps she would like some company, he said.

She said she would like that very much.

The girl had a folding canvas chair in a bag of her own. She retrieved it from the bridge deck, and together they followed the winding path until they reached the main entrance to the festival grounds. Truhler offered to treat the girl to a thirty-five-dollar ticket, but she already had one. They found a grassy knoll in the back with a clear view of the stage and set up. He offered to buy her a beverage. Beer, or perhaps a Jack Daniel's Country Cocktail. She liked the idea of a Black Jack Cola.

"You are old enough to drink, aren't you?" he asked.

She giggled at the question. "Of course I am, silly."

"I thought that meant she was over twenty-one," Truhler told me. "I didn't realize until later that the drinking age in Ontario is nineteen." I asked him if it mattered. He said it did. "What kind of guy do you think I am?" I didn't say.

They sat through several acts—I was surprised to hear Minneapolis blues band Big Walter Smith and the Groove Merchants was among them—and downed several cocktails that Truhler said didn't affect him at all. Toward late afternoon, the girl slid a blunt wrapped in cherry-vanilla paper from her purse and lit up. After several tokes she offered the blunt to Truhler. He took a long drag, hoping the people around him wouldn't notice that the thin cigar had been hollowed out and filled with grass. They passed the blunt back and forth until they could no longer hold it without burning their fingertips. The girl sealed the remains inside a plastic 35 mm film canister and dropped it into her purse. Truhler laughed. He asked the girl where she got the canister. He hadn't seen a roll of film in years.

The next thing Truhler remembered, he was naked and lying facedown on a bed in a motel room.

He woke up slowly, so slowly that at first he didn't realize he was awake. He kept his eyes closed. There was a throbbing pain above his eyes, and he knew from experience that when he opened them, the pain would increase. He remembered the cocktails and he remembered the dope and then he remembered the girl and wondered if she was still there. Truhler swept his arms slowly across the mattress, pleased that his fingers did not find her—it would be so much easier if she was gone. He touched his own body and found that he was naked. It didn't entirely surprise him. He was cold. He reached out for a sheet or bedspread to cover himself, but his hands came up empty.

He opened his eyes. The dull pain in his forehead increased, as he knew it would, followed by a stabbing pain at the base of his skull. He closed his eyes, reached back, and rubbed his neck. His fingers found a bump that was sensitive to the touch. Where did that come from, he wondered.

Truhler rolled onto his back and opened his eyes again. There were cracks in the ceiling. A bare lightbulb in a chipped fixture glared at him. That wasn't right, he told himself. He raised himself up on his elbows and glanced around the room. Truhler didn't know where he was, but it sure as hell wasn't the pristine and elegant Prince Arthur Hotel.

He thought about the girl. What was her name? Hell, did she even tell him her name? Truhler couldn't remember. He called out. "Hey." Maybe she was in the bathroom. "Hey." There was no answer. He collapsed back on the bed.

Truhler had never suffered a blackout in his life, he told me. Not once. He said that sometimes his memory had become a little fuzzy, especially when he was a kid and hitting the booze like he would live forever. Yet waking up in a strange room without knowing how he got there—that was a new experience, and he wondered if the dope had something to do with it.

He called out again. "Hey."

He sat up and looked around. It was definitely a motel room, and not a very expensive one. Regulations and pricing information were attached to the back of the door. There was a battered credenza with a TV and cable box mounted on top. A table tent next to the TV advertised X-rated pay-per-view movies with the promise that the titles of the films wouldn't appear on the bill. The drapes of the window were tightly closed. A small wooden table stood in front of the window. There was a wooden chair set on either side of the table. He could see that his clothing was piled neatly on top of one of the chairs and the girl's clothes were just as carefully stacked on the other. Truhler wondered about that for a moment. If he had screwed what's-her-name, the girl, he couldn't imagine being tidy about it.

He stepped off the bed. His foot touched something wet and sticky on the floor. His first thought, was that he had stepped into a spilled drink. He looked at the floor. It was a lake of blood. The girl floated below him in the lake. She was naked and curled into a fetal position with her hands clutching her throat. Her throat was deeply slashed; he could see a black hole beneath her fingers. Her lifeless eyes were open. They seemed to stare at him.

Truhler screamed and fell back onto the bed. He frantically wiped the blood off of his foot with the bedsheet and screamed some more. The instinct for self-preservation kicked in, and he covered his mouth with both of his hands to keep from screaming again, praying that no one had heard him; that no one would come knocking on the door demanding to know what was wrong.

Had he killed the girl?

He couldn't remember.

Truhler began to tremble with a chill that had nothing to do with the cold and his own nakedness. They'd blame him, he knew they would. The cops would come and they would see the girl and they would see him and they would point their fingers and say, "You did it."

Except he could not have killed her. He could not have done a thing like that.

He swept his body with both his eyes and his hands. There

was no blood. Nor was there blood on the bed except where he had wiped his foot. Yet there seemed to be blood everywhere else. How could he have killed the girl like that without getting blood on himself, slashing her throat with, with what? He looked about for a knife without leaving the safety of his island bed and found none. He tried hard to avoid looking at the girl.

What had happened? His last memory was of sitting in his canvas chair at Marina Park. John Németh, maybe the best white blues singer in the business, was holding forth beneath a blue-and-yellow-striped canopy. He had been joking with the girl about her film canister. Truhler could remember all that. Then it was as if he had blinked his eyes and magically appeared in the motel room.

For a moment Truhler thought that maybe it was all just a bad dream, a hallucination brought on by the blunt. He hesitated, glanced over the edge of the bed, looked down at the girl. The nausea hit him like a sucker punch. Without warning, he doubled over and began to vomit. He tried to stop, only he couldn't. He kept throwing up until there was nothing left in his stomach to throw up, and then he went through several minutes of dry heaves.

He felt the icy fingers of panic gripping him, squeezing him. He had to do something—but what? Truhler covered his head with his hands. If the pain went away, maybe he could think of what to do. It didn't. He needed a cigarette. He needed a drink. He needed—he needed to get out of there. He had to run. That was as far as his thinking could take him. Get out of the room. Get away from the girl. The dead girl.

I asked him why he didn't call the police, why he didn't call for help.

"I was going to," he said, "but . . ."

"But what?"

"I was afraid."

Truhler slid off the far side of the bed and tiptoed as quickly as he could around the blood. He grabbed his clothes off of the chair and went to the bathroom. The bathroom was all white and clean and bright from the overhead light. He carefully examined his clothes and found that the blood had not splattered them. Truhler dressed quickly. He checked his pockets. He still had his wallet, his cell phone, his cigarettes, the card key to his room at the Prince Arthur, his money—he counted his money and found that it was all there.

He tried to tell himself it was a dream. It had to be. Then he asked, Why him? Why was this happening to him? What did he do to deserve this? It wasn't fair.

Truhler stepped back into the room. He searched for his canvas chair. He couldn't find it. He looked at the girl one more time. A sudden wave of anger crashed over him. Why was she doing this to him? He reached for the door handle and hesitated for fear of leaving fingerprints, then decided it couldn't be helped.

"I just had to get out of there," Truhler told me.

He stepped out onto a second-floor balcony, carefully closing the door behind him. Truhler noticed the room number for the first time. Thirty-four. It meant nothing to him. He stood outside the door and waited, he didn't know for what. It was night. His cell told him it was two thirty in the morning. All he could hear was the low rumble of an air conditioner. That was why it was so cold in the room, the air conditioner. He shivered. It was warmer outside, but not by much. The parking lot below the balcony was quiet and still. A dim light seeped through the window of the motel office at the foot of the metal and concrete staircase. A much brighter pink light flashed the name CHALET MOTEL and NO VACANCY just above the front door. Cars moved along the well-lit street beyond the motel's driveway, but they were few and far between.

Truhler walked the length of the balcony as quietly as possible and carefully descended the stairs. When he reached the office, he glanced quickly through the window and pulled his head away. He looked again. The office was empty. He wondered briefly if he had used his own name when he registered. He wondered if he had registered at all. The girl must have, he decided. If it had been his choice, he would have taken her to his hotel.

Without thinking any more about it, Truhler sprinted across the parking lot and began to run along the street, putting as much distance between him and the dead girl as possible. He did not know where he was. He did not know where he was going. Truhler ran for nearly a block before he realized he was making a fool of himself. People would think he'd done something wrong if they saw him running. He hadn't done anything wrong. Stop running, he told himself.

He slowed to a brisk walk. The street sign on the corner told him he was on North Cumberland. Truhler couldn't believe his luck. It was one of the few streets in Thunder Bay that he recognized. The Prince Arthur was on Cumberland. Truhler didn't know where he was, but he was now convinced that if he kept walking he would eventually find safety. He walked for several miles, passing shipyards, windowless concrete buildings he could not identify, and a variety of retail outlets, all of them closed.

Cars and trucks passed him, including one patrol car from the Thunder Bay Police Service. None of them stopped. He smoked cigarette after cigarette until the package was empty. His head throbbed and his hands trembled and he began to wonder if he was walking in the right direction. Eventually he found himself approaching Marina Park and, in the distance, his hotel. His heart leapt in his chest, and it was all he could do to keep from running again. He entered the hotel through the rear entrance, the one facing the parking lot. The desk clerk, a young woman with narrow glasses, glanced up at him and then back at whatever work she was doing. Truhler went directly to the stairway. His room was on the fifth floor, only he didn't want to wait for the elevator, didn't want to meet anyone on the elevator.

Truhler soon found his room. He went inside, making sure the door was locked behind him. He kept the lights off except for the bathroom. He stripped off his clothes and took the longest shower of his life, filling the room with a thick cloud of steam. Afterward, he took three aspirin tablets and two capsules of ibuprofen from the plastic containers in his suitcase. He swallowed them along with a tall glass of water before climbing naked between the cool sheets of his bed. He felt like crying but didn't. He had done all of his weeping in the shower.

The next morning, after a fitful sleep, Truhler dressed, packed, and drove home. During the long drive south he kept asking himself, "What happened?" By the time he reached the outlying suburbs of the Twin Cities, he decided nothing happened. This bit of self-deception lasted for about a week, lasted until a person or persons unknown sent a photograph to his cell phone. Truhler showed it to me after first making sure that

Erica was still in the backyard; we downloaded it onto my computer so I could study it later. It was taken at a high angle and showed him on the bed and the girl on the floor. Their faces were clearly visible. The girl seemed very young. After waiting twenty-four hours to make sure Truhler was properly terrified, the blackmailer called and demanded money. Truhler paid it. Then he paid it again. And again. He paid the blackmail until he decided he couldn't afford it anymore.

Truhler was upset that I wasn't particularly impressed by his story.

"I know you think I'm lying," he said.

I used to date a psychiatrist who told me one of the toughest parts of her job was getting past all the lies that patients told her; told themselves. When I asked how she could tell the difference, she said there were a number of things to look for. One was their emotional reaction to pointed questions. If they became angry or defensive, laughed nervously, or made accusations, she knew something was up. Another was their way of talking. If they spoke in a higher or lower pitch, or more quickly or slowly than usual, that could be a sign of lying. Still another clue was nonverbal body language. A shoulder shrug should never accompany a definitive statement. Wrapping legs or hands around chair legs or arms was a sign of restraint, of holding back, while leaning away might indicate lying because we lean away from things we want to avoid. She also had what she called the belly-button rule. She claimed that when we're telling the truth we generally point our belly buttons toward our audience. When we're lying, we turn away. If our belly buttons face the door or exit, it's because subconsciously we want to escape.

Yet my favorite clue was the simplest. She said patients were usually being honest when they said, "You may not believe me, but I'm telling the truth." When they said, "I know you think I'm lying," they nearly always were.

Jason Truhler did all of these things, all of them with the most sincere expression on his face. Still, there was nothing to be gained by calling him a liar.

"Tell me about the blackmailer," I said. "Any idea of who he might be?"

"No."

"How did he contact you?"

"The first time he called my cell phone."

"Did you recognize the voice?"

"No. He only called that one time. After that it was text messages and e-mail. But . . ."

"But what?"

"He sounded black."

"Don't let the ACLU hear that. They'll accuse you of profiling. Does your cell have caller ID?"

"Yes, but it never gives me a name, just a number. I hit recall after the first time. A recording said to please leave my message and then repeated the number. When he texted me, the numbers were different every time."

"Probably using prepaid cell phones."

"He's smart," Truhler said.

"Not necessarily. Cash is careless. It requires someone to pick it up, transport it, possibly launder it, deposit it—the FBI will be the first to tell you, always follow the money. The fact that the blackmailer isn't using electronic transfers makes me question his sophistication. Let's talk about the girl. Are you sure she was dead?"

"Of course I am."

"Did you feel for a pulse?"

"No. God, McKenzie. She was dead, okay? The blood—Jesus Christ, the blood."

"Okay."

"Don't you think I would have known if she was—if she was still alive?"

"I don't know. Would you have?"

His eyes bulged in anger, and then diminished as he thought it through.

"What are you trying to say?" he asked.

"Let me tell you a story. Guy walks into a bar. Maybe he's on a business trip. Maybe he's in Thunder Bay, Ontario, for the blues festival. Could be he's leaning on the stick, minding his own business, and the sexiest woman he's ever seen sits next to him, and he offers to buy her a drink. Or she's sitting at a table all alone and crying, and the guy, being a gentleman, decides to comfort her. In any case, the guy and the girl meet, they talk. She asks questions, and he tells her things—such a pretty girl he can't help himself. He tells her he's alone. He tells her he's a big shot in—exactly what do you do for a living, Jason?"

"I work in agribusiness."

"Lucrative, is it?"

He closed his eyes. "Yes," he said softly.

"Yeah, and he tells her that, too. After a while it's his place or hers, usually hers. Pretty soon the guy and the girl are doing—doing what? They're being polite to each other. Isn't that what you said before, that you were being polite? Suddenly there's a knock on the door, and an angry man, usually a husband, is standing there with his hand out."

"What are you talking about?"

"That's the original version of the badger game. It dates back to the nineteenth century. Hell, it probably dates back to the beginning of time. Nowadays, you don't usually get an angry husband, though. Instead, the grifters more often confront the mark after the fact with photos or audiovisual. This works best with husbands or prominent businessmen afraid of scandal, and you're neither of them, of course. For single guys like you there's the threat of a rape charge; the woman claims the encounter wasn't consensual, that it was rape, and she's going to call the police. Or the girl is underage, which brings on a whole different set of problems. Are you sure the girl was old enough to drink, Jason?"

"Jesus Christ."

"This version—I have to admit that this version shows imagination."

"Jesus Christ."

"I wish you'd stop saying that," I said.

"Goddammit!"

"Yeah, that's much better."

"You think it's just one big, enormous fraud."

"A guy with a camera being in the right place at the right time suggests planning."

"What if—"

"What if the girl is really dead?"

"Yeah."

"I don't know, Jason. What if?"

"I didn't kill her, McKenzie. You have to know that."

"The only thing I know for sure is that someone took a photograph and it wasn't you."

Truhler went to the kitchen window. After a moment, he said, "Rickie's coming back."

"She's been very patient waiting all this time," I said.

"Look, I don't care about the girl."

"What do you care about?"

"I just want the blackmail to stop."

"Only two ways to do that. Get rid of the reason for the blackmail or get rid of the blackmailers."

"Kill them?"

"No. Let's be clear about that, Jason. If you're looking for a hitter, you've come to the wrong place."

"What can we do?"

I didn't like the way he said "we" but let it pass.

"When is your next payment due?" I said.

"They'll probably contact me Tuesday or Wednesday."

I chuckled at that.

"What?" he asked.

"Give me time to work, wouldja? It's Sunday."

"I know."

"All right. First, we'll find out if a crime has actually been committed."

"How?"

"The newspaper."

"What newspaper?"

I heard the door open behind me.

"Thunder Bay has a population of over one hundred and twenty thousand," I said. "I bet it has a daily newspaper."

"Newspapers are dead," a voice said. "Everything is online now."

I heard the door close. I turned to see Erica stamp her feet and unwind the scarf around her neck. She had her mother's black hair, high cheekbones, and narrow nose and her father's eyes and tapered chin. Her generous smile was up for grabs.

"It's getting colder," she said.

"Well, it is Minnesota in November," her father said.

"Yes, but this is the first cold day we've had since August."

We all laughed at the joke. It had been an odd November, with days like summer; this following a summer with days that reminded everyone of early winter. It was enough to make you wonder if all those environmentalists screaming about climate change might not be onto something.

There was a little more chitchat before Erica's father decided it was time to leave. We all moved to my front door. Truhler was the first to reach it. He opened the door and stepped through it.

"I'll be in touch," he said.

"Sure," I told him.

He gave his daughter a glance over his shoulder and then looked hard at me before continuing toward his car. I think the look was supposed to warn me to keep my mouth shut.

What a jerk, my inner voice said.

"Are you going to help my father?" Erica asked.

"Yes."

"Promise?"

"Yes."

I was surprised when Erica curled her arm around mine. She was rarely that familiar, at least with me. We walked out the door and across the porch together.

"How come you and Margot have never, you know?" she asked.

"What are you talking about?"

"She thinks you're a hunk, a hunk of burning love."

"Oh, for goodness sake."

"Seriously."

"Oh, you're being serious?"

"McKenzie, seriously."

"I love your mother, Erica. It's as simple as that."

She uncurled her arm from mine. She said, "I'm counting on that, you know," and walked quickly to her father's car.

TWO

Despite Erica's cynicism, I discovered that Thunder Bay had two newspapers—the *Chronicle Journal* and the *Post,* although the *Post* had apparently been transformed into tbnewswatch. com. Oh well.

I searched the archives of the *Chronicle Journal* first.

A Thunder Bay man charged with first-degree murder after human remains were found in a burned-out car earlier this month will be back in court next week.

A 49-year-old Thunder Bay man is charged with second-degree murder following an incident at a North Edward Street apartment.

A Thunder Bay man with a personal history blighted by dysfunction and criminal behavior will spend the next chapter of his life in prison as the result of the beating death of a Geralton teenager.

*The death of a 37-year-old woman in Thunder Bay this
week could once again label this community as the murder capital of Canada.*

I spent some time with the latter story. It seemed that Thunder Bay had been the scene of six homicides that year, and since
statistics are compiled on a per capita basis, the city was fast
approaching the designation of most murders per 100,000 resi-
dents. People were outraged. One citizen, unswayed by the fact
that Thunder Bay had a total of only nine killings in the past
six years, was appalled by the community's horrific criminal
record and wondered what the police were doing with all that
tax money they were being paid.

"Hell," I said aloud. "A half-dozen murders is just a bad
three-day weekend in the Twin Cities."

The *Chronicle Journal* listed the killings in chronological
order. None of them involved a young woman in a motel room.

I turned to tbnewswatch.com. It was a bit more sensational
in its reporting than the *Chronicle Journal* but provided no
additional information. I tried the Web site of the Thunder
Bay Police Service. The cops were asking for help in three un-
solved murders that occurred in 1984, 1992, and 2005. There
were no reports concerning missing persons uploaded on any
of the Web sites.

"I need to go up there," I said aloud. "Just to be sure."

"You're doing what?" Nina wanted to know.

"Sweetie, it's not my idea. Besides, I'm not actually doing a
favor for Jason."

"Then who are you doing it for?"

"Erica."

"Bullshit."

If there was any doubt that Nina was angry, that settled it. She almost never cursed.

"See, this is why I called instead of telling you in person," I said.

"Dammit, McKenzie."

"Erica asked me to help her father. What was I supposed to say?"

"You were supposed to say no."

"How could I do that?"

"By reminding her that you're my boyfriend, not hers."

"You keep saying that you don't want to marry again, yet there's a real chance that one day I could become Erica's step-father. Tell me again how I'm supposed to say no."

"Marriage, McKenzie? Do you really want to bring that up now?"

"I'm just reminding you that I love you desperately and that there is nothing I wouldn't do to make you happy, so if you want me to blow off Erica's old man I'll do it—just as long as you're standing next to me when I tell her."

"I . . ."

"Yes?"

"I don't think I want to do that."

"Me, neither."

"Just out of curiosity, what kind of trouble is Jason in?"

"I'm kinda sorta sworn to secrecy on this one."

"Is that right?"

"Kinda sorta."

"You're not going to tell me?"

"If you really want me to, I will."

Nina thought about it for a few beats.

"No," she said. "I don't want you to break a promise for me."

"You're the only one I would do it for."

"I appreciate that."

"I'll give you a hint, though. When you two were married, did Jason go off on his own a lot, take trips by himself?"

"Let me guess. This is about Jason wanting to be alone with the music."

"Something like that."

"The thing is, McKenzie, he was never alone for very long. It's why we're not married today. One of many reasons, actually."

"I figured. The truth is I'm not sure Jason's in any real trouble. He's paying a heavy fine for making some bad choices, which he richly deserves, by the way. If I'm right, though, he should be able to walk away from it."

"What are you going to do?"

"Scoot up to Thunder Bay tomorrow, check out a few things, and come back the following day."

"While you're doing this favor for Jason, would you mind doing one for me?"

"Sure."

"Bring me some donuts."

THREE

Early the next morning I drove north. I preferred Highway 61, the legendary roadway made famous in song and story, if only for the sights, but the road was interrupted by Interstate 35 between Wyoming, a small town just north of the Twin Cities, and Duluth. Once upon a time, Highway 61 was as important a thoroughfare as Route 66. It stretched from Thunder Bay in Canada nearly seventeen hundred miles south to the Orleans Parish Criminal Court Building in New Orleans, following the Mississippi River for most of the distance, and giving travelers an up-close and personal look at middle America. 'Course, that was before the interstate freeway system was built; before people decided they needed to get where they were going at the speed of light. Now Interstate 35 dominates. Drivers navigate it at seventy miles an hour in most places without seeing a thing worth mentioning. Certainly that was true of I-35 between the Cities and Duluth, just one long, dull ribbon of concrete decorated only by off-ramps and the obsequious outdoor advertising for Indian casinos.

The view improved greatly once I-35 intersected Twenty-sixth Avenue East in Duluth. That's where it became Minnesota Highway 61 again and veered northeast. Suddenly there was plenty to see, mostly the rugged northern shoreline of Lake Superior, but also a stunning succession of lush forests, waterfalls, lighthouses, resorts, and small, curious towns. Unfortunately, somewhere between the Twin Cities and Duluth I had driven from fall into bleak winter. The gale-swept waves of Lake Superior began to break against the shore with an almost frightening ferocity. The trees had lost most of their leaves, becoming little more than gray skeletons amid a smattering of dull green fir trees, their amazing red and gold colors reduced to a thick brown carpet at the forest floor. Resorts that did not offer cross-country or downhill skiing were shuttered for the season, and the crowded tourist towns had become virtually empty of traffic. Certainly that was true of Grand Marais, a port city that could trace its history back four hundred years. I had hoped to lunch there on a fresh herring burger at a café with the unlikely name of the Angry Trout, only the café was closed. However, a bakery with the even more implausible name of World's Best Donuts—which just might, in fact, make the world's best donuts—was still open, and I devoured an assortment of cake and raised donuts. Yes, I know it wasn't a particularly healthy meal, but they are the tastiest Nina and I have ever had. That's why she requested that I bring some home, which I vowed to do on the return trip.

Just north of Grand Marais the world changed again. Snow appeared, first as scattered white dust, then in small, isolated patches—a reminder of things to come. Wind slapped my car from both the right side and the left. The temperature dropped to freezing. I could see the breath of the Canadian customs officer at the Pigeon River Border Crossing as he asked the requisite questions—where was I going, what was the purpose of my trip, how long was I staying, was I bringing in any food, did I have a gun? I wasn't carrying, yet I was glad I had driven my Jeep Cherokee just the same. The false bottom in the trunk of my Audi might have raised embarrassing and unnecessary questions.

Once across the border, Minnesota Highway 61 became Ontario Highway 61 and wound forty-five miles to Thunder Bay. Technically the City of Thunder Bay did not exist when Highway 61 was built in the early twenties. It was cobbled together in 1970 with the merger of the communities of Fort William, Port Arthur, Neebing, and McIntyre, and it showed. It sprawled over 131 square miles, which made it larger than St. Paul and Minneapolis combined, if that's how you measure size. It didn't have a central business or residential district, but it did have two downtowns, and while the Twin Cities had built up, Thunder Bay built out, so it was mostly flat. I didn't see a single building that was more than five stories high and precious few of those. One of the five-story buildings was the Prince Arthur Hotel.

The Prince Arthur was located in what had once been downtown Port Arthur. It certainly seemed impressive from the outside. I didn't venture inside despite the cold. Instead, I parked in the hotel's lot, hoping the Cherokee would not be towed away as threatened by the sign next to the entrance, and crossed to the pedestrian bridge leading to Marina Park. It was my intention to retrace Jason Truhler's steps, although I had no idea what that would tell me.

The bridge was enclosed, its walls covered by city-sanctioned graffiti, so I did not feel the bite of the brisk wind until I reached the concrete zigzag ramp at the far end. The grass and flower beds were coated in a thin layer of frost, but the park's sidewalks were dry and clean. So were the bowl, ramps, and railings where the skateboarders performed their death-defying stunts, although there were none while I was there. Only a handful of boats remained at their slips in the marina, and the restaurant and stores of the converted railroad station to my right were closed for the season. I stood looking out at Lake Superior. The steel-tinted water, the wind-whipped waves, and the snow-dusted Sleeping Giant in the distance would have made me shiver even if it hadn't been so cold.

I zipped my jacket to my throat and made my way to the second pedestrian bridge, the one that separated the marina from the park. Truhler had said there was a fountain, but that, too, had been shut down. There were no ducks to be seen, either. When I reached the middle of the bridge, I turned to face the Prince Arthur. It certainly was possible for someone to pick a mark out of the crowd, possible to carefully study him while he crossed the pedestrian bridge and descended the ramp, possible to accost him before he could reach the blues festival. I didn't think that was what happened, but it could have.

I followed the concrete sidewalk to where Truhler would have entered the park. It didn't take long to locate a knoll facing the empty bandshell where he and the girl might have set up their chairs. I had not been to the Thunder Bay Blues Festival; however, I have been a frequent visitor to the Bayfront Blues Festival in Duluth, and I knew how it worked. The entire area is enclosed within a temporary fence lined with canvas to discourage non-ticket-holders. ('Course, you can't do much about the music; when the wind is blowing right, you can clearly hear the Bayfront blues in downtown Duluth.) There are no ushers, no fixed seats, and no bleachers. Spectators are encouraged to set up their chairs or spread out their blankets wherever they think they have a clear view of the stage. Enclaves form; friends signal to each other with all manner of colorful flags, banners, pennants, ensigns, and kites. My favorite was a street sign that proclaimed the intersection of Three Chords and the Truth. Any aisles that form in this throng are purely accidental, making it virtually impossible to move about without being seen by thousands of witnesses. Of course, there is a difference between being seen and being noticed. An asphalt roadway—Marina Park Drive—bordered the rear of the park not far from the knoll. It occurred to me that a couple of guys could have helped their apparently drunken friend from his chair on the knoll, out the gate to a waiting vehicle, and driven off without anyone being alarmed. I didn't believe that was what happened, but it could have.

I returned to my Jeep Cherokee and drove slowly north on Cumberland, passing all the landmarks that Truhler had mentioned. Eventually I found the Chalet Motel and pulled into the parking lot—it was exactly 3.9 miles from the Prince Arthur according to my odometer. The Chalet was two stories high with all of the room doors facing Cumberland. Looking out the windshield, I could see the number 34 printed in gold on a door located midway along the second-floor balcony. I told myself that a couple of guys might have been able to help their drunken friend out of a vehicle in the parking lot and carry him up the staircase, along the balcony, and into room 34 without being noticed by any of the Chalet's guests or management. I didn't believe it happened that way, either—but yeah, it could have.

It was a small office and cramped. There was a table with a half-full coffeepot, sugar cubes, nondairy creamer, and foam plastic cups against one wall, the table flanked by two chairs. On the opposite wall was a rack filled with slick tourist brochures. Between them was a high counter topped with even more brochures. It could have been the waiting room for an auto repair shop for all the ambience it evoked.

A small, thin man dressed in a white short-sleeve shirt that was buttoned to the throat greeted me. His complexion and accent suggested India or maybe Pakistan. He had been sitting behind the counter and watching a TV about the size of a hardback novel. He turned off the TV and stood when I entered.

"Good afternoon," he said. "I am Daniel. How may we accommodate you?"

I liked how he said that—accommodate.

"Good afternoon, Daniel," I said. "I'd like accommodations for the night."

"Single occupancy?"

"Yes."

Daniel opened a drawer and retrieved a registration form. He placed both it and a pen on the counter in front of me and requested that I fill it out. The form had blanks for the usual information, including the license plate number of my vehicle.

"Please, I will need to see a credit card and a photo ID," he said.

I gave him both.

"Do you require a credit card from all of your customers?" I asked.

"It is policy. You may pay in cash if you like." It seemed important to him that I know that. "But we require a credit card also."

"In case there is damage to the room or I try to skip out on the bill," I said.

"It is so."

I offered my hand. "I'm McKenzie."

The manager shook it without hesitation. "Daniel Khawaja."

"Khawaja. It that Pakistani?"

"It is a Kashmiri name. Kashmir is claimed by Pakistan, India, and China, so the choice is yours. I prefer to believe it is a Canadian name."

"Have you been here long?"

"Since I was a boy. My parents emigrated just in time to vote for the city's new name following amalgamation. They preferred Lakehead. Thunder Bay won by five hundred votes."

"This was in the sixties?"

"Nineteen sixty-nine."

Daniel processed my card. While he did, I turned to the rack. There were brochures for an amethyst mine, the longest suspension bridge in Canada, Fort William Historical Park, the Sleeping Giant, Kakabeka Falls, and a dozen additional tourist attractions. I seized the one promoting the Thunder Bay Blues Festival.

"This looks like fun," I said.

"It is the biggest event of the year."

"Really?"

"All the motels will be filled. If you want a room, you must register in advance."

"How far in advance?"

Daniel thought about it for a moment, then said, "At least a month and a half. Sometimes sooner."

"Is that right?"

"It is so."

Daniel gave me a credit card receipt to sign and slid a key across the counter, not an electronic card like most motels and hotels use, but an actual key attached to a plastic tag with the number 15 embossed on it. I left it where it was.

"I'd prefer room thirty-four if possible."

I saw it—the slight flinch, the whites of Daniel's eyes widening. The signs were just barely detectable, and probably I would have missed them if I hadn't been watching intently.

"Room thirty-four?" he asked. His voice was calm and unaffected. He did not look away.

"It's my lucky number."

"Lucky number?"

"It's the number Kirby Puckett wore."

"I do not know this Kirby Puckett."

"He played center field for the Minnesota Twins when they won the World Series in '87 and '91."

Daniel shook his head.

"Baseball," I said.

"Ahh. The baseball. I follow the hockey."

Well, my inner voice reminded me, *it is Canada.*

"We have the Fort William North Stars," Daniel said. "It is Junior A hockey."

"We used to have the Minnesota North Stars until they moved to Dallas. Now we have the Minnesota Wild."

"I wish we had a professional hockey team."

I flashed on the Wild's record over the past decade.

"So do we," I said.

Daniel covered the key with his hand and slowly slid it off the counter. He replaced it a moment later with number 34.

"I hope you will be most comfortable," he said.

Everything in room 34 was clean, neat, and in its place. The bed was impeccably made; the towels hung just so in the bathroom; the wastebaskets were empty. Yet the air seemed heavy and thick with the coppery scent of blood. I knew that it was just my imagination, but it took a few minutes before I could breathe normally just the same. I set my overnight bag on the table in front of the window—the same table and window that Jason Truhler had described. I didn't even remove my coat before I opened the bag and pulled out a large envelope. Inside the envelope was a copy of the photo that Truhler had downloaded onto my computer. I had printed it out in glorious color on photo-quality paper and put it into the envelope without looking at it. Now I was looking, tilting the photograph this way and that, using it to align myself in the room until I was standing approximately where the photographer must have stood when he snapped it. There was the table and chairs, the credenza and TV, the chipped light fixture, the king-sized bed with Truhler lying on top, his head turned so that he was facing the camera and clearly identifiable. Beneath him on the floor was the girl. She was also facing the camera. My eyes went from the photo to the floor, and for a moment I thought

I actually saw the girl lying there, her lifeless eyes staring at nothing, her naked body surrounded by a dark red stain spreading across the green carpet.

I closed my own eyes and tried to imagine the girl facing her killer as he moved toward her. I guessed that it had to be someone she knew, someone she would have allowed to get close enough to slash her throat. The killer would have had to come through the door. Would it have been locked? I turned to face it. There was no spy hole. If someone knocked, the girl would have had to open the door to see who it was. There was a door guard and chain with a chrome-plated finish that would have caused an intruder some trouble—if it had been set. I turned the knob, swung the door open, and then let go of the knob. Once open it did not close on itself the way many motel room doors do, yet once it was shut it locked automatically, which meant the girl had probably opened the door to her killer. Assuming she had been killed. More likely, I thought, she had an accomplice or two in the room with her all the time, helping set the stage for Truhler, snapping photographs until they got the shot they wanted.

I leaned against the door, staring at the spot at the corner of the bed where the girl had fallen, and considered the possibilities. The blue carpet was well scrubbed and—

"Wait a minute," I said.

I went to the spot and knelt, running my hand over the carpet. I looked at the photo and then the carpet and then set the photo on the carpet and looked at them both together. For an instant I felt a thrill of fear electrify my body. Up until that moment I was convinced that Jason Truhler had allowed himself to be victimized by a variation of the old badger game, and I couldn't think of anyone who deserved it more. Now I wasn't so sure.

The carpet was green in the photo, my inner voice told me. *Now it's blue.*

Daniel was sitting behind the counter and watching his TV when I entered the office. He switched it off and stood just as he had before.

"Yes, Mr. McKenzie?" he asked.

"I would like to talk about the room."

"You are not comfortable?"

I leaned against the counter and smiled. The smile was from uneasiness. I was about to make some serious allegations, felt I had to make them, even though I knew that I was probably full of crap.

"You replaced the carpet," I said.

"Yes," Daniel said. The word came out slowly, like air from a tire.

"It used to be green. Now it's blue."

"You have stayed in room thirty-four before? I do not remember—"

"When did you replace it?"

"Why do you—"

"Was it after the Fourth of July weekend? Following the blues festival?"

"Yes, but—"

"Did you change the carpet in all the other rooms?"

"No. I—"

"How many rooms did you replace the carpet in?"

"Why do you ask these questions?"

"Why did you replace the carpet?"

"No more. I do not know why you ask these questions. You must tell me why you ask them."

"I have a friend who stayed in room thirty-four during the blues festival."

"Who is this friend?"

"You tell me."

"I do not understand."

"The person who rented room thirty-four during the blues festival, was it a man or was it a woman?"

Daniel moved quickly to a file box. For a moment, I thought I had him, but he hesitated.

"It is against policy to reveal such information," he said. "Why do you ask for such information?"

"I have evidence that a murder was committed in that room."

"Murder?"

A man walked into the office, a black bag slung over his shoulder. He was about thirty-five with deep brown eyes, an unkempt brown mustache and beard, and a brown ponytail streaked with gray. His grin suggested that we weren't saying anything that he hadn't heard before.

"Did you commit the murder, Daniel?"

"Outrageous."

"Why are you covering it up?"

"You say these things—outrageous."

"If you just answer my question—"

"Outrageous. I answer no questions. You will leave. You will leave my motel."

The man's grin broadened into a smile. He crossed his arms

over his chest, revealing the beginnings of a tattoo that started at his wrist and disappeared under the sleeve of his leather jacket. His eyes flicked from me to Daniel and back to me again.

"You are making this much harder than it needs to be," I said.

"You will leave immediately," Daniel said.

"Listen—"

"You will leave or I will call the police."

"Don't worry about that. I'll call them myself."

"Did I come at a bad time?" the bearded man asked.

I ignored the question and brushed past him through the door, slamming it behind me. The door slam was just for dramatic effect. I wanted Daniel to think I was angry and indignant instead of what I really was, embarrassed.

I went to my Cherokee. Once inside and with the engine running, I fished my iPhone from my pocket and used the maps application to locate the Thunder Bay Police Service—it was on Balmoral Street, about six miles away. I put the vehicle in gear and drove off. I could see Daniel dealing with the ponytailed customer through the office window as I passed.

"You could have handled that better," I told myself.

FOUR

I was expecting a Royal Canadian Mounted Policeman wearing a red coat and a nifty hat. After much rigmarole I was passed off to a woman wearing a brown pantsuit and a white turtleneck sweater. Her eyes were blue, her hair was blond, and she was tall and trim enough to make me feel both small and out of shape. I had to look up at her when she rose from the chair behind her desk and offered her hand.

"Detective Constable Aire Wojtowick," she said.

I shook her hand and told her who I was.

"Wojtowick, is that Polish?" I asked.

She motioned me to a chair next to the desk.

"Slovakian," she said. "Why do you ask?"

I flashed on the Kashmiri motel owner.

"You have quite a melting pot up here," I said.

"Every ethnicity that you have in the States you'll find in Canada."

"I didn't know that."

"That's because Americans rarely think beyond their own borders. You are an American, right?"

I balanced the envelope on my knee.

"Yes," I said.

"I guessed as much when the sergeant downstairs said you were making a nuisance of yourself."

"I didn't mean to. I'm just looking for information."

"Such as?"

"To start with, I'd like to look at your missing persons reports."

"That information is not generally available to the public."

"Will it help that I was on the job for eleven and a half years with the St. Paul Police Department in Minnesota?"

Wojtowick held her thumb and index fingers about an inch apart.

"It impresses me that much," she said.

"I occasionally work as an unlicensed investigator."

She closed the distance between her thumb and finger to about a quarter inch.

"I'm trying to solve a murder," I said.

"Whose murder?"

"I don't know."

"Mr. McKenzie, I am the most junior member of the Criminal Investigation Branch of the Thunder Bay Police Service. It took me many years to achieve this position, and I was forced to vault many hurdles that less gifted but more masculine colleagues were not. I'd hate to jeopardize it now by squandering time and resources listening to lunatics. It would behoove you, sir, to tell me—and tell me quickly—why I should not throw you out of here."

"Do you know Bobby Dunston?"

"Who?"

"He has the rank of commander in the Major Crimes and Investigations Division of the St. Paul Police Department. He used to be a lieutenant, but they don't have lieutenants anymore, and it used to be called the homicide unit, but apparently they don't have homicides anymore, either. Anyway, you'd like him. He'd like you. You both sound very much alike."

"Mr. McKenzie."

"I'll tell you what I would tell him—think how much fun it would be to solve a murder that your superiors didn't even know you had."

Whatever bluster I had quickly evaporated while Wojtowick sat straight in her chair and glared down at me, the fingers of her right hand drumming a monotonous rhythm on the desktop. She was a powerful woman, older but not pining for her youth, and without a hint of conflict or doubt in her eyes. She stared at me for what seemed like a long time.

"Here's what you do," she said. "When you leave this place, take a left out of the parking lot, then take another left on Central Avenue. Follow Central to Memorial Avenue and take another left. Keep at it until Memorial becomes Algoma Street. After a couple of miles you'll see a large building surrounded by a huge lawn. That's the Lakehead Psychiatric Hospital. Check yourself in. We'll call your friend Bobby. He can come and visit."

"Yeah. Well, listen, Detective, I'm about to piss you off."

"It's Detective Constable, and you've already done that."

I opened the envelope, slid out the photograph, and dropped it on the desk in front of her. Wojtowick looked closely without touching it, then fixed her eyes on me.

"Tell me this is Photoshopped," she said.

"The man on the bed says it's not."

"Start talking, McKenzie, and I mean right now."

I withheld nothing except Truhler's name. Wojtowick didn't like that at all.

"This is Canada," she said. "Not the United States. You don't get to make that decision here. If you prefer, I'll confiscate your passport and incarcerate you as a material witness. You can remain in jail until—"

"Jason Truhler," I said.

"What?"

I repeated the name and gave Detective Constable Wojtowick his address and phone number. She seemed genuinely surprised that I gave him up so easily and said so. I shrugged it off. I had promised I wouldn't reveal Truhler's secrets to Erica and Nina. I said nothing about the Thunder Bay Police Service. I figured I had done my bit by holding out as long as I had under Wojtowick's relentless interrogation. My conscience was clear, and if Truhler didn't like it, he could go entertain himself.

Wojtowick said, "You spoke to the owner of the motel?"

"Daniel Khawaja."

"What did Mr. Khawaja have to say?"

"Nothing. I botched the interview."

Wojtowick raised an eyebrow.

"Most men I know don't admit to their mistakes," she said.

"What can I say? I'm a helluva guy."

"A motel room eighteen weeks after the fact, I'd doubt that there'd be much for the scenes of crime unit to look at."

"Scenes of crime unit?"

"You've been conditioned by American TV to call it CSI. I hate TV. Except for *Ghost Whisperer*. I love that show."

"I've always been partial to *Sons of Anarchy* myself."

"Why am I not surprised? Come with me."

I followed Wojtowick out of her office, she didn't bother to close the door, and together we made our way down the corridor. She walked with purpose, her stride long, firm, and quick— I had to hurry to keep up with her. She may not have been a Mountie, yet I had no doubt that she always got whatever man she went looking for.

Wojtowick led me to a large room filled with computer terminals. Several officers were sitting at the computers, but we found an idle unit in the corner. After logging on, Wojtowick called up a list of missing persons reports. It was in alphabetical order and distressingly long. Instead of going through them one at a time, Wojtowick started loading preferences into the search engine, starting with female. That eliminated only about a third of the names. I thought it would get rid of at least half, and I said so.

"How long were you on the job again?" Wojtowick asked.

Next came race—Caucasian; age—eighteen to twenty; weight—one hundred ten pounds, hair—blond; eyes . . .

"What color were her eyes?" Wojtowick asked.

"Brown."

Finally the date—July 5 to the present.

There was one match, an eighteen-year-old who went missing in Greater Sudbury in October, but she wasn't our girl. Wojtowick eliminated the date from the search preferences and increased the age from sixteen to twenty-four and came up with seven more possibilities that we quickly dismissed. Next she eliminated hair color. That produced eleven additional candidates that we checked one after another. None of them matched the girl in the photograph, either.

"These are all the reported missing persons in Canada," Wojtowick said. "Could she have been an American?"

"She could have been Portuguese for all I know."

"That's not helpful, McKenzie."

"Yes, of course she could have been an American. If it's just an elaborate scam like I suspect, it probably originated in Minnesota."

"Based on what you told me, your Mr. Truhler claims it didn't."

"I think Mr. Truhler is trying to make himself out to be more innocent than he really is."

"Let's have a chat with Mr. Khawaja. I'll do the talking this time."

Standing in black leather boots with two-inch heels before the registration desk, Wojtowick looked like she could have played small forward for the Timberwolves, and God knows Minnesota's NBA franchise could use one. Daniel was obviously intimidated more by her height than he was by the credentials that she showed him. Not me. I like tall women. 'Course, I've always been ambitious.

"I have done nothing wrong," Daniel said. He said it several times. "I do not know why McKenzie says these things about me."

"Would you relax?" I said. "You act like we're accusing you of murder or something."

"Outrageous," Daniel said.

"Mr. Khawaja," Wojtowick said. "Am I pronouncing that correctly?"

"Yes."

"Mr. Khawaja, we are interested in room thirty-four. Now, I understand that you replaced the carpet in the room immediately following the Thunder Bay Blues Festival."

"Is that a crime?"

"Did you replace the carpet?"

"Yes."

"Why?"

"I am replacing the carpet in all of the rooms. I did ten rooms last year and ten this year, and I'll do the rest next year and the year after."

"How many rooms do you have?"

"Forty."

"Why only ten at a time?"

"It is all I can afford."

"Mr. Khawaja," she said, "are you replacing the carpet according to any pattern?"

"I replace the carpets that are most worn first. Why are you asking me this?"

"Is there any particular reason why you replaced the carpet in thirty-four?"

"It was badly damaged. Too damaged to clean."

"Damaged by what?" I asked.

"Vomit," Daniel said. "Vomit and wine. Someone dumped an entire bottle of red wine on the carpet. What is this about? You must tell me. Do I need a lawyer?"

"What happened to the carpet?" Wojtowick asked.

"The workmen took it away."

"Where?"

"I don't know. They put it in the back of a truck and carted it off."

"Then you didn't replace the carpet yourself."

"No," Daniel said. "Please, Constable . . ."

Wojtowick turned toward me. She made a "come here" gesture with the fingers of her hand. I gave her the envelope. She opened it, removed the photo, and slid it across the counter to Daniel. I didn't think it was possible for a man with his dark complexion to turn white, yet he nearly managed it. He backed away from the photo until his spine was pressed hard against the wall behind him.

"What, what?" he chanted.

"This photograph was taken in your room thirty-four," Wojtowick said. "We believe it is a phony, but we must be sure."

"Phony?" Daniel spoke the word as if he didn't know what it meant.

"Fake, fraud, hoax," I said. "Unless—you didn't find any dead girls in your room and try to cover it up, did you?"

"Cover up?" They seemed to be additional words that Daniel didn't know.

"Mr. Khawaja?" Wojtowick said.

"I do not know what is happening."

"Please look closely at the photograph. Mr. Khawaja? Please."

Daniel stepped forward reluctantly.

"Is this room thirty-four?" Wojtowick asked.

"It, it could be. Half of the rooms have the same layout, and the other half, it is the same layout only reversed, with the door on the other side."

"You said the carpet was damaged by red wine."

"I thought it was wine, there, where she . . ." He pointed at the girl. "It was red wine. I have seen spills before. I was sure it was red wine. The smell. It was red wine. I am sure."

"It probably was red wine," Wojtowick said. "Mr. Khawaja? It probably was red wine. We believe the photograph is a fake. We believe that you are a victim of a hoax."

"Hoax?" Daniel asked.

"We do?" I asked.

Wojtowick drove the tip of her elbow into my rib cage. Yeah, she could play pro ball, I told myself as I fought to regain my breath.

"Mr. Khawaja, do you recognize the girl?" she asked.

He shook his head.

"Mr. Khawaja, I would like to see the registration form of the person who rented room thirty-four just before you replaced the carpet. Can you give that to me?"

Daniel nodded and went to his file. He produced the card and set it in front of Wojtowick. It was identical to the card I had filled out. I read it over Wojtowick's shoulder. It listed the name James Linck on Maryland Avenue in St. Paul. Truhler lived in Eden Prairie, I reminded myself. There was a handwritten notation in the corner of the card: 5/21. I asked Daniel about it.

"That is when the reservation was made," he said. "It was made by telephone. The caller, I told him he was lucky because usually I am full for the festival by then."

Wojtowick continued to question Daniel while I made a call.

"Did you contact Mr. Linck concerning the damage of your property?" she asked.

"I tried," Daniel said. "I could not get through. The phone number he gave me—it was not in service."

"What about his credit card?"

"It was false as well."

"You didn't know that when he registered?"

"He gave me the card number to hold the room when he registered over the phone. When he arrived, he paid in cash, so there was no need to check the card. I only ran it after I saw the damage." Daniel glanced at the photograph again and stepped back. "That is why now I ask to see credit card as well as photo ID. McKenzie knows."

"Do you remember anything about this man? What he looked like?"

Daniel shook his head. "I get many guests."

"Could he have been black?" I asked.

Daniel shook his head again.

"Do you have security cameras?" Wojtowick asked.

"We never saw the need."

My call went through.

"Bobby," I said.

"Hey, McKenzie, what's going on?"

"The guys were wondering where you were Friday night. They think you'd rather spend time rubbing shoulders with felons and miscreants than play hockey with us."

"What are you talking about? Half the guys in the locker room are felons and miscreants."

"True, very true. So, Bobby, I was wondering if I could ask you to run a Minnesota license plate number for me."

"McKenzie, the St. Paul Police Department does not exist for your personal convenience. If you want to run a license plate number, I suggest you contact Minnesota Driver and Vehicle Services. It'll cost you all of nine dollars and fifty cents."

"I don't have the time."

"That distresses me terribly. Honestly, it does."

"Bobby, I am standing next to Detective Constable Aire Wojtowick of the Thunder Bay Police Service in Ontario, Canada. You'd like her. She'd like you. You should talk."

I handed the phone to Wojtowick. She looked at it, then at me, then pressed the receiver to her ear.

"This is Detective Constable Wojtowick," she said. "I'm sorry I do not recall your name . . . Commander Dunston, we have a situation here . . . Is that so?" She looked at me again. "He has not committed any crimes that I am aware of, but I am sure I can think of something to hold him on . . . I would much rather have him deported."

"Wait a minute," I said.

"Was he really a police officer?" Wojtowick said. "Still, it does make me question your professional standards . . . You are most kind." Wojtowick recited the license plate number that Linck had written on his registration card. "Thank you."

About a minute passed.

"Yes, Commander," Wojtowick said. She wrote whatever Bobby told her into her notebook. "Thank you, Commander . . . So I have been told from time to time." She laughed heartily at whatever Bobby told her. "Is that right? . . . I'll keep it in mind. Good-bye, Commander . . . You, too."

She handed the phone back to me.

"What did he say?" I asked.

"The license plate number is registered to a sixty-seven-year-old female who lives in your city of Bemidji."

"No, I meant what did he say that made you laugh?"

Wojtowick turned toward Daniel, showing me her back.

"Mr. Khawaja, do you check the license plate numbers people write on the forms against their motor vehicles?"

He shook his head.

"Start."

He nodded.

"If it is not too much trouble, I require the name of the firm that replaced your carpet. Can you give that to me now?"

"Yes, of course." Daniel went to his Rolodex and produced a business card that he handed to the detective. "Dooley Brothers. It is a reputable firm."

"I'm sure it is."

Wojtowick slid the photograph back into the envelope and held it up for me to see.

"I'm going to keep this," she said.

"Okay," I said.

"We're done here."

"We are? Don't you want to go up to room thirty-four?"

"To look at what? Mr. Khawaja, I apologize for the inconvenience we have caused you."

"What about this?" Daniel pointed at the envelope.

"I will contact Dooley Brothers to see if we can find the old carpet. At the moment this is the only evidence that suggests a crime has been committed in your motel, and I do not trust it. I believe you are a victim of an elaborate hoax, as I said earlier. A hoax"—she turned toward me—"that originated in the United States." Daniel was visibly relieved by what Wojtowick told him. "If you are telling me the truth about all this, there is nothing for you to be concerned about."

"I am," Daniel said. "I am telling the truth."

"Then I apologize for alarming you."

"Yeah, Daniel, I'm sorry, too," I said. "Don't worry. I'll find another motel."

Daniel waved his hand in front of his face as if he were scattering smoke. Or maybe it was a bad odor.

"It is all right, Mr. McKenzie. You may stay."

"Thank you."

He waved his hand some more. I took that as a sign that I was to get out of his sight.

It was only five thirty, yet already night had fallen, as had the temperature. I could see our breath in the light of the streetlamps as the cars whizzed past the motel parking lot.

"Did you get what you're looking for?" Wojtowick asked.

"No."

"What exactly are you looking for?"

"The girl, I suppose. If she's dead, then it's murder, and I will personally deliver Jason Truhler into your hands to do with as you please. If the girl is alive, than it's extortion pure and simple, and she'll be the one who's in trouble. I'm hoping she's alive. When I get back home, I'll check some more missing persons reports."

"I'm sure your friend Commander Dunston will enjoy that."

I crossed my fingers and held them up for Detective Constable Wojtowick to see.

"We're like this," I said.

"He said you are tenacious, your Commander Dunston did."

"One of my lesser virtues," I said.

"When are you leaving?"

"First thing in the morning."

Wojtowick slipped a business card from the pocket of her coat and put it in my hand. I returned the favor by giving her my cell phone number, which she jotted down in her notebook.

"I'll check with the fraud unit tomorrow to see if they've had any complaints similar to the one you're investigating," she said. "I will also attempt to locate the carpet. I will inform you if we learn anything. In the meantime, please let me know what you discover on your end. I do hope you find the girl."

"Thank you."

"When you find her, you might mention that the Thunder Bay Police Service would like to have a word."

"Can you arrest her if Jason Truhler refuses to sign a complaint?"

"This is Canada, mister, and Truhler isn't the only victim. There's also Daniel Khawaja and the Chalet Motel."

"Tell me something—what makes you think the scam originated in the States?"

"You tell me," Wojtowick said.

"The reservation. It was made from Minnesota. It was made seven weeks before Truhler got here, which means they were expecting him."

"They were expecting someone, anyway. It didn't necessarily have to be him. Any mark might have done just as well."

"There's one way to check his story."

"How?"

"Contact someone at the Prince Arthur Hotel. Find out when Truhler made his reservation there and for how many guests."

"Good idea. I'll do that."

Wojtowick gave me a nod and started moving across the parking lot toward her car. I called to her.

"Are there any good restaurants in town?"

"A few."

"I'd be happy to buy you dinner."

She gave me a rueful smile and shook her head.

"Commander Dunston was right about you," she said. "You are an incorrigible flirt."

A few moments later she drove off. I watched her taillights receding into the darkness.

I heard a woman's voice. It was loud and distinct. "I'm lost," it said. A second voice replied. It was mine. My voice said, "Where are you?" The first voice said, "How the hell should I know—I'm lost." "Who are you?" I asked. The voice said, "Oh, for God's sake, who do you think?" Then I woke up. It wasn't a particularly satisfying ghost moment, but there you are. Still, I discovered that the sheets were soggy with perspiration and my heart was beating fast. I wondered what had been going on in my dream before the voices woke me. I listened hard, only there was nothing more to be heard.

I flipped the pillow to the dry side and closed my eyes. Sleep didn't come, and I didn't think it would, at least not for a while. If I were at home I'd saunter down to the kitchen for a glass of milk—that was usually enough to tire me out. In room 34 of the Chalet Motel, where a young woman might or might not have been brutally murdered, I reached for the TV remote. It was on the nightstand next to the bed; the sliver of streetlight that peeked through a crack in the drapes gave me enough to find it. I had used the remote to turn off TSN–Canada's Sports Leader— just hours before. There was no ESPN in Canada, the barbarians. I turned on the TV and switched to the Weather Network, a poor cousin of our own Weather Channel. The crawl at the bottom told me it was 3:14 A.M. It also told me that it was minus 3.3° Celsius in the City of Thunder Bay, Ontario. I did the math in my head just the way I was taught in high school: −3.3 multiplied by 9, divided by 5, plus 32 equals 26.1° Fahrenheit. That made it seem warmer, but not by much, so I used the equation for converting Celsius to Kelvin and came up with 269.85°. Toasty.

I flipped back to TSN. None of the scores from the evening before had changed; both the Wild and the Timberwolves still lost. When I became bored enough, I switched off the TV and rolled over. I heard voices again. Only this time they seemed to originate outside the room instead of inside my head. I went to the window and pulled the drapes back an inch. Two men were walking side by side along the balcony. One looked like the man who had entered the office while Daniel and I were quarreling. The other was smaller and wore his blond hair biker style, flowing down his back. They spoke quietly. I couldn't make out what they were saying, yet I heard their voices just the same. It made me wonder.

"If the girl had screamed, someone would have heard her," I told the room. "Why did no one hear her?"

No one in the room replied.

FIVE

I was awake by seven o'clock, an altogether uncivilized hour for a man to be up and about—and I had done it two days in a row now! Personally, I don't think people should get up before 10:00 A.M. or go to bed before midnight. I've been told those are the hours that most people keep in France. However, I went to Paris with Nina not long ago, and I don't believe it's true.

By seven thirty I was on the road. I stopped at a Robin's Donuts. I was tempted to order a Bismark or a French Cruller, but felt I would be betraying the World's Best Donuts in Grand Marais, where I intended to stop on my way south. Instead, I settled for a Sausage, Egg, and Cheese Brekwich that tasted suspiciously like a McMuffin—that is, not very good. I sat at a table and stared out the window. I had such a long way to go, and I was already tired. I drank a lot of Robin's Coffee, resisting the impulse to pollute it with cream and sugar. It tasted much better than the sandwich.

For some reason I was thinking about gas. My Jeep Cherokee was parked just beyond the window. I needed to gas up before I drove much farther. Probably I should give it a wash, too. It was pretty grubby after the long drive from the Cities. You could tell by the contrast where a hand had rubbed off the dirt just above the hinge of the tire carrier on the back. After I bought the Cherokee a few years ago, I had a heavy-duty rock bumper and swing-away tire carrier put on. This not only freed up storage space inside the rear compartment—which I rarely used—it gave the vehicle a tougher, more rugged look—which, of course, was essential, even though I almost never took the SUV off-road.

I sipped more coffee and finished off the Brekwich and continued to stare at the handprint. It took a while before my brain caught up to what my eyes were seeing. Yet when it finally did, all my internal alarms blared at once.

There's a handprint above the hinge of the tire carrier of my Jeep Cherokee, my inner voice shouted.

I could make out where the thumb and the fingers had rested.

Where did that come from?

I could have made it when I scraped the frost off my windows that morning, I told myself. I could have leaned against the frame . . .

No. The handprint was made with a right hand. I held the ice scraper in my right hand.

It looked like the print had been made by someone who had been leaning against the vehicle—the hand had come out to steady him, to keep him from losing his balance. It had to come from someone who was tampering with the Cherokee.

Had anyone been parked next to the SUV in the Chalet Motel lot?

I closed my eyes. In the image that formed behind them, the Cherokee was alone.

Funny thing about adrenaline—suddenly I wasn't tired any-more.

The self-service car wash required "toonies"—Canadian two-dollar coins—and I had to dash across the street to an IDA drugstore to buy a few. The woman seemed reluctant to ex-change them for my American money, which made me wonder just how sound the dollar was these days. Before returning to the car wash parking lot, I studied the street carefully. If some-one was watching they were well hidden.

I crossed the street and went back to the Cherokee. Fantas-tic thoughts reverberated through my imagination as I started it up and drove it into the car wash.

What if there's a bomb? my inner voice asked.

It would have gone off when I started the car or when I drove out of the motel parking lot.

Are you sure?

No.

Pumping the toonies into the coin mechanism allowed me to close the front and back doors of the car wash. It was when I was hidden from view that I went to the wheel carrier. I found nothing. I got down on my knees and searched under the bum-per and inside each wheel well. Still nothing.

Getting kinda paranoid in your old age, aren't you, pal? my inner voice asked.

"Probably," I said aloud.

I went back to the wheel carrier and searched again. This time I cautiously ran my fingers along the black metal brackets and crossbars. I felt it before I saw it, a black pouch made from the same material they use in body bags. It had been carefully hidden between the crossbar and the wheel, attached with black electrician's tape. I would never have known it was there if I hadn't been searching for it.

I cut the pouch free with a pocketknife and opened it. There was a clear plastic bag inside. I could hear blood rushing in my ears and my own heavy breathing. My sight narrowed until I could see only what I held in my hands. By weight, I guessed it to be about three quarters of a pound of cocaine—make it a third of a kilo. The price of coke varies in the Twin Cities. If you're buying from a black kid in the less desirable blue-collar neighborhood of Frogtown, you might pay seventy-five dollars a gram; from a lily-white kid in upper-crust Lake Minnetonka, it'll cost you twice that. Anyway, figure an average of a hundred dollars a gram and I was holding thirty-five thousand dollars. It seemed like someone was paying an awful lot of money to set me up.

Who?

It had to be Daniel Khawaja.

If it is, then he's a moron.

Given that I already had expressed my reason for coming to Thunder Bay to a detective constable of the police service and that nothing had come of it, to call the cops now—anonymously or not—and report that I was transporting drugs would have been silly. It would be like hanging out a sign announcing that I was on the right track. 'Course, criminals have done dumber things. Except, if it was a setup, why hadn't I been arrested when I claimed the Cherokee or when I drove out of the parking lot? Unless the call had been made to the Ontario Provincial Police and they were waiting to jump me when I left the city and headed for the border.

Ahh, the border. Customs.

I slipped the cocaine out of the pouch, broke open the plastic bag, dumped it over the drain, and used the power hose to flush it, vinyl pouch, plastic bag, electrical tape, and all. Afterward, I searched the Cherokee as if my life depended on it. When I discovered nothing more, I cleaned the vehicle inside and out. By the time I was finished, it sparkled just like it had the day I drove it off the lot. All that was missing was the new car smell.

I approached the Pigeon River Border Crossing as if I were driving up to a parking lot ticket booth—that is, I was trying real hard to act casually. I powered down my window and handed the border agent my passport. Icy air slapped me in the face. I was sure that was what made me shiver.

"Good morning," I said.

"Good morning," the agent said.

He took my passport and examined it. It seemed to me that he examined it for a very long time. Meanwhile, a second border agent appeared out of nowhere and approached the rear of the Cherokee. In front of the vehicle and off to the right a third agent stood. It seemed to me that his hand was resting awfully close to his gun.

"Open the tailgate, sir," the agent in the booth said.

"Certainly."

I opened my car door.

The agent said, "Stay in your car, please."

The snap of his voice startled me, and I quickly closed the door. I had no intention of leaving the Cherokee. I opened the door to merely make it easier to reach the release lever on the floor between the door and my seat. I pulled the lever.

The agent in back of the Cherokee swung the wheel carrier out of the way, opened the rear hatch, and peered inside. The agent in the booth started asking the obligatory questions. "Do you have anything to declare?" I answered directly and succinctly. You do not joke with border guards. You do not behave rudely. You do not complain about the wait, question the procedures, dispute the legality of a search, debate border policy, or demand your rights as a citizen no matter how intrusive the guards might be. You do not rant about the government. You do not wear LEGALIZE MARIJUANA T-shirts. If you are smart you speak only when you are spoken to. For the most part, fear of terrorism has made border guards virtually untouchable. No matter which nation they hail from, they are tiny gods on earth with the power to ruin your vacation or your life with little provocation. So I sat there, with my mouth shut, waiting and watching, until the agent in back of the Cherokee closed the tailgate and returned the wheel carrier to its proper position, the guard in front of the car strolled away, and the agent in the booth returned my passport.

"Welcome home," he said.

My heart leapt in my chest, and I felt a kind of warm tingling throughout my body. The same sensation had overcome me only once before and under similar circumstances. It was the first time I had left the country, flying down to Jamaica for a couple of weeks. When I returned, a female customs agent at Miami International Airport said the same thing—"Welcome home"—and I felt a moment of almost overwhelming euphoria, even though I hadn't missed being home at all.

"Thank you," I said.

I let my breath out. I had been holding it in for a while without realizing it. A few moments later, I was heading south on Highway 61, the border crossing receding in my rearview mirror.

"That went well," I said.

Then I thought about the cocaine.

"What the hell?"

Five hours later, I parked the Cherokee inside my garage next to the Audi. I gave the wheel carrier a shake before I left, as if I were daring something to happen. Nothing did. Once inside the house, I set my overnight bag and the carton of donuts on the kitchen table. I gazed out the window to see if the ducks had flown south while I was gone. They hadn't. The sight of them filled me with both pleasure and disappointment. I was glad that the ducks had seen fit to adopt me. On the other hand, hanging around so late in the year, they were pushing their luck. In Minnesota, winter was always just around the corner.

The clock above my sink read three fifteen. I was anxious to get Jason Truhler off my plate before I saw Nina, so I went to my home office and started making phone calls, although my first call had nothing to do with him.

"For cryin' out loud," Clausen said. "They're ducks. You don't think they know when to fly south?"

Doug Clausen worked for the Minnesota Department of Natural Resources. I had known him since college.

"You said they'd be leaving any day now," I said. "That was a week ago."

"It was four days ago, and nothing's changed. Dang, McKenzie. How come I only hear from you when you're worried about your dang ducks?"

"I'm just wondering what's going on."

"Yeah, you and all the dang duck hunters. I told you, the unusually mild weather has stalled the duck and goose migration from Manitoba all the way to Mississippi. It's that simple."

"But what's caused the mild weather? Is it global warming?"

"I don't know from global warming. It's an evolving science, and it's in its infancy. I do know that it's an El Niño year, when there's a warming of the central and eastern tropical Pacific waters, which brings rain to the Southwest and warmer winter weather to the northern states."

"Still . . ."

"Look, if it makes you feel any better, there's a change in the weather approaching. The migration forecast is for a major movement of dabbling ducks. Want my advice? Watch the Weather Channel."

It had been about six years since I put in my papers at the St. Paul Police Department, and I still had plenty of friends there. One of them was a sergeant working in the missing persons unit named Billy Turner, the only black man that I knew personally who played hockey. He gave me about half an hour of his time, meticulously combing his databases, including his lists of unclaimed and unidentified bodies. Nothing matched the description of the dead girl in Thunder Bay.

I had sources across the river, too. Unfortunately, the Minneapolis Police Department was suffering through one of its periodic scandals—this one revolving around members of the SWAT team who were moonlighting as armed bank robbers—and paranoia had set in. That made it tougher to find someone who would sell me unauthorized information. However, a little groveling and the promise of a couple of unmarked fifties bought exactly what Billy Turner had given me for free—nothing.

Next I tried the Minnesota Bureau of Criminal Apprehension. Unlike the local cops, the BCA had a Missing Person Clearinghouse, a Web site that requested the public's help in identifying and locating missing persons. The site listed twenty-eight missing persons, another eighteen that were considered runaways, two nonfamily abductions, and three unidentified bodies. One of the unidentified bodies, tagged Female 004, came close to matching the description of the girl in Thunder Bay, but the dates were wrong. Female 004 had been found naked in a drainage ditch four months before the blues festival.

I called Truhler.

"Who knew you were going to the Thunder Bay Blues Festival?" I asked.

"What do you mean?"

"It's a simple question. Who knew that you were—"

"I don't know," Truhler said. "A lot of people, I guess. It wasn't a secret."

"When did you decide that you were going?"

"I had always planned on it."

"When did you make your reservation at the Prince Arthur Hotel?"

"May."

"When in May?"

"First week, second week, I don't remember. Why?"

"The reservation for the room at the Chalet Motel was made May twenty-first."

"I don't know the exact date. I'm pretty sure I made my reservation before—oh, I get it."

"What do you get?"

"The people who did this to me, they knew I was coming."

"Seems like," I said.

"What about—did you find out about the girl?"

"I don't know about the girl. You tell me."

"I don't know her, I keep telling you."

"You might not know her," I said, "but she and her friends knew you."

"She had friends?"

"At least one—the man who registered at the motel."

"Then it's what you said, a, what did you call it, a badger game?"

"All I know for sure is that there is no evidence that a girl was killed in room thirty-four of the Chalet Motel in Thunder Bay, Ontario, on or around the Fourth of July. Nor can we find evidence that anyone matching the girl's description has gone missing in Ontario, Canada, or Minnesota since then."

"What should I do?"

"What do you mean?"

"When they call demanding more money. What should I do?"

"That depends."

"On what?"

"On what you're not telling me."

"Nothing, nothing at all, McKenzie. I've told you everything, I swear to God."

I sincerely doubted that, only there wasn't anything I could do about it.

"Well, then," I said. "When they call you . . ."

"Yeah?"

"Tell them to do their worst."

Truhler hesitated for a moment.

"I'm not sure I want to say that," he said.

"Then say nothing."

"Nothing?"

"Good-bye, Jason."

Daylight Saving Time had expired on the first Sunday in November, so even though it was only 5:00 P.M. when I left the house, the trees were already black silhouettes against an orange-red sky. I took the Audi, leaving my Jeep Cherokee in the two-car garage, and worked my way out of the neighborhood. I'm a St. Paul boy, born and raised, and proud of it; I had no desire to live anywhere else. Unfortunately, after I came into my money, I moved to Falcon Heights, a first ring suburb. It was an accident. I thought I was buying a house in one of the more affluent St. Paul neighborhoods. It wasn't until after I signed an offer sheet that I realized I was on the wrong side of Hoyt Avenue. I've been getting crap about it ever since from Bobby Dunston and some other friends.

I was on Highway 280 and heading for eastbound I-94 when my iPhone played the Ella Fitzgerald–Louis Armstrong cover of "Summertime." I don't like to talk on my cell and drive at the same time, so I let voice mail pick up the message. Ten minutes later, I parked in the lot outside Rickie's. Before going inside, I checked my messages. There was a report from my private security firm. Someone had broken into my home.

There were two St. Anthony police cars and a cruiser from the security firm parked in front of my home when I arrived. There were also about a dozen of my neighbors standing around and shaking their heads. Not long ago they presented me with a petition bearing nearly fifty signatures demanding that I move. I can't say I blamed them. I was a far cry from Benjamin Hoyt, the pioneer preacher the avenue was named after, and the kidnappings, murders, and shoot-outs that had occurred since I moved in certainly constituted a "detriment to the community," as the petition suggested. Still, they seemed to be getting used to me. A couple of neighbors broke into sincere applause when I sprinted across my lawn toward the assembly of officials gathered in my driveway. One of them shouted, "Hey, McKenzie. Who did you shoot this time?"

Those kidders.

Sergeant Martin Sigford of the St. Anthony Police Department was the first to greet me.

"What the hell, McKenzie," he said.

Falcon Heights didn't have a police department. Instead it had a contract with the St. Anthony PD to provide services. Sigford had been to my house on several occasions.

"I coulda sent a couple of rookies," he added. "Seeing it's you, though, when the alarm sounded I hightailed it over here expecting gunplay, expecting who knows what? Instead, all I get is a simple break-in, and not even your house. It's your garage. How disappointing."

"Sorry 'bout that, Marty," I said.

"Mr. McKenzie, your house seems locked up tight." That came from a member of my security firm. "We must ask you to check the premises, of course," he added—but then, he had a report to file. "In the meantime, if you would examine your garage."

Sigford led the way toward the two-vehicle structure; there

was also a portal for a boat and trailer, but I added that on a couple of years ago. The garage itself had been constructed long before society discovered that it was dangerous to put windows in. That's how the thieves gained entrance—they broke the window of my side door and reached in to unlock it. From that instant, they had less than five minutes to take what they wanted before the St. Anthony Police Department responded to the alarm my security system broadcast. Guards from the security firm arrived moments later.

"No one was observed in the vicinity when we arrived," Sigford said. "We checked with your neighbors. They didn't see anyone, either. The unsups must have known they tripped your alarm as soon as they broke the glass, although, if they had known about the security system, why did they break in at all?"

Together, we stepped inside the garage. The light was already on.

"That was us," Sigford said.

I searched quickly. Lawn mower, snow blower, bikes—everything seemed to be in its proper place, and that's what I told the cops. I didn't mention that the wheel carrier on the back of my Jeep Cherokee had been swung open and then closed, but not latched.

"What were they after, I wonder," Sigford said.

"I have no idea," I told him.

"Sure you're not holding out on me, McKenzie?"

"Why would I do that?"

"Force of habit."

SIX

Nina Truhler lounged behind her desk, her feet on the blotter, eating donuts. Her office, if you could call it that, was located just off the downstairs bar at the jazz club that she had named after her daughter. It was small and cramped and filled with enough cartons and boxes that it resembled a storage closet. The only thing that suggested someone actually spent time there was the twelve-inch-high trophy—a gold figure with sword extended mounted on a marble stand—that Erica had won at the St. Paul Academy Invitational Fencing Tournament last year and given her mother. I sat in the only other chair in the room. I was eating a donut as well.

"These are amazing," Nina said. She was licking brown sugar off her fingers as she spoke.

"Ambrosia," I said.

"At least one good thing has come of your helping Jason."

"Two. The donuts—"

"And?"

"I scored a few points with Erica."

"Rickie has always liked you."

"I'm not altogether sure that's true. I'm the guy courting her mother. How could she possibly approve of that?"

"Good question. Clearly you're not good enough for me."

"All my friends who have met you say that I outkicked my coverage."

"I don't know what that means, but I like the sound of it."

Nina smiled around a mouthful of donut, her pale blue eyes bright and shiny, and glanced up toward the ceiling. Even after all the years I've known her, there are still ways she can sit, stand, turn, move, run her hand through her jet black hair, ways she can cock her head, that make me feel suddenly flushed and light-headed. Even the way she chewed her donut made me aware of just how much I adored this woman. If it hadn't been for Jason Truhler we might have married long ago. Her experiences with him had soured Nina on the institution of marriage, leaving us in a committed relationship, yet living on different sides of the city, together but apart.

Nina swallowed her donut and reached back into the white carton.

"We should save a few for Rickie," she said.

"Sounds like a plan."

"I'm sorry about the way I reacted when you said you were helping Jason."

"I understand. No need to apologize."

"I never told you much about our relationship."

"You told me enough."

"He was very abusive. Not physically abusive. It would have been easier, I think, to deal with that. Instead, he had a way of making me do things I didn't want to do, of making all of our problems seem like they were my fault, of—he had a way of

73

making me feel small. That was the worst of it. He made me feel like I was so much less than everyone else."

"The two of you did a good job raising Erica, though. Anyway, that's what Jason said."

"He's wrong. Rickie didn't get nearly as much time and attention from either of us as she should have. Jason was never around except on holidays and the occasional weekend when he could tear himself away from his bimbos. Me? I spent more time building and running this place than I ever did with her. I had to prove that I wasn't small, you see. Rickie suffered because of it. She grew up despite us."

"I don't believe that's true. I bet Erica doesn't, either."

"Rickie treats me like a dense, dull old woman who just happens to pay the bills. We get along, I suppose, but we're not as close as we should be. She keeps a lot to herself. It kills me that she doesn't take me into her confidence."

"Doesn't every mother say that about her daughter?"

"I don't know."

"She's a good kid."

"She's not a kid anymore, that's the thing. She's grown up. She's starting to make decisions that will affect the rest of her life. I'm not saying she can't make smart decisions. She's never done anything stupid; she's never been in any real trouble. It's just that she's always pushing her luck. She rarely does anything until the last possible moment. She's been working as a tutor for a couple of years and hasn't saved a dime. She stays up too late, never picks up after herself, spends all her free time on her laptop or her cell phone, won't eat unless you make her. She never dates the same guy more than twice. Well, I don't mind that so much. I married at twenty-one. If I have my way,

Rickie won't marry until she's thirty. It's just—she drives too fast, if you know what I mean."

"Erica has a perfect four-point-oh grade point average," I said. "She's a champion fencer, does charitable work, looks you in the eye when she speaks, and always finds a way to get home before midnight." I pointed at the trophy. "I was there when she gave you that. 'Thank you, Mom,' she said, and since she didn't say exactly what she was thanking you for, I presume it was everything. Sounds to me like you must have done something right."

Nina stared thoughtfully at the trophy for a few moments. The metal plate at the bottom read CHAMPION WOMEN'S ÉPÉE.

"Maybe," she said. She slid her legs off the desktop and sat straight in her chair. "I presume you mean *I* did something right, not her father."

"Of course."

"You're done with him, aren't you?"

"I certainly hope so."

"How much trouble was Jason in?"

I thought about the girl in the motel room. I thought about the telephone next to the bed.

"Without going into detail," I said, "all he had to do was pick up a phone. If he had done that, all of his problems probably would have gone away. He didn't. He was afraid. Everything escalated from there."

"He was never one for taking responsibility."

I would have agreed with her, except I didn't get the chance. Nina's chef, a temperamental young woman named Monica Meyer, who once worked for Wolfgang Puck, walked into the office without knocking, looked down at the carton of donuts, looked up at us eating the donuts, and said, "What are you two doing?"

"I'll give you three guesses," I said.

"I have beef tenderloin with truffle potato puree and red wine demi and you're eating donuts?"

I gestured up and down with my hands as if they were the business ends of a scale.

"Your cooking—donuts; your cooking—donuts; your cooking—ahh, donuts win."

"Are you insane?"

"Is that a rhetorical question?"

"Stop it, McKenzie," Nina said. "Monica's cooking is superb. Profits have gone up nearly twenty-five percent since she took over the kitchen."

"Don't tell her that. She'll ask for a raise."

"Nina gave me a raise yesterday, smart guy," Monica said. "Plus profit sharing."

"At least we both agree that I'm a smart guy."

"Sarcasm is wasted on you."

"Do I have to put up with this every time you two are in the same room?" Nina asked.

Monica pointed at the white carton.

"He brought donuts," she said.

"The world's greatest donuts," I said.

"Puhleez."

"Try one."

"Not a chance."

"Seriously, try one."

Monica looked at Nina as if she were seeking help. Nina shrugged. Monica sighed deeply.

"Fine," she said.

She reached for a glazed donut, took a small bite, and chewed carefully. Then she took a bigger bite. Then another.

"Where did you get these?"

"World's Greatest Donuts," I said.

"Can't you answer a simple question without trying to be funny?"

"I'm not kidding. That's the name of the bakery. The World's Greatest Donuts. It's in Grand Marais."

Monica looked at Nina. "Really?"

Nina nodded.

"Isn't that like three hundred miles from here?"

"Something like that," I said.

Monica took a second donut from the carton and held it up as if it were the apple Eve gave to Adam. She studied it carefully.

"I bet I can make donuts just as good as these," she said.

"Fifty bucks," I said.

"What?"

"Fifty bucks says you can't."

"You're on."

Monica spun slowly toward the door, still holding the donut in her outstretched hand.

"Monica?" Nina said.

Monica looked back.

"Hmm?"

"Why did you come into my office? Did you want something?"

"Hmm? Oh, Jenness asked me to tell you—there's a man in the bar wants to talk. He says he's your husband."

● ● ●

Nina walked on the business side of the bar, making sure it was between her and Truhler. I recognized the smile on her face—let's just say it was less than sincere and let it go at that. Truhler smiled with the same genuineness when he saw her.

"Hello, Jason," Nina said. Her voice was as cold as the ice in Truhler's drink.

"Like the man said, you look marvelous," Truhler replied. His voice wasn't much warmer. "Doesn't she look marvelous, McKenzie?"

"Marvelous," I said.

I climbed up on the stool next to him.

"Whatever else you think of me, you have to admit I have excellent taste in women," Truhler said.

"The problem, Jason, wasn't your taste," Nina said. "It was your brand loyalty."

"Ouch," Truhler said. He took a sip of his drink and then waved it at the bar. "It looks like you're doing well."

The downstairs component of Rickie's was humming with customers taking up nearly every table, booth, comfortable sofa, and overstuffed chair. The upstairs portion, which featured a full-service dining room, bar, and performance area, was standing room only—jazz and blues chanteuse Debbie Duncan was singing up there, and she always packed them in. Yet Nina replied with one of those positive-negatives Minnesotans use when they don't want people to know what they're thinking— "Not too bad."

Truhler took another sip of his drink. Nina leaned against the back wall of the bar and watched him. They looked as though they had plenty to say to each other, yet were each waiting for the other to speak first. I gave it a couple of beats before breaking the silence.

"What do you want, Jason?" I asked.

"I couldn't get you on the phone, so I took a chance—"

"I think it's shameful that you've involved Rickie in your affairs," Nina said.

"Affairs? Affairs? What does that mean?"

"You know what it means."

"What did McKenzie tell you?"

"McKenzie didn't tell me anything. He's an honorable man. But you, Jason? I know you. If you're in so much trouble that you need McKenzie's help, it probably involves a woman. A young woman."

Truhler took another pull of his drink. Apparently he couldn't talk to his ex-wife without imbibing.

"We've been divorced for so long, Nina, I'd think your anger would have run dry by now," he said.

"I have an endless supply. You saw to that."

"So it would seem."

"I don't want you in my place."

"Isn't it open to the public?"

"Management reserves the right to refuse service—"

"I came here to talk to McKenzie, not make you angry."

"Yet you do, every time I see you." Nina crossed her arms over her chest. "Every single time."

"That tells me a lot."

"What does it tell you?"

Truhler smiled then, his expression one of smug dreaminess, as though he spent a lot of time contemplating a valuable secret that no one else shared.

"People don't get angry over things they don't care about," he said.

"You don't get it, do you, Jason? You never have. I was a believer. White houses with blue trim, picket fences, two-point-four children, golden wedding anniversaries, Robert Browning—*Grow old along with me! The best is yet to be, the last of life, for which the first was made. Our times are in His hand who saith 'A whole I planned, youth shows but half; trust God: See all, nor be afraid!'* I wanted all of it. Since I was a little girl, I wanted it. You took the dream away from me, and when I see you I'm reminded of that. The loss becomes a fresh grief. As it turns out, my life is pretty good now, a vast improvement over what it was, and it seems to be getting better every day." She was looking directly at me when she said that, and like the Grinch, I felt my heart grow in size. "That doesn't mean I have to forgive you. Besides"—Nina gestured with her chin at the glass in Truhler's hand; it was half filled with amaretto and 7UP, a very sweet concoction. "You drink like a girl."

"Charming," Truhler said.

"You want to talk to McKenzie, so talk to him. Then get out."

Nina spun abruptly and walked away with long, purposeful strides.

"That woman," Truhler said. "What a—"

"Hey," I said. "You'll be making a big mistake if anything comes out of your mouth that's not a glowing compliment."

"Christ, McKenzie. You are so whipped."

"Fuck you, Truhler."

I slid off the stool and started walking in the same direction as Nina. Truhler followed close behind.

"No, no, please. C'mon. I'm sorry, McKenzie. C'mon."

He grabbed my arm. I shrugged it off.

"Erica said—"

I interrupted him again, this time shoving a finger in his face.

"You pull that card out of the deck one more time I'll make you eat it," I said.

Truhler took a cautious step backward.

"I'm sorry," he said. "I really am. I know I can be a jerk. I know I have no right to ask you for help. I don't know where else to go. McKenzie, they threatened to put the images on the Internet."

I wondered then if I'd ever truly understand myself, recognize why I do certain things, why I don't do others. Most days I'm pretty sure I have a good handle on life, that I have it all figured out. Then something will happen—like Truhler happened—and I'll realize that I don't have a clue. This has to stop, I told myself. I needed a plan, a set of guidelines to follow instead of always making it up as I go along. One of these days I'm going to find myself in real trouble and wonder how I got there.

"Sit down," I said.

Truhler went back to his spot at the bar. I followed him.

"What happened?" I asked.

"They called. I said they would."

"What happened?"

"I told them what you told me, told them there was no evidence that a girl was killed in Thunder Bay. They said there was a dead girl. They said she had been buried along with my DNA and business card. They said if I didn't pay up they would tell the police where to dig."

"They're bluffing."

"They also said they were going to post the photos they took of me and the girl on the Internet. Were they bluffing about that?"

"Does it matter?"

"If people saw them, my employers, my clients, my daughter—how could I possibly explain? I could say they were fakes until I turned blue. Do you think anyone would believe me?"

"Can you afford to keep paying?"

"No."

"Well, then. Something's got to give."

"Help me. Please, McKenzie. Help me."

"Help you do what, exactly?"

"I just want it to stop."

"Call the cops. Extortion is against the law, after all. You could put your friends away for ten years."

"It would ruin me."

"It's unlikely you're their only victim. If you put the finger on them, others will probably come to light. It may never go to trial."

"I can't take the risk. I just can't."

"Truhler—"

"Please, McKenzie."

Erica, my inner voice said.

"Dammit," I said aloud.

"What?"

"When are you supposed to give them the money?"

"Tomorrow."

"When tomorrow?"

"They're going to call, tell me the time and location. In the past though, it was always around three in the afternoon and always in a crowded place."

I glanced at my watch. It was pushing 9:00 P.M.

"We should have plenty of time to get ready. I'll call you at about eight in the morning." I winced even as I said it. I hated getting up early.

"What are we going to do?" Truhler asked.

"Follow the money."

"And then?"

"That depends on where it leads us."

Truhler thought about it for a few beats. It occurred to me that he was thinking that I might take on his adversaries, maybe even shoot them. He was mistaken.

"Thank you, McKenzie," he said.

"Nuts."

I leaned against the door frame of Nina's office and quoted Christopher Marlowe.

"Come live with me and be my love, and we will all the pleasures prove that hills and valleys, dale and field, and all the craggy mountains yield."

Nina didn't even bother to look up from the envelopes she was opening with a letter opener that looked like it could be used in trench warfare.

"Nice try, McKenzie," she said.

"One of the first things you learn as a cop, you don't get to choose the victim," I said.

"You're not a cop anymore."

"No, I'm not. Sometimes I forget."

"I don't know what all this is about, and I don't want to know unless it involves Rickie."

"That's the only reason I'm involved, so Erica won't be."

Nina thought about that for a moment. She looked up from her mail.

"Be careful," she said. "Jason—he can't be trusted."

"I know."

"I'll see you tomorrow."

"Good night."

"Thanks for the donuts."

I stepped outside the bar and took in a lungful of cool air. The wind blew a cloud in front of the moon and I lost a little of my light. The cloud passed and the moonlight came back. I noticed for the first time that it was a full moon. My psychiatrist ex-girlfriend once explained that the chemical makeup of blood was very similar to seawater and the moon pulled on it just the way it did on ocean tides. That, she said, was why we all go a little crazy during a full moon.

My car was parked in the back of the lot. I walked toward it with my head down and my hands in my jacket pockets wishing it were two days ago, wishing I could go back in time and tell Jason Truhler to solve his own problems. I should have been inside Rickie's listening to Debbie Duncan, drinking Summit Ale, and flirting with my girl. Instead, my girl was upset and I was helping a guy I didn't even like. This sucks for so many reasons, I told myself—to which my inner voice replied, *The moving finger writes; and having writ, moves on, nor all thy piety nor wit shall lure it back to cancel half a line, nor all thy tears wash out a word of it.*

Suddenly, I was sitting in the back of a mandatory poetry class at the University of Minnesota reading Omar Khayyám, the line repeating itself in my head like an unwelcome song. I blamed Nina for putting me on a poetry jag—she had started it with her Robert Browning.

"Dammit," I said aloud.

I immediately looked around to see if anyone had heard my outburst. The parking lot was full of vehicles, yet empty of people. I had just stepped into the aisle between my Audi and the car parked next to it when a man appeared, seemed to materialize out of thin air, and shoved a gun in my face.

I hate it when there's a full moon, my inner voice said.

I've spent most of my adult life on the lookout, first as a cop patrolling the mean streets and now as an unlicensed investigator or whatever else you might call me—looking for people and things that seem out of place, looking for shadows hidden within shadows, looking for trouble. Yet there I was, trapped between two cars by an armed assailant with my hands in my pockets. Could I possibly be more careless?

The man held the gun steady while a second man approached from behind. I turned my head to get a look at him. Medium height, overweight, the beginnings of a beard, long blond hair flowing down his back—adult men with blond hair make me nervous. Yet it was the gunman who commanded my attention.

"Look at me," he said.

I looked. From the light of streetlamps I recognized him. He was the man who had walked into the office of the Chalet Motel while I was quarreling with Daniel Khawaja. He was wearing the same leather jacket, the same ponytail. Blondie had been with him when they strolled past my room at 3:30 in the A.M. They must have followed me from my home after I investigated the break-in.

"Where is it?" he asked.

"Where is what?"

Blondie punched me hard in the spine. I heard myself cry out and felt my knees buckle. I had to grab hold of the roof of the Audi to keep from falling. Blondie seized my shoulder and pulled me back between the cars. I nearly fell again when he released me, but managed to keep my feet. The gunman raised his gun with one hand and pointed the muzzle between my eyes. He spoke slowly.

"Where is my coke?"

"Oh, that," I said.

I felt better, believe it or not. I now knew I wasn't a random mugging victim. The two men had targeted me because they wanted something specific. That gave me a little leverage, and time—but not much. That's something else the cops teach you: A bad situation can only get worse. If you're going to make a move, do it quickly.

"You're the guys who hid the coke on my car," I said.

Apparently that wasn't the answer they were looking for, because Blondie took a step forward and drove his fist into my kidney just above the belt line, putting some muscle behind the blow. I fell forward again, this time against the gunman. He pushed me upright, grabbed a fistful of my jacket and shirt, and shoved the business end of the gun against my throat with the other hand.

"Where is it?" the gunman asked.

"I found it while I was washing my car. Imagine my surprise."

While we were talking, I cautiously lifted my hands until they were even with my shoulders. No one seemed threatened by that.

"Where's my fucking coke?" The gunman again.

"Why did you pick me to mule your shit across the border?" I asked. "Did I look particularly stupid or what?"

He shook me by my shirt and jacket. He was a big man and strong, and for a moment I understood how a rag doll must feel.

"Goddamn you, where is it?"

"I flushed it down the drain."

The gunman's eyes grew wide, his nostrils flared, and his mouth fell open. Behind me Blondie sucked oxygen like somebody who just heard his dog died. It seemed as good a time as any to bust a move. I set myself, visualized what I was going to do, and then did it.

I grabbed the gunman's wrist with my left hand and pushed the gun away to the right, bending his arm at the elbow until the muzzle was actually pointing behind him. At the same time, I seized the hand holding my lapel and held it tight against my chest. I pivoted slightly to my right, raised my left leg, and drove my foot down against his kneecap. I heard a cracking sound followed by the gunman's scream. He dropped the gun and crumbled to the pavement, both hands reaching out to cradle his knee. I heard the gun skitter along the asphalt, yet paid it no mind. Instead, I spun around to face Blondie.

It occurred to me at that moment with agonizing clarity that I had made a monumental mistake. I didn't know if the second man was armed. If he had been—but he wasn't. He stood there, a kind of stunned expression on his face, staring at his partner. I set my kicking leg down, turned my hip toward him, and executed a side thrust kick, driving my foot hard against his rib cage—he never saw it coming. He fell against the rear quarter panel of the Audi, bounced off, and hit the ground.

I quickly searched for the gun, found it, and snatched it up. It was a wheel gun and heavy, a .357 Magnum Colt King Cobra—a fucking cannon. Blondie rose quickly to his feet, his left elbow pressed against his side. He was getting ready to take a run at me. He stopped short when I pointed the gun at him. Enough of his face was visible for me to see that he was weighing the odds. I thumbed back the hammer. It wasn't necessary. The Colt had a double action; it would fire just as easily hammer down. The gesture had the proper dramatic effect, though. He took a breath, drew back.

"Get the hell out of here," I said. "Go on. Go on."

He turned slowly and started to move across the lot. I heard his partner moan, and out of the corner of my eye I saw him writhe on the pavement.

"Wait a minute," I said.

Blondie halted. I gestured at his partner.

"Take this asshole with you."

Blondie hesitated before carefully making his way to the aisle between the two vehicles. I stepped backward, avoiding the gunman, holding the revolver steady in front of me with both hands, keeping my distance, pretending my back didn't hurt like hell. Blondie reached an arm under the gunman's shoulder and pulled him up. They both groaned with the effort.

"Have you done this often—find someone to sneak your shit into the country for you?" I asked.

They didn't answer.

"Why did you pick me?"

The gunman spoke between clenched teeth.

"I'm going to fuck you up," he said.

"The best-laid schemes o' mice an' men gang aft agley, an' lea'e us nought but grief and pain."

"Huh?"

"Robert Burns. Get the hell out of here. Both of you. Don't ever let me see you again."

The two of them moved with surprising quickness to a battered Buick parked on the street. Blondie helped his partner into the passenger seat before limping around to the driver's side. He opened the door. Before getting in and driving off, he glared at me across the roof of his vehicle.

"Hey, shithead," he said. "No one flushes thirty-five thousand dollars' worth of cocaine. They either call the cops or they keep it for themselves. You steal from us? From us? We're gonna get you. We're gonna get you good."

I should have shot him right then and there. The Colt had more than enough oomph to go through the SUV, through him, and probably through the building across the street. I didn't. Shoot someone in the parking lot of Rickie's? Nina would never have forgiven me.

SEVEN

Highway 61 sliced through St. Paul as Arcade Street, a busy thoroughfare that was nearly as old as the city itself. It served the East Side, an area reputed for its crime, drugs, low-income housing, and rough-and-tumble sensibilities. A lot of people argue that the reputation is undeserved. They point to the area's diversity, to the many neighborhoods, each with its own distinct identity and charm, and to the devoted fifth-generation families that would never live in any other part of the city. They might even convince you, until a couple of street gangs take exception with each other, or there's a raid by a joint task force on a drug operation, or the latest crime statistics are revealed.

Jason Truhler sat nervously on a bench at the bus stop at Arcade and Orange Avenue. He clutched his cell phone and a brown lunch bag in the same hand. There were four hundred and ninety-nine twenty-dollar bills in the bag. The other hand he kept pressing against the receiver in his ear like a TV reporter chatting with the anchor desk from a remote location.

"Would you stop doing that," I said. "Anyone watching will know you're wired."

Truhler dropped his hand to his lap and gazed anxiously around. The sun was behind him, yet he shielded his eyes with the flat of his hand and gazed down the street to where I was parked.

"Stop that, too," I said.

"I'm sorry," he said. "I haven't done anything like this before."

"Just relax. Everything's under control."

I hope, my inner voice said.

We were communicating with single-channel FM in-ear receivers and miniature transmitters with an eight-hundred-foot range. My transmitter was in my hand as I watched Truhler over the steering wheel of my silver Audi. His was concealed in the inside pocket of his jacket. I had leased the devices that morning from a pal who sold sensitive surveillance equipment—some of it legal—out of a secret room in the basement of his pawnshop. He told me that he was considering getting out of the snoop business because the pawnshop was doing so well. Profits were up over 18 percent because of the latest economic downturn, with cash-poor clients using collateral to get short-term loans that banks would never accept and with shoppers more inclined to buy secondhand goods at a decent price rather than pay top dollar to buy new. I would have bought an espresso machine myself while I was there except I already had two.

Afterward, we waited in a coffeehouse until the blackmailers called with instructions. I kept stretching my stiff and bruised back while we drank. Not once did Truhler ask what was ailing me.

The instructions, when they came, weren't particularly original, according to Truhler, nor did they vary much from the previous demands. I followed Truhler at a discreet distance while he went to the bank to gather the money and then to a supermarket to buy a brown paper lunch bag to put it in—he was forced to purchase a package of twenty-five. He sat in his car in the parking lot of the store until the blackmailers called again, this time with directions to the East Side. At the time, I was in the Audi eight cars down and two rows over from Truhler. If someone else had followed him, I hadn't noticed, either at the supermarket or later at the bus stop, where we'd been planted for nearly an hour.

Truhler continued to fidget on the bench. I didn't mind. He should be nervous; the kidnappers who sent him to the bus stop and told him to wait until they called would expect him to be nervous. I just wished he'd stop touching his ear, stop talking; stop giving away my position.

"Pretend you're alone," I told him.

"I was less nervous during the other money drops when I was alone," he said.

I stretched and squirmed, stretched and squirmed, trying to find a position that comforted my ailing back and failing, all the while watching for vehicles that cruised past the bus stop more than once. It was a tough job. Traffic was heavy and getting heavier. It was nearly 3:00 P.M., and just up the street the kids were being let out of Johnson Senior High School. The school was founded in 1897 and called Grover Cleveland High School until it was renamed after John A. Johnson, a former Minnesota governor whose only claim to fame was that he died in office. We played Johnson in hockey back when I was at Central, which was founded in 1866 and named after nobody. Johnson kicked our butts, but then, who didn't?

The kids flooded Arcade, some of them using the street as their own personal drag strip. A couple of teenagers joined Truhler at the bus stop. A young lady sat next to him on the bench; a few others took shelter in the Plexiglas booth behind him, although there was nothing to take shelter from. The sky was clear blue, the air about sixty-eight degrees, and the wind nonexistent. Minutes passed. A bus came. The kids got on, leaving Truhler alone on the bench.

He lowered his chin to his chest so he could speak into his pocket. "Now what?" he asked.

"Now nothing," I said. "They said to sit and wait until they called, and that's what we're going to do. And don't lean into your chest when you talk. Act naturally."

"I'm sorry."

I flicked the transmitter off so I could curse aloud and then turned it back on.

"Relax," I said.

"I'm relaxed, I'm relaxed," Truhler said, his fingers pressed against the receiver in his ear.

Oh, brother.

Minutes passed, and then a few more. It seemed longer. I kept squirming in my seat, kept stretching my back. A passenger plane flew overhead. It wasn't on one of the usual approaches to the Minneapolis–St. Paul International Airport, and for a moment I wondered if it was off course like the Northwest flight that flew 150 miles past the Twin Cities before the pilots realized they were heading in the wrong direction. Finally Truhler's cell phone rang. He answered. I could hear only his end of the conversation.

"Yes . . . Just leave it on the bench? . . . Okay, okay."

He turned off his cell.

"They said to leave the bag on the bench, walk to my car, and drive away." This time he actually looked straight ahead when he spoke. "They said they were watching."

"Do exactly what you were told," I said. "I'll take it from here."

Truhler set the bag down, rose from the bench, and walked in the direction of his car. He didn't speak. He didn't press his fingers against his ear. He didn't look for me.

Good for him, my inner voice said.

I stopped watching Truhler and instead concentrated on the brown paper bag. Sitting alone on the bench, it looked like it could have contained someone's forgotten lunch. I heard Truhler open his car door, slam it shut, and start his engine. "Good luck," he said. A few moments later, he was out of range. I turned off the transmitter and removed the receiver from my ear. No one approached the bag. Still, I thought, the blackmailers were taking a helluva risk, leaving the money in plain sight like that. What was to stop a bus rider from stumbling over it and either reporting it to the cops or taking it to the nearest Indian casino, depending on how closely they adhered to the maxim "Finders keepers, losers weepers."

Again minutes seemed like hours.

Finally a little girl crossed the street at the light. She was wearing a sweatshirt that suggested she was a student at Farnsworth Elementary School just down the block and carrying a backpack emblazoned with a Disney character. She sat on the bench, which I found odd. Didn't elementary school kids have their own school buses? Wasn't there a phalanx of teachers to make sure they got on them? Certainly there had been enough of the yellow behemoths cruising Arcade in the past half hour.

It wasn't long before the girl opened the brown paper bag. It took just a moment before she fully realized what was inside. She looked carefully around her, then stashed the bag inside her backpack. I waited for someone to rush up to her and demand the bag's return. No one did. I thought for a moment that I should retrieve the cash, then thought better of it.

The girl was meant to find the money, my inner voice said.

Nice, I thought. Very nice. The blackmailers had probably anticipated that someone—the cops, let's say—might be conducting a stakeout. If the cops rushed the girl now, what would they get? A tearful child claiming she found the money and was taking it to her parents, brother, sister, cousin, friend, teacher, or coach to ask what to do with it. If they followed the girl, like I was about to do, until she actually gave the money to her parents, brother, sister, cousin, friend, teacher, or coach and then moved in, what would they get? More tearful people, all saying the same thing. *The girl found the money and brought it to us. We were going to turn it over to the police, honestly we were.* Or: *The girl found the money and brought it to us and we decided to keep it*—finders keepers, losers weepers. In any case, no crime was committed. Nice. My estimation of the blackmailers had increased immensely.

'Course, I wasn't a cop anymore. I wasn't interested in building a case. My job was merely to identify the blackmailers and ask them, politely, to take what they'd gotten from Truhler so far and move on. Or something like that. I wasn't even carrying. My weapons were locked in the safe embedded in the floor of my basement. The Colt I took off the gunman the evening before was resting at the bottom of the Mississippi River where I tossed it on my way home—it's never wise to keep a gun if you don't know where it came from or what it was used for.

I was parked on Hyacinth, across from the First Covenant Church, the nose of my Audi facing Arcade. The position gave me a clear view of the bus stop but nothing up the street, so I didn't know if a bus was approaching or not. I just sat there and tried to mollify my growing impatience—if you've ever waited for a bus, you know exactly what I'm talking about. When it finally did arrive, it caught me by surprise, rumbling past the intersection so fast I might have missed it if I had been looking down to select a CD or change the radio station. It stopped for the girl and a couple of high school students before flashing its turn signal and sliding into the traffic lane, not giving a damn if it cut off the vehicles behind it or not. I had to wait for on-coming traffic to pass before turning onto Arcade, and then I was caught at the light at Maryland. That was okay. I preferred that the bus had a nice head start. I knew where it was going— straight down Arcade. I just wanted to make sure that I was nearby when it let the girl off.

You'd think that following a city bus would be easy, but it isn't. The problem was that it moved slowly and stopped fre- quently for unpredictable lengths of time. Eventually you had to pass it or risk looking as conspicuous as the mole on Cindy Crawford's upper lip. I made my move when the bus let out a couple of senior citizens at American Legion Post 577, Bar Bingo Thursdays at 7:00 P.M. I sped ahead, pulling into the lot at The Work Connection, an employment center on Jenks Avenue. I carefully monitored the bus's progress until it rumbled past, then got on its tail again. Soon we were passing the Seeger Square strip mall and fast approaching the bridge that spanned the Bruce Vento Regional Trail.

That's when they hit me.

An SUV sped up on my left. Someone stuck what looked to me like a Ruger MP9 submachine gun outside the passenger window. Light glinted off the black metal muzzle. I caught the reflection out of the corner of my eye.

I slammed on my brakes just as 9 mm rounds began tearing into my hood and smashing the windshield all to hell. Shards of safety glass splattered my face as I cranked the steering wheel hard to the right. All of the red warning lights on my dashboard flared at once and I heard a loud whine emanating from the engine. The Audi jumped the curb and hit a U.S. Highway 61 sign. It rode halfway up the metal post before stopping.

The SUV surged forward. The shooter leaned out of the window. I could see white forearms and white hands gripping the MP9, but not a face. He was right-handed and couldn't turn far enough in his seat to properly target the Audi once he was in front of me. He kept firing until he exhausted the thirty-two-round magazine just the same. Most of the rounds missed, gouging holes out of the bridge's concrete deck.

I tried to open the driver's side door and failed. The collision with the signpost must have bent the Audi's frame and frozen the door in place. I hammered it with my shoulder one, two, three times before it flew open. It was unnecessary. Instead of stopping to finish the job, the SUV accelerated, ran the light at Minnehaha Avenue, hung a hard right at East Seventh Street, and disappeared from sight.

I took a deep breath and leaned back against my seat. The high-pitched whine of the Audi's engine had been replaced by a solid clanking sound that reminded me of a hammer rapidly striking metal. I closed my eyes. The thugs who had accosted me in Rickie's parking lot drove a Buick, but that didn't mean they couldn't have traded up. I opened my eyes. Steam was rising from the engine in a half dozen places. I reached for the ignition key and turned it off.

I sat on the rear bumper of an EMS vehicle while a paramedic worked on my face. The cuts made by the flying safety glass weren't particularly deep, more like shaving nicks. Yet there were so many of them and the face has so many blood vessels that I resembled a character in a slasher film. The paramedic had to dab a clotting agent on nearly every cut, and by the time he finished the collars of both my shirt and jacket were stained red. I wasn't complaining, though. Just one look at the Audi—my beautiful fifty-thousand-dollar sports car—and you could see how lucky I was.

The Audi had been killed. It was still hung up on the signpost. One tire had been shredded, along with the front left quarter panel and headlight. A pool consisting of motor oil, radiator coolant, transmission fluid, and windshield wash had formed beneath it. From where I sat in the parking lot of the Seeger Square strip mall, it looked like blood—at least until the fire department doused it with a flame retardant foam that transformed it into a sickly pink color. A yellow, three-inch wide POLICE LINE DO NOT CROSS tape had been posted. A pair of cops stood outside the tape and cautiously merged Arcade's two lanes of traffic into one and directed it around the crime scene while a half dozen more stood inside the tape and examined bullet holes. I was surprised by how few gawkers there were. The diners inside the Great Dragon and Taqueria Los Ocampo restaurants couldn't even be bothered to come to the windows and look out. Then again, it was the East Side.

Two of the cops made their way up to the parking lot. I recognized them both. If I had seen them at Target Field or the Minnesota State Fair, I probably would have waved.

"McKenzie," Bobby said.

"Commander Dunston," I said.

"You all right?"

I stretched my aching back.

"Fit as a fiddle and ready for love," I said.

Bobby nodded toward the woman standing next to him, his partner of the past three years whom he once described as "young, beautiful, smart as hell."

"You know the sergeant," he said.

"Hi, Jeannie," I said.

"That's Detective Shipman to you," she said. She was smiling when she said it, though, so I didn't take her seriously.

"What happened, McKenzie?" Bobby asked.

"Well, Officer, I was minding my own business, driving down the street—"

"Don't screw with me, McKenzie. I'm not in the mood. Who shot at you?"

"I don't know."

"Guess," Shipman said.

"I can't."

"Does this have anything to do with your trip to Thunder Bay?" Bobby asked.

"I don't know."

"McKenzie, this isn't just about you." He pointed at the elementary school on the hill behind the mall. "Other people could have been hurt, too."

"I appreciate that."

"I don't think you do."

Bobby turned to the paramedic, who was packing up his equipment.

"Excuse us, please."

The paramedic nodded and moved to the front of his vehicle and climbed in behind the wheel. Shipman started to drift back to the crime scene.

"Not you."

Bobby turned back to me.

"McKenzie," he said, "I've known you since kindergarten. You're the best friend I've ever had. You're godfather to my eldest daughter. You're the executor of my estate. My mother— Mom called Sunday. She said to tell you that if you don't have any plans, you're welcome to spend Thanksgiving with the family at her place in Wisconsin."

"That's kind of her."

'There's no way that I could bring myself to arrest you."

"Thanks, Bobby."

"Sergeant Shipman, arrest McKenzie."

Shipman stepped forward while reaching into her bag for handcuffs.

"Whoa, wait a minute," I said.

"Hands on the vehicle, McKenzie," Shipman said. "You know the drill."

"What's the charge?"

"During the thirty-six hours I can hold you without a charge, I bet we'll think of something," Bobby said.

Shipman grabbed a handful of my sports jacket and yanked me off the bumper. She was surprisingly strong.

"Turn around," she said.

"You made your point," I said.

"Hands against the vehicle, assume the position."

"Bobby?"

"McKenzie?"

"I don't know who they are, but I think they're involved in drugs."

Shipman stepped back. The expression on her face suggested that she'd just hit a dinger but didn't want to gloat while she circled the bases.

I had to give them something, so I told the two cops about finding the drugs attached to my Jeep Cherokee in Canada and what happened next—the garage break-in, the assault in the parking lot of Rickie's. I asked them if they wanted to see the bruises on my back. What I didn't mention was the job I was doing for Jason Truhler. They were both shaking their heads sadly by the time I finished.

"Why didn't you call the police?" Bobby asked.

"What?"

"When you found the drugs hidden on your Cherokee, why didn't you contact the Thunder Bay Police Service? Why didn't you call your friend the detective constable? Why didn't you tell Marty Sigford when he responded to the break-in? Why didn't you call the police when you were jumped at Rickie's?"

"Why?" I asked.

"Yes, why?"

"It never occurred to me."

"Of course not," Shipman said. "Instead of doing something that might help us catch these guys, you decided to do what's easiest for you. Does that pretty much cover it? You decide what's good or bad, right or wrong, legal or illegal, and screw the rest of us. McKenzie, you used to be police. Now you're just another self-serving citizen."

Bobby and I had known each other for so long that we had developed the ability to communicate without actually speaking. I turned to him and flashed a look that said, "Are you going to let her talk to me like that?"

The look that he gave back said, "You're damn right I am."

"You're just telling us enough now to make us go away," Shipman added. "Isn't that right?"

"I told you the truth, Detective Shipman," I said.

"But not the whole truth." She gestured with her head at Bobby without taking her eyes off me. "You'll notice he hasn't explained what he's doing on the East Side."

"Yeah, how 'bout that, McKenzie?" Bobby asked.

"I was sightseeing."

Bobby dropped his chin to his chest, closed his eyes, and sighed deeply.

"You lying sonuvabitch," Shipman said.

"Prove it," I said.

"Which? That you're a liar or a sonuvabitch?"

"All right, all right, that's enough," Bobby said. "I'll catch up to you later, Sergeant."

Shipman left, yet not without delivering a parting shot. "You're lucky I'm not in charge," she said.

Bobby placed his hand on my shoulder and moved me away

from the EMS vehicle. We drifted into the middle of the parking lot. It was easy for us to see the remains of my silver Audi from there.

"You know," Bobby said, "I never did like that color."

"I did."

"What are you doing on the East Side?"

"A favor. For a friend."

"What favor? What friend?"

"I'm not at liberty to say."

"You're withholding evidence, brother."

"I'm not on the job anymore, Bobby. I'm not licensed. I'm under no obligation to tell you—"

"You say that to me? To me? After all these years? What the fuck, McKenzie?"

Bobby took two long steps away from me and then two steps back.

"You've changed," he said. "When you first started doing these favors for friends, all you wanted to do was help, and there was something noble about it. You helped and never asked for anything in return, and you never crossed the line. You were always the good guy. Always. Are you still a good guy, McKenzie? Are you on the right side of the line? Do you even know where the line is anymore?"

"I think so."

"I don't. You once told me that you do favors for friends because you want to make the world a better place. Tell me, how is that working out for you? I ask because it seems to me that the more favors you do, the less happy you are, and I'm wondering if that's because you're starting to do—what is it people say—two wrongs don't make a right? I'm wondering if you've done too many wrongs for what you think are the right reasons and it's starting to mess with you. I'm a cop. I've seen bad things. You used to be a cop. You saw them, too. Anyone who is a man would want to change those bad things—make them go away. If you try too hard, you become part of what you behold. Do you know what I mean by bad things?"

"Yes."

"That's why the cops have rules—to keep us from trying too hard. Do you have any rules, McKenzie?"

"Yes."

"I'd like to know what they are."

"I don't have them written down."

"Tell me, then."

"C'mon, Bobby."

"Do you know why I let you spoil my kids, why I let you buy Victoria and Katie stuff I can't afford? I want them to have someone in their lives besides their parents that they can depend on absolutely should the bad things ever reach out to touch them. All they have to do is crook a finger and whisper your name and you'll be there, they know that, I know that. It's a comfort to me knowing that"—he pointed a finger at me—"as long as you don't bring the bad things with you when you come."

"I admit that I sometimes play fast and loose with the rules," I said.

"You do more than that. Listen, you and I, we live on the fringe between light and dark. All cops do. We cross over into the darkness to do the job—but it's no place to live. You gotta know that. Do you know?"

"I know."

"I'm going to give you some advice, whether you want it or not. It's not my advice. It's what your father would say if he were here. Remember who you are. Remember where you came from. Remember that a man's character is judged by how he behaves when there is no one around to see."

When Bobby spoke the advice, I could actually hear the old man's voice.

"Words of wisdom," I said.

"I'll see you around, McKenzie."

Bobby started moving toward my battered Audi. I called to him.

"Don't forget hockey Friday night."

He waved in reply.

'Course, that wasn't the end of it. I still had to give a statement and sign some papers. Bobby decided that the Audi was evidence in a crime and had it towed to the police impound lot, which was fine with me. It had to be towed somewhere. I told myself maybe I'd just abandon it there. Bobby gave me a receipt for the car. When I asked for a ride home, he told me to take a cab. Shipman said if I didn't have the cash, I could take a bus, which reminded me—I had no idea what happened to the bus I had been following, the little girl, or Truhler's $9,980. If that wasn't bad enough, I received a call on my cell phone while I was outside the Subway in the Seeger Square mall waiting for the cab.

"McKenzie, this is Detective Constable Wojtowick."

"Good afternoon," I said. "Or should I say evening?"

"The sun is setting where I am," she said.

"Here, too."

"You'll never guess, but Dooley Brothers is involved in carpet reclamation."

"They're the guys who replaced Daniel Khawaja's carpet," I said.

"Yes. They're part of a group that recycles carpets, that tries to divert carpets from landfills."

"What does that mean?"

"It means they still had the original carpet from the Chalet Motel."

"After all this time?"

"After all this time, and in case you're wondering, yes, we did find the carpet that was taken from room thirty-four. I gave it to forensics, and they identified the stain in about six minutes."

"Was it wine like Daniel said?"

"No. It was a mixture of corn syrup, water, red food coloring, green food coloring, and milk."

"What?"

"Theatrical blood. What they use onstage and in the movies instead of the real thing."

"I'll be damned. What about your fraud unit?"

"They never heard of a scam quite like it, but they're going to keep a lookout."

"I don't know what to say. It looks like Jason Truhler was telling the truth after all."

"At least about that."

"What do you mean?"

"I checked with the good folks at the Prince Arthur Hotel. Truhler had made reservations for two on May seventeenth, four days before the reservations were made at the Chalet."

"For two?"

"Yep."

Dammit, my inner voice said. *The sonuvabitch did lie to you. God! If you had known that this morning, think of all the trouble you could have saved yourself. Your poor Audi!*

"I don't know what to say," I said.

"Say, 'Thank you, Detective Constable Wojtowick, for your generosity and high degree of professionalism.'"

"Thank you, Detective Constable Wojtowick, for your generosity and high degree of professionalism."

"Think nothing of it. Don't forget, McKenzie, if you find the girl, I want to know about it."

"I promise."

EIGHT

"I lied," I said.

"To who?" Nina asked. "Bobby?"

"I lied to him without even thinking about it, not a moment's hesitation. I just did it. He knew I was lying, too. That's why he was so angry."

"Why should he be different from the rest of us?"

After taking a cab home, I changed clothes. Both my shirt and sports coat were lost causes, stained with so much blood I just balled them up and tossed them in the trash. Some of the cuts started bleeding again when I washed up, and it took me a few minutes to get them back under control. Even so, my face made me look like I had been mugged by a pack of angry cats. Nina noticed it the moment I knocked on her front door. Most people would have asked what happened. She said, "What now?" I told her. She was not amused. Now she was pacing in front of the chair in her living room where I was sitting. I asked her to stop. She ignored me.

"I withheld evidence that I knew to be pertinent to his investigation," I said. "I never did that before."

"About Jason?"

"Yes."

"You were protecting Jason."

"No. Hell, no."

"Rickie, then."

"My father never in his life did a thing that embarrassed me, that made me think less of him—as far as I know. I don't want to know."

"And you don't want Rickie to know. You were protecting Rickie from the truth about her father."

"Hell, Nina, I don't even know what the truth is. Maybe your ex-husband is just a dupe. Maybe—ahh. Sometimes I feel like Yul Brynner in *The King and I*. I'm no longer positive of the things I know for sure. Maybe if someone else had been involved I would have come clean. If it wasn't just me, if it wasn't just my car . . ."

"Isn't that enough? They nearly killed you. They destroyed your Audi."

"I figure that's just the price you pay for doing the things I do."

"It seems like an awful lot of risk for so little." Nina took a deep breath and exhaled slowly. "Sometimes, McKenzie, I just want to slap your face."

"Please don't. I've already lost too much blood."

She stopped pacing and looked down at me. Somewhere inside her head a switch was turned. The expression on her face turned from anger to something else.

"Oh, hell," she said.

"What?"

Nina sat on my lap, her legs hanging over the arm of the

chair. She wrapped one arm around my shoulder, her hand resting on the nape of my neck.

"If I kiss you, will you start bleeding again?" she asked.

"I suppose you could give it a try. Think of it as a science experiment."

Nina leaned in and kissed me on the side of the mouth and then moved her lips to my cheek. She leaned back.

"Nope, no blood," she said.

"Call that a kiss?"

"Are you suggesting my kisses aren't what they should be?"

"I'm just saying the results of your experiment would have greater validity if you were more aggressive in your research."

"Oh, the things I do for science."

She kissed me again, kissed me to the depths of my soul. I sat there and took it, my eyes closed—it was like receiving mouth-to-mouth resuscitation. Suddenly the gloom that had fallen over me since the assassination attempt was lifted. I felt alive again. It seemed hardly possible that this same woman had just spent the better part of a half hour berating me for taking unnecessary risks, for dancing with danger—she actually used those words, "dancing with danger." I told her she made it sound like one of those silly made-for-TV movies on the Lifetime Channel. That made her even angrier. The kiss, however, suggested that she might be willing to forgive me my many trespasses if only I could resist saying something dumb—"A man has to do what a man has to do" came to mind. I had used that line on her earlier. I was joking at the time; I said that you could tell I was joking because I was smiling. I was never one of those guys, I insisted. Nina rolled her eyes and said, "McKenzie, you've always been one of those guys." I argued that, while I wasn't completely immune to all that macho bullshit, I usually had a good reason for what I did. The remark only antagonized her, causing her to harangue me even further. So now I just sat there and kept my big mouth shut and let her kiss me.

When she finished, she rested her head against my chest, and I gently stroked her hair.

"How does that Chinese curse go, the one you like to quote?" she asked.

"May you live in interesting times," I said.

"You're the most interesting man I know. I think that might be a curse, too."

"Yeah, but which of us is cursed? Me, or you for knowing me?"

"Both."

We kissed again. At just about the time the kissing was starting to lead to someplace more interesting, the front door opened and Erica stepped across the threshold, keys in one hand and a backpack in the other. The backpack made a heavy thud on the floor when she dropped it.

"Would you kids like some iced tea?" she asked.

Nina quickly scrambled off of my lap. She tried hard to mask her amusement from her daughter, only her eyes gave her away. I stood next to the chair, pretending the chair wasn't there and I had never been sitting in it.

"Iced tea?" I repeated.

"A couple weeks ago my mother caught me in a similar position with a boy." The expression on Erica's face suggested that she had yet to forgive her. "She asked us if we wanted iced tea and then insisted we come to the kitchen to drink it."

"I was only being polite to your guest," Nina said.

"Sure you were."

Erica and Nina glared at each other until they both felt a smile coming on, and then each turned away so the other wouldn't see it.

"I am so leaving home to go to college," Erica said.

"Good. I'll turn your bedroom into a sewing room," Nina said.

"I can see it now. You in a rocking chair with a comforter around your legs, crocheting while you watch *I Love the 80s* retrospectives on VH1, a cat sitting on your lap. We'll call him Snookums. 'Would Snookums like some iced tea?' McKenzie, what happened to your face?"

"I was cut a little bit," I said. "Nothing too bad. You won't even notice tomorrow."

Nina wouldn't let it go at that, though. Her expression changed from amusement to anger.

"Someone tried to shoot him," she said.

"Oh, no," Erica said.

"They missed McKenzie, but they wrecked his car."

"Oh, no. The Audi? They wrecked the Audi. They almost, they almost—it's all my fault, isn't it? It's my fault."

"It's not your fault," I said. "It had nothing to do with you."

"If I hadn't asked you—"

"If you hadn't asked him to get involved in your father's problems," Nina said.

"I'm not sure it had anything to do with your father," I said.

"If I hadn't," Erica said.

"If you hadn't," Nina said.

"Stop it, now," I said.

"I am so sorry, McKenzie," Erica said.

"Erica, there's no need for that," I said.

"I am so sorry."

"You should be," Nina said.

"I'm sorry."

"Nina, stop it," I said.

She turned toward me. The look in her eyes made me take a step backward.

"I need to think," Erica said.

She picked up her backpack and slowly carried it up the stairs. She was high enough on the stairs that I could only see her lower legs when she stopped.

"I'm sorry, McKenzie," she said.

"There's nothing to be sorry about," I said. I was looking directly into her mother's eyes when I spoke. "This is me, remember? This sort of thing happens all the time."

Erica disappeared upstairs. Nina stepped closer to me.

"What do you think you're doing?" she asked. Her voice was low and sharp.

"Don't you blame her for what happened," I said.

"She's my daughter."

"I don't care. If you want to blame Jason, I'll be the first to pile on, but don't you blame her."

"If she hadn't asked for your help, none of this would have happened."

"If she wasn't your daughter, I would have said no."

"So it's my fault?"

"Why are you so angry?"

"I always get angry when people shoot at you."

"I'd think you'd be used to it by now."

"Dammit. Dammit, dammit, dammit, McKenzie. Don't you make a joke out of this."

"Nina, aren't you the girl I was making out with five minutes ago? What happened?"

"I was angry when I was kissing you."

I raised my hand as if I were attempting to stop traffic.

"Wait," I said. "Give me a minute to think that through."

"Shut up, McKenzie."

Erica called to us from the top of the stairs. "McKenzie," she said. She waited a few beats before descending the staircase. I figured she paused because she thought Nina and I might be making out again and she didn't want to embarrass us a second time. I liked this girl.

"McKenzie," she said. She was carrying a laptop. "Did I ever show you my fencing photos?"

"No," I said.

"Now's not the time," Nina said.

"I thought McKenzie should see them," Nina said. "Would you like to see them, McKenzie?"

Should—she said should, my inner voice told me.

"Yes," I said.

She set the machine on a coffee table. I sat on the sofa next to her. Erica had already opened a file and was now riffling through the electronic images. I watched them appear and disappear on the large screen, not at all sure what I was looking for. Nina stood in front of the coffee table, her arms crossed over her chest. She seemed as confused as I was.

"These were taken at the St. Paul Academy Invitational last year," Erica said.

She paused at a shot of a large gymnasium floor filled with white-clad swordsmen dueling across gray strips measuring about fifteen meters long and one and a half meters wide. An electrical cord ran from the hilt of each sword to a plug attached to the fencer's white jacket. From there the cords extended to a reel attached to the floor that gave out and took in slack depending on the movement of the swordsman, then from the reel to an electronic box on the scorer's table that kept track of the competitor's touches.

"Mother," Nina said, "may we have some iced tea?"

Nina hesitated for a moment.

"Sure," she said.

When her mother disappeared into the kitchen, Erica brought up the next shot. It showed both her and another young woman sitting on folding chairs and mugging for the camera. They were wearing white knickers and white jackets that closed around the throat. Erica's companion looked like she was about fourteen. She had bright brown eyes and hair the color of roses and wheat that was tied in a ponytail with a red ribbon. Erica was pretending to pull the ponytail. It was the girl's hair that set the alarm bells ringing.

After a few moments, Erica went to the next photo.

"Go back," I said.

She did.

I studied the young woman some more.

"Who is this?" I asked.

"Her name is Vicki Walsh," Erica said. "She went to Johnson."

"Johnson Senior High School? She looks too young."

"She's a year older than I am. This was taken last January."

"How do you know her?"

"From fencing. There's only about a dozen girls in the entire state who are any good at épée; that's the sword I use. We see each other at all the tournaments, and most of us are friendly. We're not friendly on the strip, no way. Before and after, though—it's like we're members of the same exclusive club, you know?"

"Tell me about the girl."

"The others and I teased Vicki because she looked so young, and she would tease us back, saying how sad it was that we were already past our prime, that we already looked like old women. She was smart. You talk to someone and you know right away if they've ever read a book before. I guess she wasn't all that good in school, though; didn't have the grades like I do. Vicki said something about missing a lot of time when she was fifteen and that she never really caught up—I guess she was sick or something. She never said. On the other hand, Vicki said that she had been accepted by Cornell University. You don't get into Cornell with just good looks. She had a lot of personality, always smiling. Even when she lost, when I beat her for the trophy at SPA, she smiled. I liked her a lot."

Erica turned in her seat so she could look me straight in the eye.

"So did my father," she said.

From the sound of her voice, I guessed it took a lot for her to tell me that. It took a lot more for me to keep from wrapping my arm around her shoulder and hugging her to my chest, but Erica wasn't looking for comfort.

"Your father knew Vicki Walsh?" I asked.

"He came to the tournaments. He would joke around with my friends, with the other girls."

"He joked around with Vicki?"

"Yes."

"Why are you telling me this?"

"It's because of Vicki that my father is in trouble, isn't it?"

"What makes you say so?"

"The last time I saw Vicki was at the University of Minnesota in late June. We were working out with the college guys. They let us do that. Fencing is a big club, like I said. Anyway, she seemed kind of tense during practice; what's the word—preoccupied. That wasn't like her. I thought she was in trouble."

"Pregnant?"

"Why do people do that? If a girl seems depressed, the first thing they think is that she's pregnant?"

"It happens even in the best families."

"No, not pregnant—but something. Anyway, she asked if I had plans for the Fourth of July. I said a bunch of us were going down to Harriet Island for Taste of Minnesota, listen to some free music and watch the fireworks. I said she should come with us. She said she couldn't because she was going up to Canada. I said where in Canada, thinking it might be Toronto, which is like my favorite city in the whole world. I know a great French restaurant in Toronto. Only she said she was going to Thunder Bay."

Erica paused to stare at Vicki's photo some more.

"That was the last time I saw her," she said. "I figured Vicki went off to Cornell like she said. We weren't close friends or anything. She didn't owe me a good-bye. I wrote on her Facebook wall, but she never got back to me. I thought she was so busy in college that she didn't do Facebook anymore. That's okay. Like I said, it's not like we were close friends. I didn't think anymore about her until . . ."

"Until your father mentioned that he was having problems."

"He said he got into a little trouble up in Thunder Bay during the Fourth of July weekend. A very wise man once told me that he didn't believe in coincidences."

"That would be me."

"That would be you. Is my father in trouble because of Vicki?"

"Yes, I think he is. I just don't know how much trouble."

"Enough that people are shooting at you?"

"That might be completely unrelated to this."

"Are you saying it's a coincidence?"

"I'm saying . . . I don't know what I'm saying."

"Will you still help my father, McKenzie? Will you please, even after what happened?"

"I'll try, Erica."

"I've always liked that you call me that. Rickie is a child's name, and I'm not a child anymore. My mom, my dad, my oldest friends, they've known me since I was a child, so I pretty much have to take it from them. Only you've never treated me like a child. To you I was always Erica. You don't know how much that's meant to me."

Nina called from the kitchen.

"Are you two done conspiring? Is it okay for me to come back into the room?"

Erica closed the laptop and stood.

"It's all right, Mom," she said.

Nina entered the room empty-handed.

"Where's the iced tea?" I asked.

She was looking at her daughter when she said, "I must have forgotten."

"I'm sorry, Mom," Erica said. "Sorry to keep things from you. I made promises I shouldn't have made."

"What can you do? He's your father."

Erica walked to her mother and hugged her with one arm while keeping the laptop pressed to her side with the other.

"What's this for?" Nina asked.

"Nothing," Erica said. "Nothing at all."

She spun around and headed for the stairs. She called to me as she climbed them.

"You know, McKenzie," Erica said, "I didn't get a choice of parents. I don't know if I would have changed anything if I had."

When she was out of sight, Nina said, "What did you and Rickie talk about?"

"Honestly, Nina," I said, "you should stop calling her that."

I hadn't planned on punching Jason Truhler; hadn't considered it once during the sixty minutes it took to drive from Mahtomedi, the suburb northeast of St. Paul where Nina lived, to Eden Prairie, the suburb southwest of Minneapolis where Truhler lived. Yet when he opened the door to his town house, looked at me with a mystified expression on his face, and said, "McKenzie, what the hell do you want at this time of night?" I lost it. Granted, in Minnesota it's considered extremely discourteous to call or visit after 10:00 P.M. On the other hand, I had nearly taken a bullet for this lying bastard. So I drove my fist into his midsection just above the cloth belt keeping his robe closed.

The force of the blow drove Truhler three steps backward and down onto the carpet, his knees drawn up, his hands clutching his stomach. I entered the town house, closing the door behind me.

"What . . . what . . . ?" Truhler coughed and gasped for air. For a moment I thought he might vomit. "It's not . . . it's not . . ."

"It's not what?" I asked.

I caught movement in front of me. I looked up just as the girl started to scream. She was standing under the arch that led to a darkened corridor, wearing only pearls around her neck and high heels on her feet. She looked like she'd started high school last week.

Truhler rolled to his knees and slowly stood up, using an outstretched hand for support. I noticed for the first time that he was naked beneath his robe.

"Oh, for God's sake," I said.

"It's okay . . . okay," Truhler said. He moved toward the girl. "Don't, don't . . . be frightened. It's just a minor misunderstanding."

The girl must have believed him, because she soon stopped screaming and started to giggle instead.

"I thought you were just showing off when you said you were involved with dangerous people," she said.

Dangerous? my inner voice asked. *You got that right, honey.*

Truhler took a deep breath, regained some of his composure.

"Everything is fine now," he said. "Go back to bed."

"What about . . . ?" The girl gestured at me with her chin. At no time did she make an effort to cover herself.

"I know who he is. It'll be fine."

"He looks so mean . . ."

I do not. Do I?

"The scratches on his face."

Yeah, well . . .

"It'll be fine," Truhler said.

The girl giggled some more. I thought I saw her wink.

"Will he be staying?" she asked.

Truhler seemed annoyed by the question.

"No," he said. "He'll be leaving in a minute. Now go back to bed."

The girl was reluctant to leave, and Truhler had to take her elbow and escort her down the corridor and out of sight. Words were exchanged. The girl giggled again.

I sat on a plush sofa pushed against the wall. There was a glass coffee table in front of it. On the coffee table I found a razor blade, a short straw, and a small mirror. The mirror looked as if it had been licked clean. I pointed at the drug paraphernalia when Truhler returned to the living room.

"You're a cliché, you know that," I said. "How old is that girl, anyway?"

"She's legal," Truhler said.

"By legal do you mean she's eighteen?"

"What do you want, McKenzie?"

I had no intention of looking up at Truhler while we spoke.

"Sit down before I knock you down," I told him.

Truhler found a chair as far away from me as he could get and still be in the same room.

"What happened at the drop?" he asked.

"Besides getting shot at and having my car destroyed?"

I gave him the basics. When I finished, Truhler looked at the ceiling and sighed with the same dramatic flourish as he had in my kitchen.

"I take it you didn't get my money back," he said.

"Golly gee, Jason, I'm really sorry 'bout that."

"So why are you here?" he asked. "You could have told me all this over the phone."

"Does the name Vicki Walsh mean anything to you?"

"Oh."

"Oh. Did you think I wouldn't find out who she was?"

"I didn't think it mattered who she was."

"That's an interesting attitude to take. I'm sure the cops will be very impressed."

"I didn't kill her."

"You took her to Thunder Bay."

"Yes, but . . ."

"But what?"

Truhler glanced at the opening to the darkened corridor. He left his chair and moved to another, this one across the coffee table directly in front of me. He folded his hands in his lap, leaned toward me, and whispered. Guilty people do that. They whisper even when there's no one around to overhear.

"I didn't kill her, McKenzie. You've got to believe me."

"Why? Because you've been so truthful up until now? You made reservations at the Prince Arthur Hotel for two—in May."

"I took Vicki to Thunder Bay, I admit it, but I didn't know I was going to take her when I made the reservations. I didn't know who I was going to take."

"The blackmailers made their reservations four days after you did. They knew who you were going to take."

"McKenzie, I didn't tell you about hooking up with Vicki because I knew you wouldn't approve."

"She was your daughter's friend."

"See, I knew you'd react that way, a straitlaced guy like you. That's why I didn't tell you. Everything else happened exactly the way that I said it did, though. I woke up and she was dead. I know you think I'm lying, but it's true."

There's that tell again, my inner voice reminded me.

"You left her there," I said.

"What else was I going to do? It's not like we were a couple or anything."

"I got a long lecture from the cops today about doing the right thing. You should have heard it. It might have done you some good."

"C'mon, McKenzie. She was a tramp."

"She was eighteen years old."

"Yeah? So? McKenzie, Vicki wasn't some innocent kid that I seduced. You know how we hooked up? We hooked up on the Internet. I found her on a Web site for prostitutes that a friend told me about. I didn't even believe it was her when I first saw the picture. At the fencing tournaments, she always had her hair in a ponytail and she wore one of those white tunics, jackets, whatever they call it, no makeup. In the picture on the Web site, her blouse was open so you could see her tits, and her hair was down and her lips were red and—"

"What Web site? What are you talking about?"

"C'mere. Let me show you."

Truhler led me from his living room into a home office. He

had an L-shaped desk; an eMachine had been positioned on the base of the L. The power was on. Truhler called up a search engine and typed in an address. The page that popped up on the monitor displayed a shot of an attractive young woman; I would have placed her age at about sixteen. She had dark eyes and black hair that fell to her bare shoulders. There was something extraordinarily touching about her. Beneath her photo was an empty field labeled MEMBERS and another that read PASSWORD. That was it—no explanation of the site and no directions on how to become a member.

Truhler typed in his name—ColdWeatherFriend—and a password that appeared as bullet points. A moment later a new page filled the screen. This one had the title My Very First Time. Beneath it were photographs of twenty women displayed in a grid, four down, five across. Each of the women was identified by a first name only; all of them seemed impossibly young. They were posed provocatively, with shirts unbuttoned and skirts hiked to there, yet despite that they exhibited a kind of innocence that I found intriguing—a trick of the photographer's light, I decided. That opinion changed abruptly when Truhler moved the cursor to the woman called Tasha and clicked his mouse.

In attempting to define pornography, Supreme Court Justice Potter Stewart famously said, "I know it when I see it." Tasha's page left no doubt. There were a half dozen photographs of her, each of them more raw than the one before. A prop was placed in each photo to emphasize the woman's youth—a doll, a teddy bear, a plaid private school skirt, a canopied bed trimmed in pink. Yet any semblance of innocence was gone baby gone.

According to the copy beneath the photos, Tasha had earned a four-out-of-five-star rating from her clients. There was a navigation key that allowed viewers to read the woman's vital statistics, another that displayed comments posted by her clients, and still another that allowed clients to post a comment. Beneath that, there was a navigation key that read: ARRANGE TO MEET TASHA.

"Show me Vicki's page," I said.

Truhler leaned away from the computer screen.

"It's gone," he said. "They took it down a few weeks ago."

"Not after Thunder Bay?"

"No, but I checked a couple of times since I got back, and there didn't seem to be any activity. No new guys were posting comments after being with her."

"Tell me how this works."

"The Web site? Well, you just can't sign up, that's the first thing. You have to be recommended by a friend who'll vouch for you. Then the company checks you out to make sure you're not a cop, not a degenerate, and that you have money to pay before they give you a confidential membership name and a password."

"Apparently their definition of degenerate is different from mine."

"Are you going to judge me now?"

"They're kids, Truhler."

"They're not kids. They look like kids, but they're not. They're all older than eighteen. They're all adults."

"To a twelve-year-old eighteen might be an adult. Not to guys our age."

"The law says—"

I held up a hand to stop him.

"I don't want to hear it," I said. "I really don't. Just tell me who does the checking for this company, who's in charge."

"I don't know."

"What do you mean you don't know?"

"It's run by a woman. Her name is Roberta. She's about fifty years old. That's all I know. The company is very security conscious. Names aren't exchanged."

"You're saying they know who you are, but you don't know who they are."

"It's not important for me to know."

"Truhler, did it ever occur to you that these are the people who are blackmailing you?"

He shook his head as if the idea were just too outrageous to contemplate.

"They wouldn't jeopardize their business. They wouldn't kill their own employees," he said.

"First of all, their business is making money from shnooks like you. Second, Vicki Walsh isn't dead."

"What?" Truhler stood and stepped away from the desk. "What?"

"The stain on the carpet where she was supposedly killed was caused by theatrical blood—the stuff they use in slasher films."

"What? What?"

"You've been played, pal."

Truhler sat down again.

"I don't believe it," he said.

"Are you sure you can't identify your friends at—what is this Web site called, My Very First Time?"

He shook his head.

"Well, then you're screwed."

"Not if we can find Vicki. If we can find Vicki—"

"We?"

"McKenzie, you've got to help me."

"You keep telling me that."

"Please."

I didn't want to help Truhler, a man who abused children; the only people who should be involved with eighteen-year-old girls are eighteen-year-old boys. Erica—I figured it would crush her to learn about her father, only he was a jerk and she was going to find out sooner or later. Probably she knew already; she's the one who put me onto Vicki Walsh. Vicki; she looked so young, so sweet. A prostitute. A year older than Erica, she had to be nineteen by now, maybe twenty. She had to know what she was doing. My Very First Time, exploiting young women, pimping them to old men. Someone should do something about that. I could pick up a phone, give Bobby a call. An online prostitution ring, surely that constituted a major crime, right? And what about the guys who shot up my car, who nearly shot me? They didn't need to do that. That was unnecessary. Someone should do something about that, too.

Does it have to be me?

A man's got to do what a man's got to do.

"No, not this time," I said. "I've done my bit for God and country."

"McKenzie, please."

I left the office and headed for the door. Truhler followed, begging me to reconsider with each step.

"What am I going to do?" he asked.

"My advice, call the cops, call a lawyer. I know people. If you want a few names and phone numbers, I'll give them to you."

I opened the front door. Truhler grabbed my forearm. I shook it free.

"Rickie will be disappointed," Truhler said.

"Maybe so, but Erica will understand."

"What's that supposed to mean?"

"Jason," the girl called from the darkened corridor. "How long are you going to beeeeeeee?"

"Erica is more mature than most of the women you know," I said.

I turned and crossed the threshold into the cool night air. The girl's giggling followed me out the door.

It was eleven thirty by the time I reached my home in Falcon Heights. By midnight I was sitting in my favorite comfy chair and watching *SportsCenter* on ESPN, a bottle of Summit Ale at my elbow. At twelve forty-five my phone rang.

"McKenzie, it's Erica."

I felt a thrill of fear at the sound of her voice. The last time Erica called me in the middle of the night was never.

"What's wrong?" I asked.

Don't let it be Nina, don't let it be Nina, don't let it be Nina, my inner voice chanted.

"It's my father," she said.

NINE

Fairview Southdale Hospital in Edina was a half hour drive from Truhler's town house yet it was the nearest health-care facility with an emergency room, so that's where the paramedics took him. Nina and Erica were in the waiting room when I arrived. Nina looked angry, Erica looked frightened, and the young woman I had met earlier, she of the pearl necklace and high heels, looked like this was the best roller coaster ride she had ever been on. She giggled and waved when I entered the room.

"I know you," she said.

She started to stand. I pointed at the chair, and she settled back down again.

"I'll be right there," I said.

She smiled. I thought she might giggle some more. She covered her mouth with her hand, though, and made no sound.

Nina and Erica were sitting on the other side of the waiting room from the girl and watching intently. Nina crossed the room to meet me. I thought she might need a hug, so I opened my arms to her. Instead, she grabbed the lapel of my jacket and pulled me close. She spoke in an urgent whisper.

"Did you do this?"

"Did I do what?"

"Put Jason in the hospital?"

Another man might have been angry at the question; another might have been hurt. I was neither. Given our history together, and her certain knowledge of the sort of things that happen when I involve myself in other people's problems, I heard Nina's inquiry not as an accusation but merely a request for information.

"No," I said. "I did not. Of course I didn't." I spoke loudly enough for Erica to hear my answer. Afterward I dropped my voice so only Nina could hear. "Although the thought had crossed my mind."

Nina gestured toward the young woman who was watching us from a chair on the other side of the room.

"Who's your friend?" she asked. Her voice wasn't nearly as low as mine had been.

"We weren't formally introduced," I said. "I met her briefly at Jason's earlier."

"Another one of Jason's sluts. Why am I not surprised?"

"How long has she been here?"

"I don't know. She was sitting there when I arrived. The police were talking to her earlier, so I thought she might have something to do with Jason, but when I went to say hello she blew me off."

We made our way to the line of chairs positioned against the far wall where Erica was sitting.

"How are you doing, sweetie?" I asked her.

"What happened," Erica said.

"I don't know. I was going to ask you the same question."

"We got a call from the hospital," Nina said. "They said that Jason had been hurt. Apparently he listed me as his emergency contact."

"Was he badly hurt?" I asked.

"We don't know," Nina said.

"The woman at the desk said that a doctor would tell us in a few minutes," Erica said. "That was half an hour ago. She's been ignoring us ever since."

I glanced at the young woman. She was still wearing the pearls under a white shirt, but she had changed shoes. She looked like she wanted to come over and talk.

"Let me see what I can find out," I said.

I crossed the floor to where she was sitting.

"Hey," I said.

"Hi."

"We haven't been formally introduced."

I offered my hand, and she shook it without rising from her chair.

"I'm Caitlin," she told me. "Caitlin with a *C*. My friends call me Cait. That's also with a *C*. You're McKenzie."

"How long have you been here?"

"A couple of hours. I came in the ambulance with Jason. The lady you were talking to, is she the other woman?"

"I think you're the other woman."

"I'm not," Caitlin said. "Jason said there wasn't anyone else. If he was lying, that's not my fault, is it?"

"How old are you?"

"Does it matter?"

"Just curious."

"I turn twenty next January."

"Are you in school?"

She snickered as though she had never heard a sillier question.

"Jason isn't seeing anyone else that I know of," I said. "The woman"—I couldn't bring myself to use Nina's name—"is his ex-wife."

Caitlin thought about it for a moment.

"That's nice," she said, "that they can still be friends."

"Yeah, it's wonderful. Can you tell me what happened?"

"You mean after you left?"

"Yes."

She looked up at me and smiled. "I told the police—did I tell you that the cops questioned me?"

"What did you tell them?"

"After you left, Jason came back to the bedroom and said he wanted to do it again, and I said, 'Where's your friend?' because I was hoping you'd be joining us. I thought that would be fun, only Jason, he didn't like the idea at all, the three of us, and then someone was knocking on the door, and Jason was like, 'I wonder what that asshole McKenzie wants now.'" The girl put her hand over her mouth. "I shouldn't have said that."

"It's okay," I said.

"So Jason goes to the door, and I kinda follow him because I was hoping it was you, and Jason opened the door, only it wasn't you."

"Who was it?"

"I don't know. Two guys. I never heard any names."

"What did they look like?"

"They were icky. One was short and had long blond hair that looked like it needed a shampoo and a trim, and the other guy was tall and he had long brown hair that he had in a ponytail. They both had straggly beards, and they were both wearing leather biker jackets."

"What did they want?"

"I don't know. When I saw it wasn't you I went back to the bedroom."

"What happened next?"

"There was some shouting, and I heard Jason yelling, 'Don't kill me,' and I'm like whoa! I crept back down the corridor, and I saw Jason lying on the floor and the two biker dudes standing over him. One of them was holding a pipe, it looked like a pipe, and he was holding it—there was a handle, like one of those grips that they put on the handlebars of a bicycle. And his partner pointed me out and said, 'Whaddaya think?' I knew what he was thinking right away, so I ran back down the corridor to the bathroom to lock myself in, except I stopped in the bedroom for my cell phone first and I called the cops, only the two guys, they never did anything to me, they just left."

"Then what?"

"I stayed on the phone like the woman said, the woman at nine-one-one. She was really nice. I stayed on the phone until the police came, and then I answered their questions and got dressed and came on the ambulance here to the emergency room with Jason. I didn't think it would be right to just leave him, you know? So I came here and talked to the cops some more, and now I guess I'm just waiting to see if he's okay. You know, Jason said he was involved with dangerous people, but I thought he was just trying to impress me. Did I tell you that before?"

"Yes."

"I thought I did."

I took her hand and gave it a pat.

"It was good of you to stay with Jason," I said. "It was a classy move."

"You really think?"

"I do."

She giggled as I patted her hand again.

I recrossed the waiting room and sat next to Erica. Nina was in the chair on the opposite side of her daughter.

"What did she have to say?" Nina asked.

"Her name is Caitlin," I said. "With a *C*."

"And?"

"Someone attacked Jason in his home; she doesn't know why. She called the police and got Jason to the hospital."

"How virtuous of her."

"I thought so."

If our conversation had any effect on Erica, she kept it to herself.

We sat, without speaking, for another half hour. Finally a doctor wearing blue scrubs beneath a white lab coat stepped into the room, a chart in his hand. He read from the chart as if he were calling passengers to a waiting bus.

"Truhler?" he asked.

"Yes," Nina said.

The doctor couldn't be bothered to move to where we were

sitting, or to even meet us halfway. Instead, he waited for us to join him. He spoke to Nina.

"You're Mrs. Truhler?"

Nina didn't bother to correct his misassumption.

"Yes," she said.

"Your husband suffered a concussion," the doctor said. "However, a CAT scan indicated no swelling of the brain or bleeding. There is no apparent memory loss or confusion. His vision, hearing, balance, coordination, and reflexes seem normal. We will keep him twenty-four hours for observation."

"Is he going to be all right?" Erica asked.

"I believe that is what I just said."

The doctor turned to walk away.

"Wait a minute," I said.

He stopped, but he wasn't happy about it.

"Your shitty bedside manner aside," I said, "can we see him?"

The doctor shrugged away the question. "Talk to the nurse," he said.

As he walked down the hospital corridor, a man dressed in a black sports coat brushed past him. The jacket bulged beneath his left armpit where he carried his gun.

"I'll be dammed," he said. "Rushmore McKenzie."

I stared into his face, trying to place him.

"John Brehmer," he said. He offered his hand. "When we met a few years ago, I was a deputy with the Carver County Sheriff's Department."

"That's right." I shook his hand. "Deputy Sergeant Brehmer. I remember. You helped me out. I never did thank you. Sorry about that."

"That's okay. I wasn't looking for thanks."

"You're with Eden Prairie now?"

"The criminal investigations unit. I made the move a couple years ago so I could work plainclothes. So tell me, what's your connection to all this?"

"Just a friend of the family."

"Yeah? What do you know about what happened tonight?"

I gestured toward Caitlin. She was standing near her chair, watching.

"Only what the girl told me," I said.

"Do you know the two men who assaulted Mr. Truhler?"

"Not at all."

The smile on Brehmer's face didn't shift so much as a centimeter. Yet I knew he didn't believe me.

"Ms."—he glanced at his notebook—"Ms. Brooks said you left just before the two suspects arrived."

"That's true."

"Did you see them when you left?"

"No."

"See any vehicles lingering in the vicinity?"

"No."

"Do you have any idea who they could be?"

"No."

"Mr. Truhler didn't mention that he was expecting guests?"

"No."

"How about you, Mrs. Truhler?" Brehmer asked.

"I don't know anything about it," Nina said.

"Do you know any of Mr. Truhler's associates?"

"Jason and I don't live together," Nina said. "We've been divorced for eighteen years. I've spoken to him just once in the past twelve months."

Eighteen years, my inner voice said. *That meant Jason divorced Nina while she was pregnant with his daughter. Or maybe it was Nina who did the divorcing. You really ought to get your facts straight.*

"I don't even know why we were called here," Nina added.

Brehmer didn't attempt to venture a theory. Good for him, I told myself. A cop needs to garner as much information from the family as possible, yet he doesn't want to get involved with the family. There is nothing more dangerous than a domestic dispute.

"Did you interview Jason?" I asked.

"Just finished," Brehmer said.

"What did he say?"

Brehmer held up his notebook for me to read. The page was empty.

"Apparently no one came to Truhler's door and no one assaulted him," Brehmer said. "It's all been just one terrible misunderstanding."

"I've come across misunderstandings like that myself over the years," I said.

"Except they're never really misunderstandings, are they? What's going on, McKenzie?"

"I don't know, John. I really don't."

Throughout the conversation, Erica had remained a silent bystander. Now she spoke up.

"Excuse me, Officer," she said. "Do you believe we had anything to do with the attack on my father?"

"I have no evidence to suggest that."

"Then please get out of the way."

Brehmer gave Erica a hard look, but she held her ground.

He switched his gaze to Caitlin, and she took a step backward. His eyes came back to me.

"You owe me one," he said.

"I know I do."

"I'll be in touch."

My inner voice spoke to me as I watched him heading for the exit.

You did it again, it said. *You lied to a cop, lied to his face, without thought, without hesitation—the second time within twenty-four hours.*

Nina and Erica headed down the corridor toward the room where Jason was being treated after assuring the woman at the desk that they were, in fact, family. I excused myself and went to where Caitlin Brooks was standing.

"I didn't want to intrude," she said. "I have to know, though. Is Jason all right?"

"He suffered a concussion."

"Oh my God." Caitlin's hand came to her mouth. "That's really serious."

"Not necessarily."

I must have had three concussions in the past couple of years, and they haven't done me any harm. At least none that I'm aware of.

"Apparently it was a minor concussion," I said. "The docs say Jason'll be fine. They're just keeping him overnight as a precaution."

"Can I see him, do you think?"

"You'll probably be better off coming back in the morning."

"Because of what's-her-name, the lady?"

"That's one reason. Listen, do you have a ride?"

"I can call somebody."

I glanced at my watch. It was past two thirty. I pulled a wad of cash from my pocket and peeled off two fifty-dollar bills.

"Here, Cait, why don't you take this and get a cab home. It'll be easier."

Caitlin took the bills.

"What do you want for it?" she asked.

"What do you mean?"

"I mean what do you want me to do for the money?"

"Nothing. Nothing at all."

She looked from the bills to me, back to the bills, and then to me again.

"Amazing," she said.

Jason was sitting up in bed and smiling at Erica, who was holding his hand, and Nina, who was standing at the foot of his bed.

"My best girls," he said. Nina looked like she didn't care for the label; Erica didn't seem to mind at all. "And McKenzie, too," he added, when he saw me enter his room.

"You and I need to have a conversation," I said.

"Not now, McKenzie." Truhler touched his forehead. "I have a terrible headache." He touched his stomach. "I have some nausea, too. The docs said to watch for nausea." He put his hands behind his head and settled against the pillow. "Besides, it's so late."

"Now," I said.

"It is awfully late," Erica said.

"Sweetie, I need five minutes to speak to your father. Alone."

I didn't say "Now." She heard it just the same. Erica kissed her father's cheek and said she'd be back to see him in the morning. Nina followed Erica out of the room. She never said a word.

"What do you want, McKenzie?"

There was a clip resembling a clothespin attached to Truhler's index finger. A thin cord ran from the clip to a monitor that flashed his heart rate—71 beats per minute. When I approached the bed, the number increased to 74.

"Let's talk about the men who hit you upside the head," I said.

"I never saw them."

I pointed my finger at him like a gun. His heart rate jumped to 80.

"Don't even think of lying to me again, you sonuvabitch," I said. "The guys who hit you are the same ones that jumped me at Rickie's. Probably they're the ones who tried to shoot me out on Highway 61, too, so you better start talking and you better talk fast."

"Don't yell at me, McKenzie. This isn't my fault. It's your fault. It's your fault for flushing the coke. If you had turned it in like a good little citizen, none of this would have happened. Now they think you stole it; they think I'm in on it. They saw you leaving my house."

"Who are they?"

"My suppliers, I guess you'd call them."

"You're dealing coke?"

"I'm not dealing." Truhler's heart monitor hit 84. "I wouldn't call it dealing."

"What would you call it?"

"I give most of it away. I give some to friends, but mostly I give it to business associates, to clients."

"You give it away?"

"You have no idea how business works these days."

"What are we talking about? A dozen grams a week?"

"Something like that. Maybe two dozen. Maybe a little more."

"You're a fucking ounce dealer."

"Dammit, McKenzie. I'm not a dealer. I'm not making any money from it, if that's what you think. Whenever I charge anybody, I only charge what it costs me. Eighty dollars a gram."

The heart monitor flashed 88.

"All right," I said. "Take it easy. Relax."

Truhler's heart rate slowly dropped to 78.

"Tell me about the two guys who attacked us," I said. "Why did they conceal the coke on my car?"

"I'm really sorry about that, McKenzie."

"I bet you are."

"I am. I am sorry. What happened, they were my suppliers, like I said. Only because of the blackmail I was paying, I ran short of cash. I couldn't pay them for the coke. They said maybe they could work something out, like if I arranged to transport the coke across the border for them, they'd give me a piece."

"You sent me to Thunder Bay to mule your shit?"

His heart rate increased again.

"The blackmail thing is real," Truhler said. "It is. When you said you were going up there, though . . ."

"You thought you'd take advantage of the situation," I said.

"I thought it was harmless. You shouldn't have known anything about it."

"Unless I got busted at the border."

"I said I was sorry."

"Jeezus, Truhler."

I stepped away from the bed. Truhler's heart rate decreased.

"Tell me about these guys," I said. "Who are they?"

"Big Joe and Little Joe."

"Last names, please."

"That's how they were introduced to me—Big Joe and Little Joe. I don't know their last names."

"Who introduced you?"

"Roberta."

"Roberta? Roberta who runs the My Very First Time online prostitution ring, that Roberta?"

"Yes."

"Oh, this just keeps getting better and better."

"They used to drive the girls around, drop them off, pick them up; protect them, I guess. I found out they were dealing on the side, so . . . Roberta found out, too. She fired them. Roberta thinks drugs, that's trouble she doesn't need."

"Roberta is right."

"What are we going to do, McKenzie?"

"There's that we again."

"The Joes, they think we're in it together. They think we ripped them off. I told them what a Boy Scout you are, that it's all just a misunderstanding, only they don't believe it. They said they want their money or the dope. They said they'll be back. McKenzie, what if they—what if they go after Rickie or Nina next?"

I had to give Truhler credit. He knew exactly which of my buttons to push.

"Do they know about Erica and Nina? Did you tell them that you have a daughter and an ex-wife?"

"No, but . . ."

"But what?"

"They can find out, can't they?"

Yeah, they can.

"How do I contact these people?" I asked.

"I don't know."

"How did you get your girls? How did you get Vicki Walsh?"

"The only way is through the Internet, through my account, only they don't work for Roberta anymore."

"Did they say they would contact you again?"

"Well, yeah. Big Joe did. He said he'd let me think about what we had done for a while, then he'd come back. That was when he hit me with the pipe. 'Call it a convincer,' he said. He used those exact words; said it was in case I thought to try something smart. He didn't need to do that, McKenzie. He didn't need to hit me."

No, he didn't, my inner voice said. *Which means he probably wants to hit you, too, McKenzie. You shoved a gun in his face; you stomped on his knee. It's unlikely he'll accept an apology.*

"When he contacts you," I said, "tell him you'll pay the money. I figure the amount at thirty-five thousand. If he thinks it should be more, let me know."

"I don't have the money," Truhler said.

I didn't believe him. I said, "I'll pay the money," just the same.

"You will?" Truhler asked.

Hell no, my inner voice said.

"That should work," Truhler said. "What about Vicki? Oh, no, I just had a thought. What if they're working with Vicki?"

"We won't know until we find her. Until I find her."

"Thanks, McKenzie."

"One thing."

I moved to his bed and leaned in close. His heart monitor started racing.

"Listen to me," I said. "Listen to me very carefully. I'm going to say this slowly, so there's no confusion. If anything happens to Nina, if anything happens to Erica, if their hair is so much as mussed because of this bullshit, you are the one I'm going to take it out on. Understand?"

By the time I had finished, Truhler's heart was pumping over 90 beats a minute. An alarm rang, and a nurse dashed into the room.

"What's going on here?" she wanted to know.

If Truhler had an answer for her, I didn't wait to hear it. Instead, I brushed past the nurse and stepped into the corridor.

Nina and Erica were waiting for me. If they had heard any of my conversation with Truhler, they didn't show it. Erica crossed her arms when I approached.

"Don't you have school tomorrow?" I asked.

"I keep telling her," Nina said.

"I'm going to take the day off," Erica said. "I doubt I could concentrate properly anyway."

"Rickie . . ."

"I have a four-point-oh average, Mom. You don't think I can afford to take one lousy day off?"

"I could kill your father for getting you involved—"

"Yeah, yeah, yeah," Erica said. She stepped past her mother, effectively shutting her off. If she had been my daughter I would have called her out for her rude behavior, but she wasn't. In-

stead, I stood there, my feet apart, my shoulders squared, looking like a gunfighter waiting for his opponent to make a move.

"What are you going to do?" Erica asked.

"I don't know."

"You made me a promise. Are you going to keep it?"

"What promise?" Nina asked.

"He promised that he would help Daddy. Are you going to
help him, McKenzie?"

"I keep all my promises, Erica."

She stared at me for a few beats while her eyes welled up
with tears.

"My father doesn't," she said.

She turned and reached for her mother. Nina pulled Erica
close and hugged her fiercely.

TEN

I probably was the only person in the state of Minnesota who was happy that the temperature dipped to its November average—thirty-three degrees with a wind waffling down from the northwest to remind us that while the calendar might say it's fall, winter had begun. The chilly weather allowed me to conceal my Kevlar vest beneath a sweater. 'Course, the vest and the sweater—not to mention the distressed brown leather jacket that I wore to cover the 9 mm Beretta I had holstered just behind my right hip—made me look like the Before photo in a diet ad. Still, a man has to do what a man has to do.

Let's not go through that again, my inner voice said.

Yeah, okay, I told myself.

After getting dressed, I made sure the prepaid cell phone I bought at Best Buy was charged. I had my iPhone, of course. Yet while anyone could reach me on my home phone—it was listed in all the directories—only a precious few had my cell number; at least they were precious to me. There was no way I was going to give it out to the various miscreants I expected to encounter while I searched for Vicki Walsh, including Truhler.

Still, I used my landline when I made my first call. Nina answered on the fifth ring.

"Hello?" Her voice sounded blurry and faraway.

"Hey, it's McKenzie."

"McKenzie? Do you know what time it is? It's, it's— McKenzie, it's eight o'clock. Are you out of your mind?"

Nina owned a jazz club that closed at 1:00 A.M. Even on a trouble-free night it might be two or two thirty before she reached her home and usually an hour later before she crawled into bed. To her, 8:00 A.M. was the crack of dawn. Truth be told, I agreed with her. I'd probably still be in bed myself if not for the mobile alarm clock that I bought online. The clock was mounted on wheels. When I hit the snooze button it jumped off the table and rolled across the room. I had to get out of bed and chase it down in order to turn off the alarm.

"I'm sorry I woke you," I said. "Actually, I was looking for Erica. Did she go to school after all?"

"No. Just a sec."

I heard Nina set the phone down, and then I heard nothing for nearly three minutes. Finally Erica picked up the phone. She sounded as chipper as a songbird.

"Sorry if I woke you," I said.

"Oh, I've been up for hours. I usually get up at six so I can be at school by seven to practice music. I would have slept later, but my internal clock wouldn't let me."

"Why didn't you answer the phone, then?"

"I figured it was school wondering where I was. It's hard to pretend that you have a contagious, life-threatening disease when you're answering the telephone."

"Yet people do it all the time. Erica, I need a favor."

"Really? A favor from me?"

"Tell me how to gain access to Vicki Walsh's Facebook page."

"Why do you want to do that?"

"If I'm going to find her, I'll need clues."

"I could send you a link and a password."

"Please do."

I didn't need to give Erica my iPhone number or e-mail address. She was one of the precious few.

I dropped the prepaid in my jacket pocket and headed for the door. I opened it and looked around carefully before stepping out. Big Joe and Little Joe knew where I lived, and I didn't want to be surprised by them as I had been in the parking lot at Rickie's. I didn't particularly like slinking around my own house; still, a man has to do what a man has to do.

Really, my inner voice said. *Again?*

Despite what I promised Truhler, I had no intention of giving a couple of drug-dealing thugs thirty-five thousand dollars. So what if I could easily afford it? It wouldn't be enough to make them go away peacefully. Besides, there was a principle involved. Bobby Dunston had accused me of not always knowing where the line was, and maybe he had a point, but I certainly knew that paying off the Joes would put me on the wrong side of it.

On the other hand, I had no idea how else to deal with them. I couldn't prove that they planted dope on my car in Canada, that they broke into my garage, that they jumped me at Rickie's, or that they were the ones who shot up my Audi. At the same time, it was obvious that Truhler had no intention of bringing charges against them. He was either afraid or concerned that his own involvement in drugs would be discovered or he simply didn't want to lose his connection, take your pick. That left the cops out of it.

On yet another hand, I couldn't just sit back and wait for them to come after me, either.

What to do, what to do?

In the meantime . . .

It took nearly an hour to negotiate the morning rush hour traffic, not a pretty sight in the Twin Cities, working my way from Falcon Heights to the Eden Prairie Police Department. The department was located on the first floor of the Eden Prairie City Center, a building with all the charm of a dental clinic. Before going inside, I hid the Beretta under the seat of my Jeep Cherokee for fear it would cause a ruckus with the building's metal detectors. Besides, there was a sign attached to the front door—THE CITY OF EDEN PRAIRIE BANS GUNS FROM THESE PREMISES—and you know me, I'm not one to challenge authority.

The cop sitting behind the bulletproof glass partition gave me a hard look when I asked to see John Brehmer, maybe because I failed to say Officer Brehmer or Sergeant Brehmer or Detective Brehmer. I would have except I never did get his official title.

"Does he know what this is regarding?" he asked.

"Tell him it's McKenzie. He'll know."

The cop made a call. A couple of minutes later the secured door leading into the cop shop opened. Brehmer stood on the far side of the threshold, holding the door open and chuckling as if I were a sight gag in a TV sitcom.

"I'm surprised to see you, McKenzie," he said.

"I don't know why. It's like you said, I owe you one."

"Come on back."

Brehmer released the door after I passed him, and it shut of its own accord. I followed him to an island made from four desks shoved together. We found a couple of chairs.

"Seems you've put on weight since I saw you last night," he said.

"What can I say? I'm a glutton for mini-donuts."

"I thought it might be the body armor you're wearing. You are wearing body armor under that bulky sweater, aren't you?"

"You're a lot more observant than I remember."

"Talk to me, McKenzie."

"The two men who roughed up Jason Truhler last night, they're called Big Joe and Little Joe. I don't have last names."

"I know them."

"Yeah?"

"Couple of North Side asswipes who decided to export their bullshit to the suburbs—Big Joe Stippel, Little Joe Stippel."

"They have the same name?"

"They're brothers. Their old man thought he was quite the comedian; called himself True Joe Stippel. He named his eldest son Joe Two. The kid got whacked by some bikers during a drug deal gone sour a while back. The Joes had terrorized North Minneapolis for years. They were into everything—drugs, guns, armed robbery. Their biggest claim to fame, though, they had a real estate business, if you want to call it that. What they'd do, they'd force people out of their homes, buy the property cheap or acquire it through a quitclaim deed, no money changing hands at all, then resell it at a profit or, more often than not, burn it down for the insurance money. If you're dealing with them, you're smart to be wearing body armor."

"What are they doing in your jurisdiction?"

"According to my contacts, the Joes had partners, a couple of hard-core pyromaniacs named Backdraft and Bug, short for Firebug, who did all the heavy lifting. Apparently the Joes stiffed them on a job. Backdraft called them out in the parking lot of a bar, and True Joe beat him with a claw hammer and then he and his sons pissed on him. Backdraft was beat so badly that he couldn't feed himself anymore, couldn't dress himself. This didn't sit well with Bug, but before he could express his outrage, the MPD grabbed True Joe up for assault with arson as an aggravating factor. Apparently he attempted to cut out the middleman and set fire to a house while someone was inside it. The courts sentenced him to twenty-seven months in Oak Park Heights. He served three days before he was shanked.

"Meanwhile, True Joe's boys fortified their house with four-by-eight-foot steel sheets weighing five hundred pounds each so they could get a night's sleep. Two days after their old man bought it, someone tried to blow a hole through the armored house with C4. That's when his boys decided they needed a change of scenery. Unfortunately, they picked us. Do you know how Eden Prairie got its name? An East Coast writer, back in eighteen fifty-something, called it the garden spot of the territory. Get it? Garden of Eden? Hasn't been that for a long time. Could be, though, if we could get rid of pricks like the Joes."

"Maybe I can help," I said.

"I'm listening."

"The Joes are smuggling coke across the Canadian border.

Some of it was lost in transit. That's what prompted their dis-
agreement with Truhler."

"Truhler is dealing?" Brehmer asked.

"Let's say he is being forcefully encouraged to participate."

"Is that true?"

"It could be."

Brehmer studied me carefully.

"Are you here to make a deal for Truhler?" he asked.

"I am not authorized to do so, but here's the thing, John—I
might be able to get Truhler to come forward if someone else
came forward with him."

Liar, liar, pants on fire, my inner voice said.

Brehmer studied me some more.

"Whom do you have in mind?" he asked.

"Caitlin Brooks," I said. "She was there when Truhler was
attacked. She can identify the Joes."

"Why would she?"

"Caitlin is a working girl."

"That's my impression as well."

"Perhaps we can offer her an incentive."

Brehmer clucked at the idea.

"If the Joes have any gifts at all, it's in witness intimida-
tion," he said. "Last March, Big Joe knifed a gangbanger in
the parking lot of the Eden Prairie Center. There were twenty
witnesses. None of them came forward, including the guy
who got knifed. There's a reason for that. Three months earlier they robbed a Christmas drug party, got away with prod-
uct and cash. Afterward they went to the homes of each and
every one of the witnesses; showed up in the middle of the
night and threatened to kill anyone who talked and their

families. What could I possibly offer a little girl in return for standing up to that? A walk on a ninety-day misdemeanor? C'mon."

"I might be able to convince her."

Brehmer smiled and nodded his head. "Okay," he said. "Now I get it. Now I understand. You didn't come here to deal for Truhler. You came to get the girl's address."

"Yeah," I said. I saw no reason to lie to Brehmer any further— he saw right through me. "Are you going to give it up?"

Brehmer considered the question for a moment.

"Yes," he said. "Do you want to know why? Because as far as Eden Prairie is concerned, no crime has been committed, not by the Joes, not by Truhler, certainly not by Caitlin. There's nothing I can do but sit here and twiddle my thumbs, and I hate that, hate not being able to put away pricks like the Joes. You, on the other hand, have a knack for disrupting the status quo, and like the man once said, in confusion there is opportunity. Just remember, you owe me."

Caitlin Brooks lived in a tastefully decorated two-thousand-dollar-a-month apartment less than five minutes away from the Eden Prairie cop shop. She greeted me at the door wearing a pink sweatsuit that made her look so young I nearly asked for her mother. I told her so when she let me in.

"That's my fortune," she said. She spoke with her mouth full of English muffin smeared with grape jelly. "Looking young enough that old men can pretend they're screwing their grandchildren. It's why I get top dollar. Do you want some breakfast?"

I thanked her for the offer but declined.

"I'm sorry I look like crap," she said. "I was just about to go for a run."

I told her that she looked just fine.

"You're a nice man," she said. "Your face looks much better. Can't hardly see any scratches."

I thanked her for noticing.

"So, why are you here, McKenzie? Change your mind about the hundred dollars? Want to get your money's worth?"

"Caitlin with a *C*," I said. She smiled broadly. "I need your help."

Caitlin circled a glass coffee table and sat on a sofa that looked like it cost as much as her monthly rent, tucking her feet beneath her. There was a copy of Brian Freeman's latest thriller on top of the table.

"I bet it's the Joes," she said.

"You knew who they were when they came to Truhler's last night," I said.

"Oh sure. A couple of psychos. They used to work for Roberta until she discovered that they were scaring the clientele. Didn't help that they were dealing drugs, either. Roberta hates drugs."

"Why didn't you tell the police who they were?"

"I didn't think Jason would like that. I know Roberta wouldn't have. It's one of her rules—no police intervention."

"Roberta is your employer?"

"She's more like a facilitator. She puts people together, kinda like a matchmaker."

"For how much?"

"A third."

"That seems like a lot."

"No, it's fair," Caitlin said. "She runs the Web site, screens the clients, collects the money. That limits our exposure, you know? If no cash changes hands, then the cops can't call it solicitation, can they? They have to call it voluntary relationships. Plus, she takes care of us, protects us, makes sure we have health care, that we're always being checked for STDs. I have no complaints."

"How long have you been working for her?"

"Since the day after my eighteenth birthday. That's another one of Roberta's rules. All the girls, we might look like kids, but no one works for her who isn't at least eighteen. I had to show her my birth certificate. It's about the law, I guess. Soliciting for prostitution of a minor is serious business. You can go to jail for twenty years. For someone who's not a minor, eighteen or over, a good lawyer can get that down to a gross misdemeanor, and Roberta has good lawyers."

I bet, my inner voice said.

"Where did you meet her?" I asked aloud.

"Mall of America. I was sitting there by myself, being angry at the world, I don't even remember why, and she sat down and started talking, made me laugh. If she had been a guy I would have bolted right away because that's what they do, guys, they cheer you up, they schmooze you, tell you how misunderstood you are, how beautiful you are, they buy you clothes, dinner. Pretty soon they love you, they need you, they can't live without you. Next thing you know, they're turning you out because they need this, they need that, and only you can help them. You end up doing lousy twenty-dollar tricks in an alley somewhere."

"How is Roberta different from them?"

"With Roberta I can get anywhere from six thousand to

seventy-two hundred a week depending on how many dates I go on, and I keep two-thirds. With some pimp, I might not be able to keep any. Plus, I've been in the nicest hotels and some of the nicest homes in Minnesota, once even on a yacht on Lake Minnetonka. She makes it clear anytime you want to call it quits, just let her know and she'll take you off the Web site, no questions asked. In fact, she's always telling us, save your money, have a plan, go to school, start a business, get married cuz you can't do this forever. Like I said, I've got no complaints."

"If you don't mind the work," I said.

"It's not so bad. For a while I thought I might give adult films a try, but that's brutal. There's no money in it anymore. You can't make a living because of all the amateur stuff on the Internet, all the pirating. They pay what? A thousand to eighteen hundred a sex scene, yet you only get a couple of scenes in a film and only a couple of films a month, if you're lucky. You don't get to say who you'll have sex with, either. This is much better. With Roberta I make four thousand dollars for fifteen hours of work and I don't have to sleep with anyone I don't want to. You know, it's funny they call it that—sleeping. No one ever sleeps. Not ever. That's not the information you wanted to know, though, is it? You want to know about the Joes."

"I want to know about Vicki Walsh."

Caitlin flinched.

"Vicki," she said. "How do you know Vicki?"

"I don't. I want to, though. You seem surprised."

"It's just that, Vicki Walsh, that's a name out of the past."

"You know her?"

"Well, sure. She was one of the girls, for a couple of months, anyway. I didn't know her well. I don't know any of the girls well. We worked a couple of parties together in June, though. She seemed nice."

"What happened to her?"

"She quit. She had a gig somewhere up in Canada, and when she came back she quit. That's what Roberta said. I hadn't actually seen her since just before she left. Sometime before the Fourth of July. I know Roberta was upset. She liked Vicki a lot. At least that's the impression I got. I know she kept Vicki's profile up on the Web site a lot longer than she had for anyone else who retired."

"That's surprising, isn't it? That Vicki would retire so soon?"

"It's not for everyone, what we do," Caitlin said. "This is a choice for us. The prostitutes who work the streets, most of them are being forced into it, you know? Some guy is making them do it, or they need money for drugs, or whatever. It's a bad situation. It's not the same with call girls—I suppose that's the category you'd put us in. People say we're being exploited, but call girls are partners in the exploitation. It's just a way for us to make a lot of money in a hurry. In olden days they called us courtesans, and no one thought it was particularly immoral. Madame de Pompadour was a courtesan, you know. So was Theodora, who was empress of the Byzantine Empire. There's this economics professor at the University of Chicago who said hiring call girls is like renting trophy wives by the hour. That's no different than what Louis the Fifteenth did, or Justinian the First."

"I'm impressed by your grasp of history," I said. I meant it as a compliment, only Caitlin didn't take it that way.

"I don't go to college, okay? That doesn't mean I'm dumb." She pointed at Freeman's book. "I read." She took a deep breath.

"People judge. They think if you do what I do—I just got tired of believing the things they teach in high school. You know what I'm talking about, that through hard work and persever-ance you can become whatever you want. It's not true, you know. You don't believe me? Ask all the people who lost their jobs when the housing market collapsed and now can't get them back, the jobs they should have. The American Dream. It might be a dream for all those rich bastards who screwed up the economy in the first place, but for the rest of us . . . Anyway, you need to have the right mindset for what we do. I guess Vicki didn't have it."

Good for her, my inner voice said.

"Do you know where I can find her?" I asked.

"Vicki? Gosh no. I have no idea. Why are you looking for her?"

"It has something to do with Jason Truhler."

"That dweeb? You meet so many people in my business that are pretending to be something they're not. It's kinda sad."

"If you can't help me, I'd like to talk to Roberta."

Caitlin thought that was awfully funny. When she stopped laughing, she said, "No one talks to Roberta."

"Not even you?"

"Sometimes, when she calls me first. Otherwise, everything is done over the Internet."

"How do I get her e-mail address?"

"Do you have an account with My Very First Time?"

"No."

"Then you don't get her e-mail."

"You could help me."

Caitlin shook her head vigorously. "Nuh-uh," she said. "Not

about this, McKenzie. I could send her your name and number. If she calls you she calls you. I can't give out her e-mail, though. That's one of Roberta's rules."

Caitlin and I left the apartment building together. When we reached the front door she said, "You're a nice man, McKenzie. You can visit anytime."

Caitlin started jogging down the street. I watched her go while I made my way to the Cherokee. A horn sounded as a car passed her, and not because she was in the way.

It occurred to me once I climbed inside the SUV that it was possible Vicki took Roberta's advice. She could have gone to college. I used my iPhone to call Cornell University in Ithaca, New York. I told the admissions department that I was an employer checking on the job application of a young woman who claimed to be a student there. After a few minutes, an administrative assistant informed me that the enrollment application of a Vicki Walsh of St. Paul, Minnesota, had been accepted by the school last April and that Vicki indicated the same day that she would be attending classes in the fall. However, Cornell had not heard from her since. Vicki never completed the paperwork necessary to register, nor did she show up for the fall term.

"Ms. Walsh is not a student at Cornell University," the assistant said, "although she would be most welcome should she wish to begin classes in the spring."

Next, I called Johnson Senior High School in St. Paul, pretending to be a member of the admissions department at Cornell University. I explained that Ms. Walsh had been accepted by the school but hadn't showed up for the fall term. The university was attempting to contact Ms. Walsh to remind her that she was welcome to attend classes in the spring; however, the phone number she listed was not in service. The counselor supervising students with last names *U–Z* remembered Vicki— "a wonderful student with a great attitude," she said—and she was happy to help me out. She gave me both an address and a phone number. I called the number. I let it ring ten times before hanging up. I decided to drive out there.

Vicki's last known address was on a high hill above Seeger Square, on Greenbrier Street three blocks down from the John A. Johnson Elementary School. It made me aware that the locations for the money drop and the ambush were not chosen randomly. This was her ground.

I parked in the driveway between the Walsh residence and the house next door. The Walsh house was narrow and ugly; a two-story built in the early years of the previous century. It had been built to last like everything else in those days, yet the best intentions of the builders couldn't keep it from decaying along with the rest of the neighborhood. I walked across the tiny yard and up the six steps to the front porch. The floorboards creaked beneath my feet as I moved to the door. There was no bell. I knocked and waited. I knocked again. When no one came to the door I glanced at my watch. It was well past noon on a Thursday.

Some people work for a living, I reminded myself.

I left the porch, but before I could get to my Cherokee, a car pulled to a stop in front of the house. A woman got out. She stared at me across the roof of the car. I gauged her age at about forty-five, an overly plump woman with a blond dye job and skin that, at this time of year in Minnesota, suggested she was a frequent patron of the tanning salons. She didn't ask who I was. Instead, she demanded, "What do you want?"

"Mrs. Walsh?" I asked.

She ducked into the car and quickly emerged with two large white plastic shopping bags with bright red circles printed on the sides. She walked past without looking at me.

"Walsh is my ex-husband's name," she said. "My name is Clementine Lollie. If you want Tim, he's not here. He hasn't been here for years."

I followed Clementine onto her porch. When she fumbled with her door key, I said, "Let me get these for you," and took the bags from her hands. She stared at me for a moment as if she had never seen an act of consideration before. She opened the door, reclaimed her bags, and said, "Wait here." I half expected her to slam the door in my face. She didn't. Instead, she emerged from the house a few minutes later, locking the door behind her.

"The house is a mess," she said. "Besides, I have to get back to work." Clementine moved to the railing of the porch and rested her thigh against it. "What can I do for you, Mr. . . . ?"

"McKenzie," I said.

"What can I do for you, Mr. McKenzie? If it's about that asshole Tim, I haven't seen or spoken to him in almost fourteen years."

"I'm looking for Vicki Walsh."

"You're in luck, McKenzie. I haven't seen or spoken to Vicki since the Fourth of July."

"Do you know where she is?"

"Nope. She packed her bags, said she was going to Canada, and left. Haven't seen her since."

"She just disappeared?"

"Yep."

"You didn't call the police?" I knew she hadn't or I would have seen the missing persons report, yet I needed to ask.

"She was eighteen and graduated from high school. I no longer had any legal obligations toward her. That was the only reason she stayed with me once she got out of the hospital anyway. Legal obligations. So the hell with it. If she doesn't want to stay here with me, good riddance. Besides, it's not like we were close or anything. We barely spoke to each other after she seduced my husband."

"Vicki seduced her father?"

"No, no, hell no. Even she wasn't that depraved. No, her father, Tim, he's been gone forever. Carson Lollie was my second husband, Vicki's stepfather."

"You're saying that Vicki seduced her stepfather?"

"Came on to him like gangbusters. Carson never had a chance. Once I found out, I couldn't stay married to him, of course not, I mean . . . well, how could I? Had to divorce him. Now look at me. Look at where I live."

"You blame Vicki?"

"That little slut, yeah, I blame her. She's the reason I got no one to love me now. No one except bastards who want you to suck 'em off, who want to dominate you, degrade you, make you into something they'd just as readily piss on. The guys I meet, all they want is a hole to masturbate in."

"Mrs. Lollie . . ."

"I'll tell you the last thing Vicki said, her parting words as she's marching out the front door. She said she was tired of getting pushed around. From now on she was going to do the pushing. Well, good fucking luck with that. You know what? I haven't got time for this. I need to get back to work."

Clementine moved quickly off the porch and across her tiny yard. She didn't look at me again until she opened her car door, and then only for a moment before getting behind the wheel and driving off.

ELEVEN

I sat in my SUV in Clementine's driveway and worked my iPhone. As promised, Erica had sent me a link and a password, plus instructions that even someone as technologically challenged as myself could follow, all of which gave me access to Vicki's Facebook page.

It used to be, and not long ago, that you needed smart, focused Web surfing to find out what you wanted to know about a target. You had to have an aptitude for accessing both public and private records—court, motor vehicle, property taxes, health care, credit history, Social Security, and so much more. Now most of what you need to know can be found by hacking a target's Facebook page. People upload the most amazing information, everything from comprehensive résumés to explicit details about their most intimate relationships.

Something else—it's been my experience that 80 percent of what you want to know comes from human beings, not archives and databases. With Facebook you can uncover what targets have written about themselves; you can learn about their backgrounds, their personal histories, the people in their lives, and what's important to them, so when you do talk to them, you'll already know them. You'll be able to chat with them like you're old friends, like you already have a special relationship.

If that's not helpful enough, the target's Facebook page will also list an army of friends that can be ready and willing sources of intelligence. Take Vicki Walsh's page. She identified thirty-two friends—one of them was Erica. That number seemed awfully low to me. I've heard of some Facebookers who have literally thousands of friends. Personally, I don't believe it is possible to have thousands of friends. Or even thirty-two, for that matter, but that's another story. In any case, I was able to follow the chosen few on Vicki's page to their own pages, where I found their contact information.

The data Vicki supplied under INFO gave me an insight into her character:

Sex: *Female.*
City: *St. Paul.*
Hometown: *Ditto.*
Birthday: *April 23.*
Looking for: *Friendship.*
Relationship status: *It's complicated.*
Religion: *Infidel.*
Education: *Cornell University (in the fall); Johnson Senior High School.*
Activities: *Fencing, chess, and all things geek.*
Favorite music: *I like all music.*
Favorite TV: *Um, generally speaking, I don't watch TV*

(but then she listed twenty-two programs including
Star Trek—all incarnations, House, The Simpsons,
Glee, and Invader Zim, whatever the hell that was.

Favorite movies: *"Eternal Sunshine of the Spotless*
Mind," "The Princess Bride," "Spirited Away," and
the complete works of Hayao Miyazaki.

Favorite books: *She listed thirteen authors including*
Jane Austen, but no titles.

Favorite quotes: *"Forgiveness is the fragrance of the*
violet left on the heel that crushed it."—MARK TWAIN.

"You gain strength, courage and confidence by
every experience in which you really stop to look fear
in the face. You are able to say to yourself, 'I have
lived through this horror. I can take the next thing
that comes along.' You must do the thing you cannot
do"—ELEANOR ROOSEVELT.

She left Parents blank.

She also wrote, "I now present 21 random things you should
know about me:"

1. It's hard for me to talk about myself.
2. I have four piercings, two have healed over.
3. Pets I've owned include fish, hamsters, a parakeet,
   and a dog named Riley. They're all gone now.
4. I thought about being a veterinarian when I grow up.
5. I also considered being an architect, medical doctor,
   and writer.
6. I cry every day.
7. I also laugh every day.

8. I started reading to myself at age three because no one else would read to me.
9. I can't stand coffee unless there's chocolate in it.
10. I've never used illegal drugs, although plenty of people have offered them to me.
11. I have, however, used over two dozen different psychiatric medications.
12. I've never broken a bone.
13. is my lucky number.
14. The most challenging book I've ever read was "Les Miserables" by Victor Hugo. It took me a solid month, reading an hour or two a day after I did my homework.
15. I want kids, but at the same time I'm terrified that I'll raise them to be as screwed up as I am.
16. I like cherry Kool-Aid.
17. I've played violin, recorder, clarinet, flute, piano, and acoustic guitar, all of them badly.
18. I have a pathological fear of spoiled food. I can't eat leftovers that are more than a day old.
19. I've never met a man who didn't like me.
20. I've dyed my hair blue, blue-black, purple, green, and crayon red (which faded to orange). I decided my natural color is best.
21. I can change a flat tire.

I scrolled down Vicki's home page, reading all the postings. She seemed genuinely thrilled when Cornell University accepted her application in early April; she wrote that her hands were trembling when she replied by e-mail that she would enroll there in the fall. Her friends congratulated her profusely.

Denny Marcus wrote that they should take a road trip to Ithaca to scope out her new digs. Denny, as it turned out, was one of only two males included among Vicki's friends. The other was named Drew Hernick, and as far as I could tell, Vicki had exchanged no postings with him. However, she had exchanged more postings with Denny than with anyone else, male or female. In fact, her very last posting was to Denny. It was made July 2, just before she left for Canada.

According to Denny Marcus's INFO page, he was a freshman at Augsburg College in Minneapolis and worked part-time as a barista in a coffeehouse on East Franklin Avenue, not far from the campus. He even provided his work schedule. That's where I found him, working behind the counter. I recognized him from his photograph. He was three inches taller than I was and thirty pounds lighter. If you ever needed someone to sweep your chimney, he was your man.

"What can I gitcha?" he asked.

I looked up at the menu written in chalk on the blackboard behind the counter.

"What would Vicki have, I wonder?" I asked.

"Excuse me?"

"Vicki Walsh. She doesn't drink coffee unless there's chocolate in it, am I right? How 'bout a Café Mocha?"

He stared at me for a few beats before saying, "Would you like whipped cream with that?"

"Of course." I cringed even as I said it. There was a wonderful man who helped raise me named Mr. Mosley who would roll over in his grave if he saw me drink coffee with additives of any kind.

Denny made the drink and set it on the counter under the PICK UP sign.

"How do you know Vicki?" he asked.

"The question is, how do you know Vicki?"

He took my money and rang up the purchase. I dropped all of the change into the tip jar.

"We're friends," Denny said.

"Close friends?"

"Who are you?"

"My name is McKenzie."

"Why are you asking about Vicki?"

I lied. I said, "Her family asked me to help try to find her."

"I don't get it."

"Vicki's disappeared."

"What do you mean, disappeared?"

"No one has seen her since the Fourth of July."

"That's crazy."

"Do you know where she is?"

He thought about it before answering.

"Why would I?"

"You were close friends," I said.

"I suppose."

"More than close."

"What's that supposed to mean?"

"You were romantically involved, weren't you?"

Denny laughed out loud. "Don't you think it's possible for a man and a woman to be just friends without anything else between them?" he asked.

I thought about my own relationships.

"Not really," I said.

"Well, we were just friends."

"Friends with benefits?"

Denny laughed some more. "McKenzie," he said. "Did you say your name was McKenzie?"

I nodded.

"McKenzie, I'm gay."

Oops.

"Couldn't you tell?" he said.

I thought about a guy I played hockey with for thirty Friday nights out of the year every year since I graduated college who was gay and how everyone in the locker room seemed to know it but me until he put purple laces in his skates and I said, "Tommy, that is so gay," and he said, "What's your point?"

"No, I couldn't tell," I said.

"Then I must be doing it wrong," Denny said.

"When was the last time you saw Vicki?"

"Last summer."

"When?"

"July something. Look, McKenzie, if Vicki's disappeared"— he quoted the air—"it's because she wanted to disappear. Have you met her mother?"

"Yes."

"Well, then . . ."

"I just want to make sure she's all right."

Denny studied me carefully without speaking.

"Listen," I said.

"No, you listen. Vicki is fine. I got a text message from her yesterday. I got an e-mail the day before."

"Why doesn't she use Facebook?"

"She said Facebook is too consuming. She hasn't got time for it anymore."

"These messages you received, what did they say?"

"Having a wonderful time, wish you were here—whatever they said is none of your business."

"Where did she send them from? Where is she?"

"If it's so damn important, Vicki is in Ithaca, New York. She's attending Cornell University."

Either Denny Marcus was lying to me, or Vicki Walsh was lying to him. In any case, Vicki was not at Cornell. That had already been established. Cornell was where she told people she was so they wouldn't look for her.

I asked Denny to contact Vicki and have her call me. He said he would. I gave him the number of my prepaid cell; I watched him write it down. I didn't know if he would make the call, though, and if he did, if she would respond. Or even if she could respond. If Denny was lying to me—and why would he be different from everyone else—then it was entirely possible that Vicki really was dead but none of her friends noticed because they knew she was planning to leave.

I started working the index of BFFs that Vicki had posted on her Facebook page. Nearly all of them listed contact information. I sent e-mails to those who gave addresses. I told them I had been asked by the family to find Vicki—when I find a good lie I stick with it—and asked that they reply with whatever information they had. I called those who listed cell phone numbers, yet didn't get through to anyone, which surprised me. Isn't instant communication the whole point of cell phones? I left voice mails using the same lie, only shorter. Some cell phone users had taped messages that said they did not accept calls, that they preferred texts instead, which also surprised me—I just don't get out enough. So I texted them with an even shorter lie.

Staring at the tiny screen on the iPhone was starting to give me a headache. It became worse after I called Truhler. He didn't say hello when he answered. Instead, he said, "Rickie's here. Isn't that nice?"

"Just swell," I said. "Have you heard from our friends?"

"No, but . . ."

"But what?"

"You should know that I've been examined by a real doctor, not that nitwit who checked me in last night. The new doctor upgraded me to a Grade Two concussion, or maybe he downgraded me, I don't know which."

"What does that mean?"

"It means suddenly I'm having difficulty with my balance, I'm sensitive to light, I have blurred vision, they think I might have tinnitus, you know, ringing in my ears. They think I might have postconcussion syndrome. I might have headaches, fatigue, anxiety, irritability for weeks."

"What does that mean?" I asked yet again.

"It means I can't help you deal with the Joes," Truhler said. "I just can't. I'm not physically able. You'll have to do it alone."

"How convenient for you."

"You are going to pay them the money, right? You haven't changed your mind about that, right?"

"I'll do what I have to," I said. "Let me know when you hear from them. I'll give you my number." I recited the number for the prepaid cell phone, and Truhler wrote it down. At the same time my inner voice asked, *Why are you helping this guy? Why, why, why?*

"Do you want to talk to Rickie?" Truhler asked.

"Tell her I'll call later."

Thaddeus Coleman possessed more entrepreneurial spirit than anyone I had ever arrested. He never let a business setback get him down. When his face became so well known that store security guards would greet him by name, he gave up his shoplifting ring for girls, running a small but lucrative stable on University and Western. When gentrification and the subsequent increased police presence forced him out of the neighborhood, he switched to dealing drugs around Fuller-Farrington. When a trio of Red Dragons objected to the competition and put a couple of slugs into his spine, he moved to Minneapolis, where he started a surprisingly lucrative ticket-scalping operation. That's what he was doing when I entered his small office in a converted warehouse overlooking Target Field, where the Minnesota Twins now played baseball.

"Hey, Chopper."

"McKenzie, you sonuvabitch."

Coleman maneuvered his wheelchair from behind the desk and rolled out to greet me. He had earned the nickname Chopper because of the wheelchair, which he rode with the reckless abandon of a dirt-track biker. We engaged in an elaborate handshake dance that ended with me messing up.

"McKenzie, you so white," he said, which is what he always said to me. I was the one who scooped him off the pavement and got him the medical attention that saved his life. He's been a generous friend ever since, although he never did tell me what he knew about the three Red Dragons that we found executed near the St. Paul Vo-Tech a few days after he was discharged from the hospital.

"How's business?" I asked.

I found a chair in front of the desk while Chopper rolled back behind it. There was a PC on the blotter and a dozen more set up on tables against two walls. Chopper would have associates sitting at every terminal when tickets went on sale online for concerts and ball games all around the nation; sometimes he'd pay people to stand in line outside of ticket booths to buy rare small-venue events. He then sold the tickets at highly inflated prices through eBay and other outlets or directly to customers who were "in," like me.

"It's good," Chopper said. "It's all good. It's just—it's not as much fun as it used t' be, you know? 'Member when I used t' cruise up and down Target Center or the Ex in St. Paul, sellin' direct to customers—you want four, I got four—dodgin' the cops, maybe slippin' 'em a couple of Wild tickets to keep 'em from bustin' me? 'Member that? Now I sit here all day, payin' rent, keepin' books—I pay taxes, man. What is that? Not even called scalpin' no more. I'm a fuckin' broker."

"It's the state legislature's fault," I said. "It made an honest man of you."

"They shoulda never made scalpin' legal. Took all the fun out of it. You know the governor. How come you didn' help me out?"

"I know the governor's wife. It's not the same thing."

"Ahh, man. So wha' you doin' here, McKenzie? You sure ain't lookin' for tickets t' Smucker's Stars on Ice."

"I worry that you don't get out enough, Chopper. I thought

I'd buy you dinner. Chinese. I know how much you like the gai ding they serve at Shuang Cheng in Dinkytown."

"If you buyin' it's cuz you want somethin'."

"What a suspicious mind you have."

"I was watchin' the Discovery Channel—don' look at me that way. I was watchin' the Discovery Channel, and the guy says the definition of crazy is doin' the same thing over and over again but expectin' a different outcome."

"So?"

"So, if'n you invitin' me to dinner it's cuz you want somethin'. What?"

"Being that you're such an honest and upright tax-paying citizen, I realize that you're not wired the way you used to be."

Chopper gave me a grin and a head nod. We both knew that ticket scalping might be his daytime job, but Chopper had plenty of enterprises to occupy his evenings, including smuggling brand-name cigarettes from Kentucky and selling them to independent convenience stores, making a hefty profit by dodging the state's cigarette tax. He was better connected than an Apple computer.

"So you're wantin' intel," Chopper said.

"Yeah."

"You know, the cops, they pay their CIs."

"I offered you dinner."

"A ten-buck plate of spicy chicken almond ding."

"You want a combo platter? I'll spring for a combo platter."

"You so cheap, McKenzie. You got all that money, too. Jus' tell me what you wanna know."

"I need something on a couple of lowlifes named Big Joe and Little Joe Stippel."

"You fuckin' kiddin' me? The Joes? You messin' wit' the Joes?"

"You know them?"

"I know enough to stay away from 'em. Fuck, McKenzie."

"Where can I find them?"

"I don' know. I don' wanna know."

"Can you find out?" I could have asked John Brehmer, but I didn't want to go on record.

"I'd have t' be as crazy as you," Chopper said.

"Something else. Do you know a couple of firestarters named Backdraft and Bug?"

Chopper stared at me for a moment, his mouth open, before he started to laugh out loud.

"Gettin' kinda ambitious in your ol' age, ain'tcha? These are fuckin' bad people, McKenzie."

"I heard that the firestarters have a feud with the Joes. I'd like you to put the word out that I might be able to help them."

"Wha'?"

"The enemy of my enemy is my friend."

"See if I got this right. You goin' up again' the Joes and you're wantin' allies."

"Something like that."

"This is North Side shit, McKenzie. You don' want none of that. The cops these days, I don' know if it's cuz of budget cuts or what, but most cops they ride solo, you know? Watch 'em on the streets, it's one cop t' every car. Except on the North Side. They ride in pairs up there. What's that tell ya?"

"Can you help me or not?"

"You know I can, but McKenzie, I'd hate like hell t' see the expiration date on your milk carton run out."

"I appreciate that, Chopper."

He stared at me for a moment. I stared back.

"You want somethin' else, doncha?"

"If I wanted a young girl, who would I go see?" I said.

"Now you're just messin' with me."

"I would never do that."

"Wha' happened to that nice lady runs the jazz joint?"

"I'm not asking for myself."

"Tha's what they all say."

"Chopper . . ."

"Yeah, I'm jus' foolin'. Wha' you wanna know?"

"There's an upper-class operation calls itself My Very First Time, run by a woman called Roberta."

"Don' know nothin' 'bout that."

"Apparently they use the Internet."

"That ain't surprisin'. Whorehouses, the brothel, tha's long gone, man. Wha' you call a quaint anachronism. You still got hookers workin' outta bars, outta gyms, massage parlors that ain't been closed down, and out on the street corner, you're always gonna have that. More and more, though, they're usin' the Internet, includin' amateurs just lookin' for a thrill." Chopper stared menacingly at his PC. "Fuckin' computer takin' the fun outta everything."

"Anything you can get me, I'd appreciate it," I said. "If you want more than a free dinner, let me know."

Chopper smiled at me.

"Nah, no cash between us," he said. "I know that in your

world favors are coin of the realm. Let's just say you gonna owe me one."

Chopper smiled some more because he knew what I knew—owing him a favor was serious business.

It took a full half of an hour to drive my way out of downtown Minneapolis and across the river into St. Paul. I had a choice to make when I came to the I-94–Highway 280 interchange: Go home or go to Rickie's. I chose Rickie's, partly to proclaim my undying devotion to Nina and partly to mooch a free meal.

Five minutes later I took the Dale Street exit, coming to a stop at the top of the ramp. I was the fourth car from the traffic light. A shabbily dressed middle-aged man wearing glasses that were too big for his face approached each of the vehicles in front of me. He was holding up a handwritten sign—WILL WORK FOR FOOD. The way he looked into each driver's side window and then moved on, I guessed he wasn't having much luck. I powered down my window and reached into my pocket for cash. I was peeling off a twenty by the time he reached me.

"How you doin'?" I asked.

"Not bad, McKenzie," he said. "How 'bout you?"

I turned my head so quickly to look at him I nearly gave myself whiplash. I didn't know any homeless people, did I?

The man grinned broadly. His teeth were yellow, and his beard was three days old.

"Is that for me?" he asked.

He reached in and took the twenty from my hand. He stepped back and waved the bill triumphantly over his head for everyone else to see.

"You always were a generous guy, McKenzie," he said.

I couldn't help staring.

"Do I know you?" I asked.

He grinned some more and lifted his glasses so I could get an unimpeded look at his face.

"Ruben?" I asked. "Ruben Barany?" I had worked with him out of the Eastern District when I was with the police. He had five years on me, a good guy to go to for advice. "What the hell happened?"

"What do you mean?"

"What do you mean what do I mean? Will work for food? What happened to Patti, what happened to your pension?"

"Patti's good. I'll tell her you said hi."

"Ruben?"

"McKenzie?"

Ruben placed both hands on the windowsill of the Jeep Cherokee and leaned in.

"We're running a seat belt sting," he said. "Earning a little extra scratch for the state general fund. I think the law libraries get a cut, too."

"What are you talking about?"

"Cars come to a stop—we've been manipulating the traffic lights, by the way. Cars come to a stop, I look inside the waiting vehicles, identify the drivers who are in violation of the mandatory seat belt law, and alert officers down the road. We have Ramsey County and the State Patrol working with us."

"No way."

"The guys call me Homeless Harry."

"This is so wrong for so many reasons."

"It's pretty insensitive to the homeless, I admit. On the other hand, the state makes one hundred and eight bucks a citation and so far today we've written out a hundred and twelve. I'm happy to see you're wearing your belt, McKenzie."

"Sometimes I'm glad I'm not on the job anymore."

"I know what you mean. We'll be here all week. Be sure to tell your friends."

Ruben beat a rhythm on the roof of the Cherokee.

"Good to see ya, McKenzie," he said. "Don't be such a stranger."

He slapped the roof of the vehicle one last time and started walking back toward the corner. The traffic light turned green, and the cars ahead of me surged forward. I followed, calling out the window as I passed him.

"Hey, Ruben. What about my twenty?"

I had just completed dinner, for which I received no check yet left a tip equal to the price of the meal—curried chicken satay with fresh mint-soy vinaigrette. I took a great deal of pleasure from teasing Monica and had every intention of continuing to do so in the near future, but my God, the woman could cook, not that I would admit it to her.

Now I was sitting at the bar drinking Summit Ale and working my iPhone. If Denny Marcus had given Vicki Walsh my cell number as promised, she hadn't bothered to call it. I had received several replies from the e-mails and voice mail messages I had sent earlier to her friends yet learned nothing that I didn't already know. I was surprised that Vicki's friends had been so forthcoming. Only one person refused to answer my inquiries until I explained who I was and why I had contacted her. The question was, now what?

There's an art to finding a missing person, and as with most artistic endeavors, to do it well requires an enormous amount of effort. You start with the person herself, assembling every known fact about her from her style of dress to her hobbies and interests to her education to her spending habits to her employment record to her friends and family to her—well, you get the idea. The reason for all of this work was simple: People are creatures of habit. After spending a lifetime doing a specific thing in a specific way, it becomes extremely difficult if not impossible to change. It was her past that would lead me to Vicki, except that she was so young her past was not that deeply ingrained. Also, she had not been gone for so long that she might feel the need to reach out to someone she might have cared about, although apparently she had reached out to Denny Marcus.

Damn, this is going to be hard, my inner voice told me. *Maybe you should just wait until she demands more money from Truhler, only this time hire an army of investigators to help follow it.*

While I was thinking it over Nina joined me.

"Penny for your thoughts," she said.

"Nope. I need at least a nickel."

"You look tired."

"I am tired."

"Long day?"

"Very long."

"Your face looks much better."

"As compared to what?"

"This is turning into a scintillating conversation."

"Sorry. I'm just fried. I thought I'd give you a long, heartfelt kiss and then go home."

"Are you sure? Connie Evingson is singing tonight."

"She wasn't scheduled, was she?"

"No, but the trio that was scheduled was involved in a car wreck this morning outside Milwaukee. Connie graciously agreed to fill in."

"I've always liked Connie," I said.

"Just as long as you like her from afar," Nina said. She then batted her long eyelashes to tell me that she was kidding—sorta.

"I think I'll pass tonight," I said.

"You really are tired. I was thinking of coming over to your place after closing."

"I appreciate the thought, Nina, but you should probably stay away for a while. You and Erica. The guys who thumped Jason last night know where I live. I don't want you walking into harm's way."

"Jason knows who they are, doesn't he?"

"Of course he does."

"Why doesn't he tell the police?"

"It's a long story."

"I bet it isn't. I bet it's a very short story. Women."

"I hate keeping things from you," I said.

"As long as you don't make a habit of it."

I was thinking that I wasn't *that* tired after all when Monica came out of the kitchen wearing a white chef's jacket trimmed with red.

"McKenzie, you're just the person I want to talk to," she said.

"Uh-oh," Nina said.

"What?" I asked.

"Monica has been experimenting with donut recipes all day."

"How's that going?" I said.

"I am dissatisfied," Monica said.

"Want to pay me the fifty bucks now or later?"

"I haven't given up, McKenzie. I never give up. It's just that I have been unable to replicate the mouthfeel of these donuts of yours. The answer could be in the shortening, the temperature, baking time, or something in the batter itself."

I spread my hands wide and shrugged. "Yeah?"

"I want you to do me a favor," Monica said. "That's what you do, right? Favors?"

I answered slowly. "Yeah."

"I want you to get the answer for me," she said.

"The answer?"

"The recipe."

"How would I do that?"

"By any means necessary."

"Wait a minute. Are you asking me to go up to Grand Marais, break into World's Best Donuts, and *steal* their donut recipes?"

"If that's what it takes."

"Lady, I think you've had a little too much cough syrup, if you know what I'm saying."

"How hard can it be? I looked them up online. Their bakery looks like a shack."

I flashed on Bobby Dunston and the lecture he delivered the day before.

"Monica," I said, "no. Absolutely not. I mean, a guy's gotta draw the line somewhere."

TWELVE

I slept in the next morning and felt guilty about it, although I didn't know what else I should be doing. I saw Marvelous Margot through my kitchen window while I was making coffee. She was standing on her side of the pond and throwing dry corn to the ducks. She was wearing a gray hoodie with the emblem of the Minnesota Vikings on the front and blue shorts. She had terrific legs for a woman her age. 'Course, I never said that to her—woman your age, I mean. A couple of minutes later I walked a mug of coffee out to her. She drank greedily.

"How come your coffee is so much better than mine?" she asked.

"I have a seven-hundred-dollar coffeemaker."

"You and your gadgets. How long do you think the ducks will stay?"

"I spoke to my pal with the DNR," I said. "He said they'll stay until the weather changes."

"When is that going to be?"

"Hard to tell. It's an El Niño year. The central and eastern tropical Pacific waters become warmer, which translates into a warmer winter for the northern states."

"Why?"

"I have no idea, but for a second there it sounded like I knew what I was talking about, didn't it?"

"You should be very proud."

Margot drank more coffee.

"How's Erica?" she asked.

"Fine."

"Is she? The other day she seemed pretty upset about her father."

"What do you know about her father?"

"Only what Erica told me. She loves him; I don't suppose there's anything she can do about that. She doesn't like him, though, and she doesn't trust him."

"That has to be tough, having a father you don't like."

"Not everyone can have an old man like yours."

"He was an awfully good man, wasn't he?"

"He reminded me of my father. That's why I liked him so much. It's probably also why I divorced all my ex-husbands. They didn't remind me of Dad."

"You know, Margot, that might be a little unfair, insisting all these guys live up to your father."

"I don't think it's unfair to ask someone to be trustworthy, to be honest. Do you?"

"No, I guess not."

"You're a lot like your father, McKenzie."

"I wish."

"It's true."

"Except for the time he was with the First Marines in Korea, my father never purposely hurt anyone. Ever. Instead, he spent most of his life helping others. If you ever needed a favor, my dad was the guy you went to."

"That's you."

I slapped my chest with the flat of my hand.

"I'm wearing a bulletproof vest," I said. "Kevlar. I'm carrying a nine-millimeter handgun on my hip. The round under the hammer is alive."

"You're helping people, that's the main thing. You're just doing it a different way than your father."

"That's what I used to tell myself, Margot. Only the more I do it—I'm just not sure anymore."

Margot handed me the empty coffee mug and then gave me a hug, the coffee mug between us.

"I'm sure," she said.

Then again, she didn't know everything I knew.

Margot kissed my cheek.

"I'll see you later, McKenzie," she said.

As I watched her walk to the back door of her house, I heard my iPhone play "Summertime."

Steve Ritzer was sitting on the front steps of his mother's house when I drove up. He had a lighter in his weathered hands, one of those chrome pocket jobs that most smokers carried before plastic disposables became the rage. He opened the top and ran his thumb over the thumbwheel. The rough surface rubbed against the flint, creating a spark that ignited the fuel-saturated wick. He waited until the flame flared brightly before flicking his wrist to snap the top shut and extinguish the flame. He re-

186

peated the process over a dozen times while I watched from my Jeep Cherokee. Yet the show wasn't for my benefit. He was taunting the two plainclothes Minneapolis police officers that were sitting in an unmarked car across the street and three houses down and watching Bug intently.

I would have preferred that there be no witnesses to any conversation I had with Bug, but I hadn't noticed the cops until after I drove up, and by then it was too late. They were already running my plates. I could feel it.

I slid out of the Cherokee and approached Ritzer's home. There were iron bars and reinforced screens mounted over every window as well as the front door. A low cyclone fence surrounded the tiny yard. I stopped at the gate and called to him.

"Mr. Ritzer, may I have a word?"

When Chopper called me earlier, he made it clear—"Do not call the man Bug. He doesn't like it."

"Who you?" he asked.

"McKenzie."

"You Chopper's friend?"

"Yes."

He waved at me with the lighter to come ahead. I took a deep breath, pushed the gate open, and started moving across the crumbling concrete sidewalk toward him. I knew he was over sixty, but he looked twice as old. His clothes and hair were disheveled; his unshaved face carried the marks of a hundred street brawls; his breath reeked of stale beer. It was the eyes that got me, though. They were so hideously bloodshot they looked like they were bleeding. I felt better knowing that the cops were there.

Chopper was right, Bug was bad people. After he gave me

Ritzer's real name, I paid the extra bucks to have my sources with the MPD pull his jacket. I could have done it myself for a lot less money. An individual's record of arrests and contacts made by the Minneapolis Police Department can be purchased in person or by mail for twenty-five cents a page, five dollars for color booking photos. You don't even need to identify yourself. However, it would have taken a lot more time, and I'm impatient by nature. Plus, the report would have been incomplete.

Yes, it would have given me a list of "Documented Steven Ritzer Fires (suspicion or arrest)" with twenty-six entries, seven of them before I was born. It would have told me that at least one of the fires resulted in death—apparently a security guard who had been drinking on the job was unable to escape when the office building he was watching over went up. Yet it would not have told me that investigators had a more comprehensive list of a hundred and thirty-seven fires that they feel certain Ritzer started, based on MO, either alone or with his partner, Max Lucken. Nor would I have learned that investigators knew—*knew*—that the two men had been operating a profitable arson-for-hire business for decades. Or that Bug and Backdraft had admitted to being arsonists many times in the course of interrogations and taped telephone conversations with investigators, yet always without implicating themselves in any specific fire.

"Mr. Ritzer—"

Bug cut me off.

"You a white man, that's good," he said. "I figured you might be with a name like McKenzie. Only these days you can't ever be sure. 'Specially since you're a friend of Chopper's. Bad enough you got the Nig-rows and Messicans taking over every-thing without them taking our names, too."

He lit the lighter, flicked it shut, and lit it again.

"You know, Mr. Ritzer," I said, "there are cops down the street."

"Shit yeah, I know. Why you think I'm doing this for, my health? Giving the ball-yankers something to think about is all."

He smiled at me.

"It's nothing," he said. "We're all friends here, me and the pigs. Sometimes I think they're my only friends now that Maxie is—is—they fucking took a hammer to him. Hit him so hard they hurt his brain. Got him in an assisted living place, feed him, take care of him, shit! Who I got to assist me now? Couldn't live in that apartment no more. Not alone without Maxie. Had to move back here with Ma, ain't even the same place no more. Nig-rows and Messicans done took over the avenue long ago. I kept saying, Ma, you gotta get out of there, it ain't no neighbor-hood for a white woman, only she won't leave her home, so this is what I've come to, all my money going to keep Maxie in as-sisted living."

"I heard the Joes were responsible."

"Whole fuckin' family, ain't a white man among 'em doing Maxie that way. I wanted to kill that fucker myself, only the shithead got busted 'fore I could. Terrible what happened to True Joe in prison, ain't it?"

"Terrible," I said.

Bug smiled again. "Not all my money went to keeping Maxie in assisted living," he said. "Do you know what I mean?"

"I know."

"Cuz I ain't ever gonna say it."

Bug looked down the avenue at the unmarked police car and flicked his lighter.

"Ball-yankers just sitting there watching," Bug said. "Been sitting there and watching ever since—I heard someone tried to blow up the Joes' armored house. What did you hear, Mc-Kenzie?"

"I heard the same thing. I also heard that the Joes have been on the run ever since."

Bug stopped flicking his lighter on for a moment and stared at me.

"Chopper vouches for you," he said. "I done business with Chopper a while back . . ."

Don't tell me that, my inner voice said.

"That don't mean we're brothers, though. Ain't that what the Nig-rows say, you my brother? So you tell me, McKenzie, why should I believe you ain't wired? Why should I believe you ain't a pig?"

I tried to choose my words carefully.

"Mr. Ritzer, it would probably be safer for both of us if you do believe I'm police."

Bug flicked his lighter on again and slowly waved the palm of his hand over the flame, feeling its heat. He never stopped smiling.

"Max would say that, too," he said. "Anytime we talk business, he'd say, talk like there's folks listening. What do you want, McKenzie?"

"I don't want anything. I just wanted to drop by and say hello since we have so much in common."

"What do we have in common?"

"You have a friend. I have a friend. Your friend was hurt up here on the North Side. My friend was hurt down in Eden Prairie. Could be they were hurt by the same people."

"I've looked for 'em. Can't seem to find 'em. Eden Prairie, you say? Where's that?"

I was surprised by the question. Did he really not know where Eden Prairie was?

"A suburb southwest of Minneapolis," I said.

Bug nodded as if he knew all the time.

"I don't get around as much as I used to," he said. "Them people, I'd pay a lot to meet up with them people."

"No need for payment. I'd be happy to introduce you at the very first opportunity."

"What would you require in exchange?"

"Anonymity."

"When and where would this meeting take place?"

I pulled a prepaid cell phone from my pocket.

"Is this yours, Mr. Ritzer?" I asked. "I found it just over there by the curb in front of your house."

He took it from my hand and examined it casually.

"Can't say I've ever seen it before," he said.

"You should hang on to it. The guy who lost the cell might call looking for it."

"Yeah, okay."

Bug slipped the phone into his pocket.

"I should leave now," I said.

"I ain't had anyone to talk to for some time," Bug said. "Can't talk to my ma, can't talk to the ball-yankers. It gets frustrating. You come here talking to me like a person, talking to me like a white man. That goes a long way, McKenzie."

"Good-bye, Mr. Ritzer."

I left his yard, closing the gate behind me, wondering what it was I said that impressed Bug so much. I gave him a little wave as I climbed into the Cherokee. He smiled and waved back. He had resumed flicking his lighter as I pulled away from the curb.

I managed two blocks before the cops in the unmarked car pulled me over. They came at me like professionals, one to each side of the Cherokee, both officers resting their hands on the butts of their handguns—one carried a SIG SAUER, the other a Beretta like mine. I made a show of resting my hands on the steering wheel as they approached.

"Would you step out of the vehicle, please," said the cop closest to me.

"Certainly," I said.

I opened the car door and slid out of the Cherokee, again keeping my hands in plain sight. I turned my back to the cop and rested my hands on the hood of the SUV.

"Officer," I said, "I have a nine-millimeter Beretta holstered to my belt behind my right hip. The gun is registered. I have a carry permit in my wallet."

"Thanks for the heads-up," the officer said. He was not being sarcastic. He cautiously patted my hip, reached under my jacket, and removed the Beretta. I thought I heard his partner breathe a sigh of relief. The cop also took my ID. Minutes expired while everything was sorted out. Cars drove past. I expected to see expressions of curiosity on the faces of the drivers and passengers in the cars. That's usually what you get in St.

Paul. Only we were on the North Side of Minneapolis, and instead all I saw was anger and resentment. I don't think it was directed at me. Finally the officers returned my possessions.

"We know who you are, McKenzie," the first cop said. His name was Dailey. His partner was Moulton. They both worked out of the Arson Squad, an interdepartment unit of the Minneapolis fire and police departments. "What we would like to know is why you were talking with Bug."

"Just old friends reminiscing," I said.

"Bug doesn't have any friends except Maxie Lucken," Moulton said.

"He thinks you're his friends."

"He's wrong," Dailey said.

"Bug is a pyromaniac," Moulton said. "Between him and Backdraft, it seems like they've set fire to half the city at one time or another. They've been doing it for decades. Up until now, it's always been controlled. It's always been about profit. Only one person was hurt in a fire they set, and that was more or less by accident. Now . . ."

"Bug's slid a long way since Backdraft got hammered," Dailey said. He grinned at his partner as if it were a joke they shared before. Cop humor—I understood it well. "Backdraft was Bug's only friend. Now that he's drooling in his oatmeal, Bug has become a lonely, frightened old man. He drinks. When he drinks, he becomes angry. When he becomes angry, he lights fires. At least a dozen in the past month alone. He doesn't care where he sets them, either. Random targets. Most have been in the neighborhood."

"I'll tell you what his day is like," Moulton said. "Bug gets up, sits at his mother's kitchen table drinking beer until about noon, then he goes out and sets a fire somewhere close to home so he can see it when he goes back to drinking his beer."

"You can't put him away?" I asked.

"Oh, he's going away," Moulton said. "He set a fire up on Lowry, couple blocks away. We found a half can of beer at the scene. The numbers stamped on the bottom of the can matched a twelve-pack he had at home. We swabbed him and got a DNA match."

"Bug's gotten so careless, it was like he wanted to get caught," Dailey said.

"He made bail, and he's prolonging the inevitable by changing his plea, by changing his lawyer," Moulton said, "but he's going away. Probably he'll get sentenced under the Dangerous Offender statute. Ten years, easy."

"Question is, how much damage is he going to do first?" Dailey asked. "Which brings us back to the original question."

"Why were you talking with Bug?" Moulton asked.

I considered the various lies I could tell, decided to hell with it.

"I'm trying to get a line on the Stippel brothers," I said.

The two officers exchanged weary glances.

"What do you want with the Joes?" Dailey asked.

"They're leaning on a friend of mine. I want to make them stop."

The two officers exchanged glances again, and I realized that they must have been partners for a long time. They were communicating the way Bobby Dunston and I often did, without words.

"We know the Joes," Dailey said. "They haven't been around for a while."

"Gone from our jurisdiction, but not forgotten," Moulton said. "As much as we want to put Bug away . . ."

"We've been trying to put those bastards in prison for ten years," Dailey said.

"Or six feet under, depending on the circumstances," Moulton said.

"The shit they've pulled up here," Dailey said. "The people they've hurt."

"We could tell you stories, McKenzie," Moulton said.

"I've already heard some of them," I said.

"We had three witnesses lined up to testify against them on felony arson and assault charges," Dailey said. "They broke into the house of one of the witnesses, beat him, and then left him in the bathtub in a pool of his own blood."

"They put a couple of rounds through the front door of the second witness," Moulton said. "Next day both witnesses recanted."

"Who could blame them?" Dailey asked.

"The third witness disappeared," Moulton said.

"Missing in action, presumed dead," Dailey said.

Moulton tapped his chest.

"That's on us," he said. "It's all on us for not protecting them better."

"Oh, yeah, we want the Joes," Dailey said.

"Any way we can get them," Moulton said.

"That's good to know," I said.

"Last we heard, they were wreaking havoc in Eden Prairie or thereabouts," Moulton said.

"That's what I heard, too," I said.

"Should you have a conversation with the aforementioned parties, you might want to consider having it on the North Side," Dailey said.

"Yes," Moulton said.

"You'll find that there are people up here who might want to lend a hand," Dailey said.

"We don't know who those people might be, mind you," Moulton said.

"No, not at all," said Dailey.

"We wouldn't want to become involved in anything illegal," Moulton said.

"But there are people," Dailey said.

"Yes, people," Moulton said.

The enemy of my enemy is my friend, my inner voice said.

"That is also good to know," I said aloud.

"See ya around, McKenzie," Moulton said.

The two cops returned to their unmarked squad car and drove off. Dailey gave me a head nod as they passed.

"Wow," I said.

I drove off a few moments later, down Central to Lowry and then east toward the Francis A. Gross Golf Course. As I drove I was reminded of what Bobby Dunston told me about crossing over into the darkness in order to get a job done. He was right—it's no place to live.

I checked my e-mail and phone messages when I returned home. By then most of Vicki's friends had responded to my inquiries. Nearly all had the same thing to say—they had not seen or heard from Vicki since the Fourth of July. A few of them seemed genuinely concerned. One of them was named Anita Malaska. She agreed to meet me. I was heading for the door when my prepaid cell rang. It had the tinny ringtone of an old-fashioned telephone.

"McKenzie, this is Jason Truhler. I don't know what to say."

"Okay," I said.

"I mean, I don't know what to do."

"About what?"

"You know about what. About, about—the Joes called. I told them what you said about the money. They said they won't take it, the thirty-five thousand, I mean. They said they want more, to cover their time and trouble, they said."

"How much more?"

"They want fifty thousand. They said if they don't get it they'd hurt Rickie and Nina."

"How do they know about Erica and Nina?"

"I don't know, I don't know—but that's not all. They said they don't trust you. They said that you're liable to do something stupid, that's what they said."

"They may be right."

"The Joes said I have to deliver the money. They said I should get it from you and then deliver it to them alone."

That didn't sound right to me. From what I'd heard of the Joes, I was sure they would demand a pound of my flesh to go along with their money.

"When and where?" I asked.

"They said they'd tell me when the time was right. They said in the meantime you should get the money together."

"What do you think about this?"

"What do you mean?"

"Are you willing to deliver the money? Alone?"

"I don't want to," Truhler said, "but if that's what it'll take to protect Erica and Nina, then that's what I'll do."

That didn't sound right to me, either.

"I think I should be there," I said.

"No. I mean, they said I have to come alone."

"For fifty grand they might change their minds. When they call back, tell them I want to be there. Tell them your concussion makes it impossible for you to do it alone."

"My concussion?"

"Give them my number. Tell them if they don't like it, they can call me."

"McKenzie."

"Remind them that I'm the guy with the cash."

When Truhler started to protest I told him I'd talk to him soon, deactivated the cell phone, and dropped it in my pocket. I took my time walking to my car, once again making sure that the coast was clear.

Do you have any idea of what you're doing? my inner voice asked.

No.

Why should today be different from all the others?

Exactly.

Anita Malaska lived in Middlebrook Hall on the West Bank campus of the University of Minnesota—that's the dormitory inhabited mostly by students enrolled in the school's honors programs. Suffice to say I didn't room there when I was at the U.

She agreed to meet me in Middlebrook's lobby, surrounded by security cameras and student staff. She was a smart and cautious girl. I liked her even before we met. After we met, I liked her even more. Anita was wearing school colors—maroon and gold—that miraculously matched her eyes. She had red-brown hair that belonged in a shampoo commercial, a complexion from a soap commercial, and a smile that toothpaste marketers lusted after. She regarded me carefully as I sat across from her.

"You said you were looking for Vicki Walsh," Anita said.

"I am," I said. "I hope you can help me."

"I don't know how. Like I told you over the phone, I haven't spoken to Vicki for months. I thought she was at Cornell."

"She never made it."

"What does that mean, she never made it?"

"No one has seen her since the Fourth of July."

"I have."

"You have? When?"

"Toward the end of August, the last weekend of August. My friends and I were hanging around the Minneapolis River-front. You know where St. Anthony Main is? They have restaurants and parks?"

"Sure."

"It was like a last hurrah for all of us before we scattered to schools hither and yon. We bumped into Vicki on the river walk. I asked her what she was up to, because she hadn't been responding to any of her Facebook postings, and she said she had been busy getting ready for school, which is what I was doing, too. Anyway, we ended up, the bunch of us ended up going over to Tuggs for cheeseburgers and to listen to the band that was playing in the courtyard. We pretty much stayed until they kicked us out. Anyway, that's when I saw her last. August."

"Was she alone?"

"No, she was with a friend. A girl. What was her name? Kate something."

"Caitlin?"

"Caitlin with a *C*." Anita laughed at the memory of it. "That's how she introduced herself."

To get from Middlebrook to the Twenty-first Avenue ramp where I'd parked my car, I had to walk between Rarig Center, where the university held most of its student theater productions, and Regis Center for Art, where the student art exhibitions were presented. I enjoyed walking across the campus, any part of it, the West Bank on the west side of the Mississippi, the East Bank on the east side, or the St. Paul campus near the State Fairgrounds. The campus always reminded me of my misspent youth and the wonderful women I misspent it with—a couple of JO majors, a theater major, a law student, a DJ working for the school radio station, Radio K. Ahh, to be young again.

My iPhone shook me out of my reverie. It played eight bars of "Summertime" before I answered it. No name was displayed, just a phone number. It didn't belong to any of the precious few.

I spoke cautiously. "Yes?"

"Mr. McKenzie?" It was a man's voice and old.

"Yes," I said.

"This is Walter Muehlenhaus."

I stopped in the middle of Twenty-first Avenue. For the first time since all this began, I was frightened. Muehlenhaus had that effect on people.

"Mr. Muehlenhaus," I said. I couldn't bring myself to call

him Walter. Hell, up until that moment, I didn't even know his first name was Walter.

"Mr. McKenzie, an acquaintance has arranged an informal gathering at his home this evening. I would deem it a courtesy if you were to attend."

I paused before giving Mr. Muehlenhaus the answer I knew he was expecting.

"Yes," I said.

"Excellent."

"When and where?"

"Arrangements will be made. Oh, and Mr. McKenzie? I would be delighted if you brought the lovely Ms. Truhler with you."

"What else did he say?" Nina asked.

"That was it," I said. "He didn't say good-bye. He didn't tell me how he got hold of my private number. He didn't tell me what he wanted. He just broke the connection."

"What a jerk."

"Yeah, well, he can get away with it."

"Why? Because he has more money than God?"

"That's one reason. He also does favors for everyone, so everyone owes him."

"The same as you."

"No, not the same as me. I never ask for anything in return. It's a lot more than that, though. He's not just a mover and a shaker; he's the guy who tells other people what to move and what to shake. If you think of Minnesota as an immense village, he's the village wise man. He brings various parties together, settles disputes, weds interests, dispenses advice that you damn well better take, and plots, plots, plots, all the time plots. Some people whisper that he's the reason we're building a commuter train from downtown St. Paul to downtown Minneapolis and why the Minnesota Twins have a new stadium and the Vikings don't—at least not yet."

"What does he want from you?"

"Probably the same thing he wanted the last two times our paths have crossed."

"He wants you to do *him* a favor."

"Yeah. I can't imagine what it would be, though, a favor he can't do for himself."

"Guess we won't know until we ask."

"We? I take it you're coming to the party?"

"I wouldn't miss it for the world."

THIRTEEN

Nick Moncur began searching for the fountain of youth decades ago. Now he insisted he had found it.

"There's no single supplement," he said. "There's no individual herb, there's no one thing that's going to make us live longer. Nevertheless, there are many little things that when combined will add a decade or more to our lives."

Moncur claimed he found these things while conducting exhaustive research in Sardinia, a large island off the coast of Italy, Okinawa, the Nicoya Peninsula of Costa Rica, and Loma Linda, a small town located between Los Angles and Palm Springs that was largely inhabited by Seventh-day Adventists. These areas were dubbed Blue Zones by scientists and demographers—regions where people live to be a hundred or more at astonishing rates. Moncur said he identified what these areas held in common and distilled their secrets into a recipe consisting of one part diet, one part exercise regimen, and one part Confucian-inspired philosophy. Someone suggested Moncur was looking to take a bite out of a thirty-billion-dollar industry that promises to make people look or feel young. He insisted, however, that profit wasn't his motive for bringing his recipe to the masses.

"I've made a discovery," Moncur said. "I want to give that discovery to the people. It's like climbing a hill and seeing a beautiful sunset. It's better if you have someone to share it with."

All he needed was partners.

To get them he filled his Lake of the Isles home with well-heeled party guests. Black-clad waiters weaved among them, offering up twirls of scallops and skinny pasta spun onto silver forks and booze, plenty of booze. The red-walled foyer of the large house was already filled when Nina and I arrived. I recognized some of the guests—the Mound, Minnesota, actor who played Hercules on TV; an actress who went from the Chanhassen Dinner Theater to Broadway; the front man for a well-regarded country-western band, who was attired in Brooklyn cowboy chic.

'Course, the guests didn't know they were going to be solicited until they arrived. Apparently they thought they were being invited to enjoy a cocktail or two before attending a five-hundred-dollar-a-plate fund-raiser for hunger relief that Moncur had also organized. They didn't know about his plans to increase life expectancy until he circled the room like a practiced politician. I got the distinct impression that if there had been any babies present he would have kissed them.

Nina and I pressed forward. I was surprised by the amount of hors d'oeuvres she devoured and the champagne she drank. Normally I wouldn't have noticed, but she was wearing a strapless regal-blue gown that made her eyes pop like searchlights, and I couldn't keep my own eyes off of her. She made my heart flutter, and not for the first time.

"Isn't that the governor?" she asked.

"Huh?"

She punched me in the arm.

"Pay attention," she said.

I am, Nina. I am paying attention.

"There," she said.

I followed her gaze to a section of the house where the gossip columnist for the *Minneapolis Star Tribune* newspaper was stalking a man dressed in a crisp white shirt, dark tie, and dark, well-tailored suit with a small video camera. John Allen Barrett kept dodging, first to his right, then to his left, but the columnist was relentless.

"Are you going to run for president?" she asked.

"I haven't given it much thought," he said. "I already have a job."

"Are you going to run for president?"

"Right now I am only concerned with passing a balanced budget here in the state of Minnesota."

"Are you going to run for president?"

"After my term expires, Lindsey and I might think about it," he said. "We'll reach out to all of our friends around the country. We'll decide if there's a requirement as citizens that we run."

"Are you going to run for president?"

Everyone seemed amused except Barrett. Finally someone distracted the columnist, and Barrett slipped away. That's when I saw Lindsey Barrett. I knew her from the neighborhood long before she married the governor; I used to date her sister. We were friends right up until the time I did a favor for her that helped the governor out, even though he never knew anything about it. That she stopped being my pal then wasn't particularly surprising. It's like F. Scott Fitzgerald wrote in *This Side of Paradise*—she disliked me for having done so much for her. I saw the dislike in her eye when she spied me from across the room. It had been nearly two years since we last spoke, though, and her resentment—if you could call it that—must have dissipated, because it changed then, the look in her eye. It became friendly, almost romantic.

Lindsey came toward me. I slipped between the guests to meet her in the middle of the room.

"McKenzie," she said.

"Zee," I said.

Her arms came around me and mine went around her and we hugged, lightly at first, and then with more vigor.

"It's good to see you," she said.

"It's good to be seen."

We chatted for a few moments like the old friends we were, mostly about what brought us to the party. We both agreed that Nick Moncur was a hopeless narcissist who was desperate to land a spot on Oprah's couch. We didn't speak about the favor, and I knew we never would.

I introduced Lindsey to Nina. Lindsey remembered meeting her briefly at a charity function we all attended.

"What a beautiful gown," Lindsey said.

That's when Barrett showed up, having ditched the gossip columnist, at least for the time being.

"Is that my girl you're hugging?" he asked.

I realized then that my arm was still around Lindsey's

shoulder and hers was around my waist. Instead of letting go, Lindsey tightened her grip.

"You remember McKenzie," she said.

"I do," the governor said, "and"—he offered his hand to Nina—"I remember Ms. Truhler. It's good to see you again. How are you?"

Nina's eyes sparked like a welder's torch.

"I am very well, Governor," she said. "Thank you for asking."

I must say I enjoyed it. I liked that I was acquainted with the governor, that I was a friend to his wife. I liked that I rubbed shoulders with men like Mr. Muehlenhaus and Moncur. It made me feel important. On the other hand, I hadn't been invited to the party because I could afford to donate the maximum to a politician's campaign fund or because I had money to invest in snake oil. Barrett knew it, too.

"What brings you here, McKenzie?" he asked. "I didn't think this was your kind of event."

"It's a very long story," I said.

Barrett turned his head to look at the man who sidled up to me from behind. The man set a hand on my shoulder.

"Mr. Muehlenhaus will see you now," he said.

"Hmm," Barrett said. "Perhaps the story's not so very long after all."

Walter Muehlenhaus was sitting in a leather wingback chair in front of the fireplace, his ancient hands folded neatly on his lap. His face and hands were as pale as skim milk, and the flickering flames cast an eerie, almost alarming shadow across them. He reminded me of Mephistopheles in the legend of Doctor Faustus, but I decided that couldn't be right. Mephistopheles was the demon who warned Faustus *not* to sell his soul to the devil.

Muehlenhaus spoke without turning his gaze from the fire.

"Good evening, Mr. McKenzie," he said. "It is always a pleasure to see you."

"Thank you," I said.

Instead of joining him by the fire, I stopped in the middle of the room. There were floor-to-ceiling shelves filled with books on all four walls, a desk big enough to land small aircraft on, and assorted sofas, chairs, and tables, all of them made from dark, highly polished wood. Yet the room had a kind of unused vibe, as if no one ever spent much time there. I noticed a portable staircase that could be wheeled from one bookshelf to another so readers could reach the volumes at the top. There was a thin layer of dust on each step.

"You are well?" Muehlenhaus asked.

"Very well, sir," I said.

"And the lovely Ms. Truhler? I must say that is a stunning dress she is wearing."

I didn't know he saw her; certainly I never saw him.

"She is quite well, too," I said. "Yourself?"

"I am getting old, Mr. McKenzie."

"Aren't we all?"

"These days I feel I am getting older than most. Somehow, I do not believe Mr. Moncur's recipe for longevity will help me."

"I don't think Moncur's recipe will help anyone."

Muehlenhaus chuckled at that.

"No, I suppose not," he said.

"Personally, I wouldn't want to live forever," I said.

"That is because you are a young man. As you get older, your opinion will change."

"Maybe so, but I don't intend to worry about it. What is it they say? Only the good die young?"

For the first time since I'd known him, I heard Muehlenhaus laugh. He laughed until he coughed into his hand.

"In that case I shall live forever," he said. Muehlenhaus turned in his chair to look at me. The lenses in his eyeglasses had been polished until they reflected light like a mirror. "So will you."

The remark reminded me of something Muehlenhaus once said, which I'm sure was his intention—that he and I were very much alike, that we both did favors for friends. He insisted that if there was a difference between us it was merely at the level on which we granted our favors. I resented the accusation, yet I wasn't entirely sure it was untrue.

"What can I do for you, Mr. Muehlenhaus?" I asked.

Before he could answer, there was a soft rap on the door. The man who had first summoned me held it open. A woman brushed past him, and he closed the door behind her. I guessed the woman's age at about fifty despite her obvious attempts to confuse the issue. She was dressed in a long black skirt, a cranberry-colored lace top with velvet and chiffon trim, and a black blazer. She looked like someone whose skin was stretched too tight; she didn't have a single wrinkle anywhere, not even when she smiled, which she was doing now.

"Walter," she cooed. She moved quickly across the room to Muehlenhaus's side. She hugged his shoulder. "It is so good to see you again."

Muehlenhaus looked at me with an expression that suggested he was embarrassed by the display.

"Have you met Mr. McKenzie?" he asked her. "Rushmore McKenzie, this is Roberta Weltzin."

"The famous Rushmore McKenzie," she said.

She walked straight up to me, her hand extended. I shook her hand.

"The famous Roberta Weltzin," I said. I nearly said "infamous." I nearly asked her how the Web site was doing. I nearly said a lot of things that I shouldn't have. Suddenly it all seemed much clearer to me.

Muehlenhaus rose from his chair facing the fire and directed us to a trio of wingbacks near the center of the room that seemed as if they had already been arranged for our comfort. I was distressed to note how thin Muehlenhaus had become and how shaky his movements were. Make no mistake; I didn't like the man—well, maybe I did a little. In any case, I did not wish him ill.

Muehlenhaus was the first to speak after we were seated.

"Once again, Mr. McKenzie, it seems our interests coincide," he said.

"In what way?" I asked.

"I believe you are searching for a young lady named Vicki Walsh."

I stared into Roberta's surgically altered face when I replied.

"It is my understanding that she's dead."

"Then why are you looking for her?" Roberta asked.

"I am doing a favor for a friend."

"Jason Truhler," Muehlenhaus said.

I wasn't surprised that Muehlenhaus knew my business;

he knew everyone's business. I just couldn't imagine why he cared.

"Do you have a relationship with Jason Truhler?" I asked him.

"Mr. Truhler is a small man," Muehlenhaus said. "I have no dealings with him. He does, however, have dealings with others of my acquaintance. I believe that he often caters to their baser tastes."

"I know just how he caters to them, too."

Muehlenhaus must have heard something in my voice, because he said, "It would seem that neither of us is fond of Mr. Truhler."

"Why are you helping him, then?" Roberta asked.

I didn't answer. Muehlenhaus knew my reasons. That's why he asked me to invite Nina to the party, because he knew, and because he wanted to exert pressure on me without seeming to. A subtle man, was our Mr. Muehlenhaus.

"Mr. McKenzie," Muehlenhaus said. "Would it be accurate to say that Ms. Walsh is blackmailing Mr. Truhler and that you have been asked to intervene?"

"Someone is blackmailing Truhler," I said. "I don't know for certain that it's Vicki."

"Mr. Truhler is not alone. Others have also been victimized. Ms. Weltzin?"

"McKenzie, I am engaged in . . ."

Roberta paused as if she were searching for just the right word to describe her business in the most positive light. I didn't give her the opportunity.

"I know what you do for a living," I said.

The sound of my voice caused her to flinch.

"I make no apologies," she said.

"I wouldn't listen to them anyway." I turned toward Muehlenhaus. "Why am I here?"

Muehlenhaus gestured back toward Roberta with the flat of his hand.

"Someone hacked my computer," she said. "They downloaded all of my files onto a flash drive, not only those files identifying my girls, but accounting and customer files as well. Since then many of my clients have been systematically blackmailed."

"How many clients?"

"Seven that I know of so far. However, another regular had ceased utilizing our services at the same time, so I suspect that he is being blackmailed as well."

"For how much?"

"Is that important?"

"Ninety-nine eighty a month?"

"How did—"

"That's her MO," I said.

I did some quick calculating. Assuming she started extorting her victims in July and had already made her collections for November, Vicki was sitting on approximately four hundred thousand dollars. I turned back to Muehlenhaus.

"Does this involve the governor?" I asked.

"Does it matter?" Roberta asked.

"Yes."

"Why?"

"McKenzie does his favors only for his friends," Muehlenhaus said. "The rest of us can go to Hades."

Roberta hesitated as if she were weighing which answer would give her the greatest advantage. I knew it. So did Muehlenhaus.

"The truth, now," he said.

"No, it doesn't involve the governor," Roberta said.

I was glad to hear it.

"It does, however, involve a great many other prominent citizens," Muehlenhaus said. "This includes supporters of the governor as well as members of his administration."

"Fuck 'em," I said.

"Mr. McKenzie . . ."

"These are men who paid money for the opportunity to abuse children," I said. "Young women they wanted to pretend were children—yes, Roberta, I know all about your rules involving birth certificates. Honest to God, Mr. Muehlenhaus, I cannot imagine why you of all people would want to protect these bastards."

"The truth is, these men are the ones who are being abused," Roberta said. "Abused by children, if you like. Abused for money."

"If anyone can appreciate the irony, I'd think it would be you."

"No one is being forced to do anything they don't want to do. Everything that occurs is between consenting adults. The girls come and go as they please. I care about these girls. I take care of them. They know the choice is always theirs."

"No crime, no foul, is that it?"

"That's it."

"Then why is everyone so afraid of being outed?"

"I do not believe we are accomplishing as much as we could," Muehlenhaus said. "Would either of you enjoy a drink?"

"No, thank you," I said.

Roberta shook her head.

"Mr. McKenzie," Muehlenhaus said. "I do not entirely disagree with your position. However, there is much that can be lost if these attempts at extortion are not thoroughly dealt with in as quiet a manner as possible. You hold the position that these gentlemen are, what is the phrase, getting what is coming to them. It is difficult to argue against such a position. However, I am sure you do not wish to see repeated the sad case of Mr. Charles Kruger. Charles was both a friend and colleague of mine. He committed suicide a year ago after paying nearly five hundred thousand dollars to keep secret sexually explicit photographs taken of himself and a prostitute. He was not the only victim, either. Before he took his life, Charles composed a letter in which he stated that he was doing what was best for his family. All these men have families. You know this. That is why you are assisting Mr. Truhler, is it not? To protect those nearest to him? You mention the governor, whom I know you hold in high regard. Should we allow his reputation to be tarnished, his political aspirations to be compromised, by the behavior of men over whom he has no control? So many others as well, innocent men and women who will suffer should these activities come to light. Children, too. Ms. Truhler has a daughter, does she not? Certainly you have considered her well-being."

"God, you're good," I said.

Muehlenhaus smiled at me. "We have always understood each other," he said.

"What would you have me do?"

"Find Ms. Walsh."

"How do you know she's behind the extortion?"

"I didn't," Roberta said. "From what my clients told me, I was under the impression they were being blackmailed by two young men, a black man and a white man. That was until I discovered that Vicki was alive. Up until then I thought she had been killed in Thunder Bay. I thought the blackmailers were the people who had killed her, that somehow they forced her to download my files and then killed her for it. I realize now that she downloaded the files herself before she went to Canada and staged her murder as a way of deflecting suspicion."

"Who told you that she had been killed?" I asked. "Jason?" She nodded.

"And you did nothing about it," I said. "Tell me again how much you care about your girls."

Roberta cast a sideways glance at Muehlenhaus, but said nothing.

"How did you know that Vicki was still alive?" I asked. "Oh, wait. Truhler again."

"Yes."

Why are you helping this guy? my inner voice asked for the fiftieth or sixtieth time.

"What have you done to find her?" I asked aloud.

"I asked my girls if anyone has seen or heard from her, but no one has," Roberta said. "Beyond that I hired . . ."

"Hired who?"

"Two men who used to work for me. I fired them originally because they didn't have the right attitude for my kind of operation. However, in this matter . . ."

I covered my face with my hands and spoke into them.

"Oh my God, she hired the Joes," I said.

I took my hands from my face and leaned toward Roberta.

"You hired the Joes," I said.

She nodded.

"Lady, the Joes are nut jobs," I said. "They're certifiable. Didn't you figure that out the first time they worked for you?"

"How do you know so much about my business?"

I heard Muehlenhaus chuckle.

"Do the Joes know what's on the flash drive?" I asked.

"Yes."

"Roberta, what were you thinking? Forget Vicki Walsh. If these guys get their hands on the flash drive, on all those files, all hell will break loose. How can you not know that?"

"I was desperate. Clients were contacting me. They were threatening me with jail and worse. I had to do something."

"Unhire them. Make them go away."

"I'm not sure I can."

"You can try, can't you?"

"I can try, but they are very difficult men."

"Tell me about it."

"Besides, I need help."

"Perhaps something can be arranged," Mr. Muehlenhaus said.

All right, all right, all right, my inner voice chanted. *It is what it is. Where do we go from here?*

"What's the deal with Vicki Walsh?" I asked.

"What do you mean?" Roberta asked.

"What can I offer her?"

"Immunity," Muehlenhaus said.

"Immunity?" Roberta echoed.

"Yes," Muehlenhaus said. His voice left no doubt. "If she ceases her activities, if she returns the stolen property, if she leaves never to return. In exchange, she will be allowed to keep the money she has extorted, her freedom, and—Mr. McKenzie, she must be made to understand that the people who have threatened Ms. Weltzin, who would very much like to find Ms. Walsh themselves, are not to be trifled with. You and I both know that there are men in positions of power in this city, in this state, who can and will do anything to protect their positions. Ms. Walsh must return the flash drive and agree to disappear."

"In that event, will you guarantee her safety?" I asked.

"You have my word."

I regarded Roberta Weltzin for a moment. I didn't trust her as far as I could throw her, but Mr. Muehlenhaus—come to think about it, I didn't entirely trust him, either.

"When I speak to Vicki, I'll deliver your message," I said.

I rose from the chair and headed for the door of the library.

"Wait," Roberta said. "Do you know where Vicki is?"

"No. I know how to find her, though. Now, if you'll excuse me, I'm going to get a drink."

"I could offer you a snifter of Mr. Moncur's excellent brandy," Muehlenhaus said.

"Thank you, sir. However, at the risk of being blunt, I don't like the company you keep."

From the expression on her face, it was obvious that Roberta didn't like the remark at all. Then again, she wasn't supposed to.

I stopped in the doorway to the foyer and took it all in. The crowd had thinned considerably, most guests having already headed off to the charity fund-raiser. Nina was standing near the center of the room conversing with a group that included Lindsey and John Barrett. I studied her for a moment, marveling at just how beautiful she was. Black hair, high cheekbones, narrow nose, generous mouth, curves that would impress a Formula One racer—and those eyes, the most startling pale blue eyes I had ever seen made even more luminous by the rich blue of her gown. It was the eyes that caused me to notice her when she served me a club sandwich at the downstairs bar at Rickie's nearly three years ago. I had followed a suspect there. I nearly lost him because of those eyes.

Yet there was so much more to her than that. She was ungodly smart. She loved music. She was tough and resourceful. Caring and brave. She was funny—at least she laughed at my jokes, which, I realized, might not be the same thing. Even her flaws were endearing, like how even a simple cold would render her grouchy and miserable. It was beyond my comprehension how Jason Truhler could have abused her and cheated on her. I would have gladly shot him dead if she asked me to.

Nina saw me approach the small group out of the corner of her eye. Either that or she had somehow sensed my presence, because she reached out for me, wrapped her arm around mine, and pulled me close without once lifting her eyes from the face of the woman who was speaking to her. In that moment I knew, absolutely *knew,* what love felt like.

Barrett glanced at his wristwatch.

"You're going to be late for dinner," I told him.

"McKenzie, it is obvious that you do not know the value of a grand entrance," he said.

Lindsey rolled her eyes the way she had when we were kids

and her sister Linda said something particularly dumb. Lin-*duh* we had called her, as compared to Lind-*zee*.

More small talk was exchanged. Finally the remaining guests floated toward their vehicles. We drifted along with them even though we hadn't been invited to the charity dinner. The governor's security guard held open the door to the state-owned Escalade. Lindsey climbed aboard. The governor paused at the door.

"McKenzie, if you're involved with Mr. Muehlenhaus, I have some advice for you," he said. "Be careful."

"Are you saying he can't be trusted?"

"He has a way of making you feel like you're on his side. The problem is you can never be entirely sure which side he's on."

"I'll keep it in mind."

A few moments later he drove off.

Since Nina and I were all dressed up with nowhere to go, I suggested we eat a real dinner and listed a number of the Cities' more expensive restaurants, only Nina said she wasn't hungry. I recommended a couple of clubs, including rivals like the Dakota Jazz Club in Minneapolis and the Artists' Quarter in St. Paul. Nina said she had a better idea. I won't bore you with the details. Suffice to say that it involved bending if not actually breaking various rules and regulations governing the operation of motor vehicles in the state of Minnesota while I drove her home. It was because I was driving so aggressively that I didn't notice the vehicle dawdling behind us until we were working through the crowded Uptown area of Minneapolis. I took a couple of casual turns to make sure.

"What is it?" Nina asked.

"We're being followed," I told her.

She turned in her seat to look, then quickly turned back.

"I'm sorry," she said. "I shouldn't have done that. Now they know we know that they're back there."

She was so sorry that she did it again.

"That's okay," I said. "I was about to educate them anyway."

"In this?"

Nina had a point. The Cherokee didn't have anything near the get-up-and-go that my Audi had. God, I already missed her.

"Okay," I said. "Change in plan."

"So, we have a plan, then?"

"Watch and learn."

I allowed the tail to follow us north on Hennepin Avenue to the intersection of Interstate 94 and then drove east. The bright traffic lights allowed me to identify it as a high-performance German sedan. I stayed in the right-hand lane, watching the vehicle behind us intently through the rearview and side mirrors. The sedan did not attempt to speed up on us. Nor did it fall back.

"Who is it, do you think?" Nina asked.

"Someone who knew we would be at the party."

"Mr. Muehlenhaus?"

"More likely it's Roberta or one of her employees."

"Who's Roberta?" Nina asked.

I gave her a quick summary without lingering over Jason Truhler's involvement. By then we were crossing the bridge leading from Minneapolis into St. Paul.

"They probably don't want to hurt us," Nina said. "They probably just want us to lead them to Vicki Walsh."

"One can only hope."

Nina didn't speak again until we were passing the Cretin-Vandalia off-ramp.

"Do you have a gun?" she asked.

"No."

"No?"

"I took you to a party with the governor. Of course I didn't bring a gun. Did you bring a gun?"

Nina ran her hands from her thighs to her waist to just beneath her breasts.

"Sorry," she said.

The sedan began to accelerate as we passed the Snelling Avenue exit. The driver was pushing it up to seventy as we approached Lexington Parkway, but then so was I. Seventy-five. Eighty. I used my turn signal to tell him I was exiting at Dale. He followed me up the ramp. I stayed in the left-hand lane and signaled my turn. To my relief he fell back, allowing a car to ease between us. The traffic light at Dale was red, and we all slowed to a stop.

"Take off your seat belt," I said.

"What?" Nina asked.

"Take off your seat belt."

I pressed the button that released the latch, and I let my own seat belt recede into the roller above and behind the driver's door. Nina followed my lead.

Ruben Barany wasn't on duty. Instead, a shabbily dressed woman moved down the line of cars, peering inside the driver's windows. I presumed she was a uniform working for the St. Paul Police Department. She was carrying the exact same sign that Ruben had carried—WILL WORK FOR FOOD.

"Homeless Harriet," I said.

"Huh?"

I deliberately avoided eye contact when the woman approached the Jeep Cherokee, in case we knew each other, and I made no effort to reach in my pocket for a contribution as I had with Ruben. I didn't want an act of generosity on my part to persuade her to let me off. Harriet looked through my window. I was sure we made a tempting target, two obviously well-off swells dressed to the nines ignoring someone in need— I would have busted me, too.

The cars surged forward when the light changed, and I made my turn. I got half a block before I saw the light bar of a Ramsey County Sheriff's Department cruiser flashing in my mirror. I pulled to a stop along Dale Street and turned off my Cherokee. The German sedan that had been following us was forced to pass, continuing on toward University Avenue. It paused as if it were looking for a place to park, but drove on when a second RCSD cruiser pulled over the car that was directly behind it.

I unrolled the window of my Cherokee when the deputy approached.

"Can I help you, Officer?" I asked.

"Sir, you are in violation of Minnesota Statute one-six-nine-point-six-eight-six, driving without a properly fastened seat belt. May I see your driver's license and proof of insurance, please?"

I gave him both, and he proceeded to write out a ticket. He then asked for Nina's ID and wrote out a ticket for her as well. For reasons that baffled me, Nina started to laugh quietly. She laughed even louder when the deputy gave us a lecture about the dangers of driving without a seat belt. I wondered exactly how much champagne she'd had.

"Miss," the deputy said, "I'd hate to see your pretty face and that, that dress you're wearing splattered across the windshield."

That stopped her while she looked down at herself.

"What's wrong with my dress?" Nina asked.

"Well, nothing," said the deputy, and Nina started laughing again. I have no idea why he didn't drag us out of the car and start administering portable Breathalyzer tests.

After the deputy told us to have a good evening, I drove around the neighborhood to make sure that the tail was gone. I then got back on the freeway.

"What now?" Nina asked.

"I can either take you home or back to the club."

"I thought we had other plans."

"Our friends in the sedan reminded me that there is something important I need to do."

Nina sighed dramatically.

"You are going to pay my fine, aren't you?" she asked.

I told her I would, and she laughed some more.

"Honest to God, McKenzie, you always know how to show a girl a good time."

I wasn't dressed for the weather and found myself shivering slightly in the Jeep Cherokee while I waited in the parking lot outside Caitlin Brooks's apartment. She hadn't answered the lobby phone when I first arrived, and there were no lights shining in what I believed to be her apartment windows. So I waited, shivering in the dark. My driver's side window was down because I didn't want to fog up my windows. I could have rolled it up and turned on the engine, but I didn't want to risk giving myself away. I didn't know when she would return or who she would be with. I didn't think Caitlin was the type to bring her work home with her, yet you never know.

While I was waiting, I called Denny Marcus. He didn't answer his cell, so I left a voice mail. I told him it was essential that he contact Vicki and have her call me. "Tell her that Roberta knows everything," I said, adding that I could help. I threw in a few "pleases" for good measure.

Finally a limousine drove up, stopping at the curb. The driver did not get out, round the vehicle, and open the door as was customary. Instead, Caitlin opened the door herself and stepped out.

"Good night, Barry," she said.

Although it worked to my advantage, Barry didn't bother to wait until Caitlin was safely inside the building before he drove off.

Chivalry is dead, my inner voice said.

I waited until Caitlin was entering the lobby of the building before I approached her. Her clothes resembled a schoolgirl's uniform except her stockings were so high, her skirt so short, and her sheer white blouse so revealing that it probably would have earned her a week's detention in any private school in America.

"Caitlin with a *C*," I said.

My voice visibly startled her, and her hand immediately dove into the bag she carried by a thin strap over her shoulder. Maybe she was grabbing for pepper spray, maybe a gun, but when she recognized me her hand came out empty.

"McKenzie," she said. "You look nice."

"So do you," I said.

"This old thing?"

"The schoolgirl look is kind of a cliché, isn't it?"

"You'd be surprised. Why are you here, McKenzie?"

"I need you to do something for me."

Caitlin raised an eyebrow. "What?" she asked.

"I need you to contact Vicki Walsh."

"McKenzie, I don't know where Vicki is."

"Yes, you do. Tell her to call me. Tell her her life is in danger. Tell her I can help—if she calls me."

"McKenzie . . ."

"Caitlin. I know what Vicki is doing. So do you. Maybe you're in on it, maybe you're not, but you know. You and Vicki have been seen together recently, long after she was supposed to have disappeared, long after you said you lost track of her. Roberta doesn't know that you're in touch with Vicki, does she? Neither do the Joes."

Caitlin flinched at the mention of their names. Part of me was pleased that she understood the threat, the other part—suddenly I felt so low I'd have needed a stepladder to scratch an ant's belly.

"There's no reason for any of them to know about you and Vicki," I said. "Do you understand?"

"You're not nearly as nice as I thought you were," Caitlin said.

"Do you understand?"

"I understand."

"I swear, Caitlin, I mean Vicki no harm. Or you, either. Truth is, I might be the only one who can help her."

"I'll believe it when I see it."

FOURTEEN

The phone jolted me awake. I jumped out of bed and raced to the prepaid cell on my bureau, stubbing my big toe in the process. It wasn't until I was hopping on one foot and cursing loudly that I realized that my land line was ringing—Vicki Walsh didn't have that number. I managed to get to the phone before it rolled over to my voice mail.

"Hello," I said.

"And a good morning to you, too," Bobby Dunston said; I recognized his voice instantly.

"What time is it?"

"Ten o'clock. Did I wake you? Poor baby. I know how much you need your beauty sleep."

"What's going on, Bobby?"

"You tell me. You make a big deal about me missing hockey last week and then you blow us off without so much as a phone call."

"Sorry 'bout that. I was out with Nina."

"That's what we were speculating, that she dragged you off somewhere. You are so whipped, McKenzie."

There are insults, and then there are insults. When Jason Truhler said that to me, I was prepared to clean his clock. That's because he meant it in the most derogatory way possible, as if somehow it was unmanly to arrange your schedule to accommodate a woman. With Bobby it was like the line in the old Owen Wister novel *The Virginian*—"When you call me that, *smile*." I could feel his grin all the way across the telephone wire. He understood as well as anyone that making personal sacrifices is exactly what a man does for the people he cares about.

"No doubt about it," I said. "If you saw the dress Nina was wearing, you'd be whipped, too."

"Yeah?"

"Strapless."

"My, my, my, my, my. Where'd you guys go?"

"We had cocktails with the governor."

"Oh la-dee-dah."

"If I'm lyin', I'm dyin'."

"Was Lindsey there?"

When I said earlier that Lindsey was from the neighborhood, I meant Merriam Park in St. Paul, where both Bobby and I grew up, where everybody knew everyone.

"She was," I said, "but you know what, Bobby? She never mentioned your name."

"I liked her sister better, anyway."

"Listen, I'm glad you called. There's something I wanted to ask you about."

"What?"

"Let's say, hypothetically—"

"Hypothetically? It's going to be one of those conversations, huh?"

"Let's say there was a prostitution ring operating in the Twin Cities that was using the Internet to arrange trysts."

"Trysts? Is that what they call it now?"

"Let's say the Web site is called, oh, I don't know, My Very First Time dot com."

"Let's."

"Who would have jurisdiction?"

"We'd probably put together a joint statewide task force like we did when we took down My Fast Pass and Minnesota Nice Guys a couple years ago. You knew that, though, didn't you?"

"Uh-huh."

"It *is* one of those conversations. What else can you tell me? Hypothetically, of course."

"I could tell you the name of the person who's running it all."

There was a long pause while Bobby waited for me to supply the name. When I didn't he said, "And that would be?"

"What kind of deal can I get for the girls?"

"You're negotiating with me, really? McKenzie, you know better. I can't make any deals. That's all up to the prosecutors."

"I don't want this to end like it always does, with courts pounding on the supply side without touching the demand side."

"You know how it works as well as I do. The johns pay a fine; the girls do the time. Whenever we roll up a prostitution ring we get a thousand phone calls from lawyers saying their clients will be happy to cooperate, happy to pay any fine, happy to do community service, as long as they remain anonymous.

That link we set up on the St. Paul Police Department Web site that displays photographs of all the people we arrest for prostitution? How many photos of well-to-do business owners or professionals do you see on that site? If you're a john, the only way your photo is going to get uploaded is if you're caught soliciting a prostitute off the street in Frogtown or the East Side."

"I know."

"Are you going to give me that name?"

"Yes, but not just yet."

"McKenzie, do we need to have another talk about crossing the line?"

"Don't worry, Bobby, I'm still on the right side. Here's the thing, though—you and I both know that there are a dozen guys who can kill a case before it comes to trial. A cop, a prosecutor, a judge—anyone who wants to protect a friend or earn a promotion or secure political support or arrange a comfy retirement or make a couple of bucks. In this case, the woman involved is protected all the way to the top."

"So, it's a woman, then."

"I have every intention of giving you her name and a lot more, but I'd like to try to do it in a way that'll make sure the right people are prosecuted."

"How are you going to manage that?"

"I have no idea."

I listened as Bobby took a couple of deep breaths.

"McKenzie," he said, "I don't mind that you do these things, I really don't. I just wish you wouldn't tell me. It makes me feel like a co-conspirator."

"As long as they put us in the same cell, that's the main thing."

"Good-bye, McKenzie."

. . .

I spent the rest of the morning and a chunk of the afternoon waiting for Vicki Walsh to call. While I waited I vacuumed my house for the first time in about two months, upstairs and downstairs—the exertion did my back some good. I separated my dirty clothes into color-coordinated piles before deciding I could put off doing laundry for at least another week. I watched a couple of quarters of the Gophers-Hoosiers football game. I read a few chapters of E. L. Doctorow's new book. I made lunch, ate it, and cleared away the dishes. I threw dried corn to the ducks. The prepaid cell didn't ring.

My landline did ring, though, at just about the time I was considering new and improved methods of threatening Caitlin Brooks. The caller ID in my kitchen displayed the name Dailey.

"Hello," I said.

"McKenzie?"

"Yeah."

"This is Scott Dailey with the MPD. We met the other day."

"I remember."

"There's a joint on the North Side called Victory 44. Know it?"

"On Forty-fourth Avenue near Camden?"

"Why don't you come out, meet me and my partner."

"What's going on?"

"Say half an hour?"

"I'll be there."

Victory 44 was located just off leafy Victory Memorial Parkway, sometimes called the North Side's Gold Coast. I don't know why Dailey and Moulton picked it except to remind me that North

Minneapolis was far more complicated than how it was usually portrayed in police reports and on the evening news.

The restaurant was far too trendy for the neighborhood. It had putty-colored walls and an open kitchen. The cooks wore baseball caps and the waitresses had tight T-shirts with the words VICTORY NEVER TASTES TOO GOOD splayed across their chests. Four large mirrors were hung on the walls along with a couple of high-end beer signs. The bar area was filled with high tables and booths with wooden benches, while the dining area was lined with black banquettes. There was no foie gras or top-shelf tequila on the menu, yet there were plenty of designer beers and an eclectic wine list. Plus, the kitchen specialized in scratch cooking. You could get a gourmet burger with skinny house-made fries and house-made ketchup, a punchy crème fraîche–chive–Grana Padano cheese dip, tempura-quality fish and chips, fish cakes Benedict, and crispy pork belly with a crunchy vegetable salad and a tarragon-garlic pistou. Drop the place in the Uptown neighborhood of Minneapolis or on Grand Avenue in St. Paul and the hipsters would line up around the block to get in. On the North Side I'd take three-to-one that it would be gone within a year.

I found Dailey and Moulton sitting across from each other in a booth in the bar. I squeezed in next to Moulton.

"Gentlemen," I said.

"McKenzie," Dailey said. "What'll you have?"

"Summit Ale," I said. The bar didn't serve hard liquor.

Dailey waved at the bartender and placed my order. A few minutes later the drink was placed in front of me. I took a swallow.

"Okay," I said. "I'm primed. What can I do for you guys?"

In reply, Moulton slipped a photograph out of a large envelope and slid it across the table to me, topside down. I turned it over and looked at the image.

"You sonuvabitch," I said.

I flipped the photo over again and turned away. I rested my hands on my thighs, closed my eyes, and bit my bottom lip. I tried to control my breathing but it was hard.

It was a photo of a man resting on a stainless steel autopsy table. At least I assumed it was a man. There was no way to know for sure. His hair, his eyes, his face, his flesh had all been consumed by fire.

"Gives a whole new meaning to the term extra crispy, doesn't it?" Moulton asked.

"Reminds me of the blackened chicken you can get at that Cajun joint in Richfield," Dailey said.

"Mmm, yummy," Moulton said.

I would gladly have punched out both of them, or at least cussed them out, except the look on their faces told me that they weren't trying to be clever so much as they were simply trying to cope with a horrifying situation. This might have been my first charred body, but it certainly wasn't theirs.

"Who is it?" I asked.

The question was as much for distraction as anything. I was already trying to push the photograph into the vault inside my brain where I stored all of the abhorrent images I've witnessed in my life. I knew it would take some effort.

"We were hoping you could tell us," Dailey said.

"How would I know?"

Moulton produced a plastic evidence bag. Inside the bag was a cell phone. He fiddled with a few buttons. A moment later I heard my voice telling Denny Marcus to contact Vicki Walsh immediately, that Roberta knew everything and that I could help her if only she would call me.

"Oh, God, no, man, dammit," I said.

"We found the cell not far from the body," Moulton said.

"The body was dumped in the alley behind Bug's house," Dailey said. "We know Bug didn't do it. Whoever did it was trying to frame him."

"It was the Joes," I said. "It was the fucking Joes."

"How do you know?"

As far as I was concerned, all deals were off. I told the cops everything I knew. I named names. I said that I was searching for Vicki Walsh, that the Joes were doing the same. I said that I knew Denny Marcus had been in contact with her and that it was my guess the Joes somehow discovered the same thing.

"If Marcus knew where Vicki Walsh was, then he told the Joes," Moulton said. "Wouldn't have been able to help himself."

"Before they doused him with gasoline, the Joes smashed every bone in both of his feet with a claw hammer," Dailey said.

"It's the family's weapon of choice," Moulton said.

It all made me feel like weeping. Either that or doing something rough, picking a fight with the bartender, anything, only as far as I was concerned neither was an option.

Think it through, my inner voice told me. *Work it out.*

I drained my beer and demanded more, wishing it were something stronger. While I was waiting, a thought occurred to me.

"What are we doing here?" I asked. I looked from Dailey to Moulton and back again. "You guys are arson, this is homicide." I pointed at the cell phone. "This is evidence." The head of the homicide unit in Minneapolis was named Lieutenant

Clayton Rask. His office was in room 108 of the Minneapolis City Hall. I wondered aloud why I wasn't in room 108 right now being interviewed by Rask.

"We're going to give up the cell phone and the kid's ID," Dailey said. "Lieutenant Rask probably will have plenty to ask you."

"In the meantime . . ." Moulton raised his hands, palms upward.

"You guys are working it off the books," I said.

"We know the Joes' handiwork when we see it," Dailey said.

"We're going to get those bastards," Moulton said.

"This is so wrong for so many reasons," I said.

"Are you going to help or not, McKenzie?" Dailey asked.

I thought about the kid. I had liked the way he stood up for his friend. He was all right, a good guy. He didn't deserve to die the way he had. No one did.

"Hell yes, I'm going to help," I said.

After the bartender served my Summit, we drank to it.

I placed a call the moment I returned to my car. Caitlin Brooks answered on the third ring.

"McKenzie, I keep telling you," she said. "I don't know where Vicki is."

"Listen to me very carefully," I said. "Are you listening?"

"McKenzie . . ."

"Do you know who Denny Marcus was? He was a friend of Vicki's. She had kept in touch with him through e-mails and text messages. Somehow the Joes found out about him."

I heard her gasp as if she knew what was coming.

"They kidnapped him. They broke every bone in his feet with a hammer. Then they set him on fire. He was alive when they burned him—"

"Oh, please, McKenzie."

"If he knew where Vicki was, you can be sure that he told the Joes before he died."

I could hear Caitlin weeping over the phone.

"Please, please," she said.

"It's not a game anymore, Cait. This is as serious as it gets. Where is Vicki?"

"I don't know."

"Then God help her."

I waited for a few moments, hoping Caitlin would give me something. All I heard was her anguished weeping.

It was four fifteen by the time I rolled into my driveway, and the sun was already thinking about setting. I sat in the Cherokee and pondered my options. My arrangement with Dailey and Moulton made me uncomfortable. I should call Lieutenant Rask, I told myself. He didn't approve of me, but he'd like it even less if he found out I was conspiring with MPD officers behind his back. I could ask Bobby what to do, only I already knew what his answer would be. My biggest concern was Vicki Walsh. Muehlenhaus said he could guarantee her safety, yet the Joes had proven that wasn't necessarily true.

Wait, my inner voice shouted. *That isn't your biggest concern.*

"Shit," I said aloud.

I took up the prepaid cell and called Jason Truhler. His phone rang six long times before he answered.

"McKenzie," he said. "I was just about to call you. Do you have the money?"

"Shut up and listen," I said.

"Hey, c'mon—"

"Shut. Up. And. Listen."

My heart was pounding, and my breath was coming fast. My fear was palpable.

You're scaring yourself, my inner voice said.

"I'm listening," Truhler said.

"When you called yesterday about the fifty thousand, you said that if the Joes didn't get their money they would hurt Nina and Erica. If you lie to me I will kill you. I will hunt you down and I will fucking kill you."

"Lie about what?"

"When you said that to me, that the Joes would hurt Nina and Erica, was that them talking, did they actually say that, or was it you saying it to make sure I would come up with the money?"

"McKenzie, I'm desperate here. You don't know how desperate."

"Tell me the truth, damn you."

"It was me, okay? It was me. The Joes don't know that I was married. They don't know that I have a daughter. You think I'd tell them that? Give me some credit."

"Truhler, you sonuvabitch. This is serious now. People are dying."

"What?"

236

"I said it before, if Nina and Erica so much as break a fingernail, I will put you in the ground, I swear to God."

"You may not believe me, McKenzie, but I'm telling the truth."

My heart rate started slowing to normal. I believed Truhler. The way he answered corresponded with my psychiatrist ex-girlfriend's lie detection theories.

"Okay," I said.

"What's going on, McKenzie?" Truhler asked. "Who died?"

I didn't have the energy to explain it to him.

"Have you heard from them, the Joes?" I asked.

"No."

"Call me when you do."

"I will."

I deactivated the phone and leaned back in my seat. I closed my eyes and sighed slowly, all the while thinking of Nina and Erica. They were safe, I told myself. I didn't have to worry about them. That left Vicki Walsh. I had not met her, yet for some reason it was now very important to me that I protect her. I couldn't tell you why. Perhaps it was the photo that Erica had shown me, the one where she was pretending to pull Vicki's roses-and-wheat-colored ponytail.

The sun had finally set, and despite my T-shirt, Kevlar vest, shirt, sweater, and leather jacket, I felt a chill in the air. I thought of Denny Marcus and shivered even more. I heard myself quoting W. H. Auden to myself—apparently I had learned a lot in that long-ago poetry class:

> *What instruments we have agree*
> *the day of his death was a dark cold day . . .*

"That poor kid," I said aloud.

My prepaid cell phone rang, and I answered it without thinking much about it.

"This is McKenzie," I said.

"This is Vicki Walsh," a woman's voice told me.

FIFTEEN

Southdale Center is the oldest enclosed shopping mall in the country and home to over one hundred twenty specialty stores. It was built in Edina, one of Minnesota's richest suburbs, before I was born and over the decades has become more or less the center of the city. A hospital, public library, courthouse, and city historical society have all been built within a stone's throw of Southdale's gigantic parking lot, not to mention countless professional offices, supermarkets, restaurants, bars, coffeehouses, bookstores, gas stations, auto repair shops, movie theaters, computer outlets, and, yes, a second shopping mall.

I sat next to the window inside one of the coffeehouses located between the two malls and looked out at the traffic moving recklessly through the parking lot. I wasn't happy about that, sitting next to the window. I knew I made an inviting target for anyone driving by in an SUV armed with, say, a Ruger MP-9 submachine gun. Yet it was one of the conditions that Vicki demanded in return for meeting me. I might have argued with her except she insisted on ending our conversation in a hurry.

I was drinking a sixteen-ounce French vanilla almond coffee

straight while resisting the impulse to set fire to the store's PA system. It was playing an innocuous smooth-jazz cover of the Dizzy Gillespie classic "Groovin' High," surely an affront to civilized man. A good-looking black kid wearing a beige windbreaker with a blue lining moved past to a second table next to the window and sat facing me. Another good-looking kid, this one white and wearing a jacket in the green and red colors of the Minnesota Wild hockey team, sat at the table directly behind me. They were both about twenty, and each had ordered a coffee drink that was heaped with so much whipped cream and sprinkles he required a spoon with a long handle to "drink" it. I wondered briefly if the two of them were members of the same club.

Finally, Vicki Walsh arrived. She didn't look around like someone who was expecting to meet a man she had never seen before. Certainly she didn't look at me. Instead, she went directly to the barista and placed her order. I couldn't help but notice that she had changed her hair color again. Her roses-and-wheat tresses were now brilliant blond and seemed to flash like a yellow caution light. There was no mistaking her brown eyes, though, or her pretty nineteen-going-on-fourteen face. She was wearing a short, thin violet-colored sweater over a long white tank top and blue jeans and carrying a small green leather handbag that didn't match her outfit.

I watched until Vicki picked up her order, an ice-cream-and-coffee concoction that caused me to shake my head. Did kids these days even know what real coffee tasted like? Vicki glanced my way but did not acknowledge my presence. She moved with utter confidence, claiming the table closest to the door, and settled in.

240

What the hell, my inner voice said.

I picked up my coffee and stood. The two kids sitting on either side of me rose at the same time. My plan was to join Vicki
at her table, but when I took a step toward her the white kid positioned himself to intercept me. He was smiling. The black kid
moved to my left flank. He wasn't smiling. I glanced at Vicki.
She had produced a purple cell phone from her bag and was
punching in numbers. A moment later, my prepaid cell rang. I
answered.

"McKenzie—you are McKenzie?" she asked. Even over the
cell her voice was like a silk nightgown. "I'd prefer that you
remain seated at your table. I am taking no chances."

"As you wish."

I sat. The two bodyguards—if you could call them that—
returned to their tables.

"What do you want, McKenzie?" Vicki asked.

"What did Caitlin tell you?"

"She said that Denny Marcus had been murdered."

"Did she tell you how?"

I could see her hand squeezing the cell phone she held
against her ear.

"She told me," Vicki said. "Who killed him?"

"I think it was the Joes."

"The Joes? Why?"

"Roberta Weltzin hired them to find you. Apparently they
thought Denny knew where you were."

"He didn't."

"I'm sure he told them that before he died."

Vicki looked away. She continued to press the cell against
her ear, yet did not speak. Her two friends looked at her as if

they felt sorry for her, as if they both wanted to hold her in their arms and tell her it would be all right. They held their positions, though. I waited until she resumed the conversation.

"How could they have known about him?" she asked.

"I don't know. I learned about him through your Facebook page."

Vicki gritted her teeth and breathed through them.

"It's my fault," she said.

If I had been sitting next to her I might have patted her hand and told her that she was not to blame, that she couldn't be held responsible for somebody else's actions, and so on and so on. I wouldn't have believed it, of course, but I might have said it.

"Why are you looking for me?" Vicki asked. "You don't work for Roberta."

It was ridiculous to keep speaking to her across the room over a cell phone. I couldn't imagine why Vicki thought that would make her safe.

"You're right to be cautious," I said. "These two, though, they won't be able to protect you."

"They did all right the other day."

"Were they the guys in the SUV? Are they the ones who shot up my car?"

"You didn't answer the question, McKenzie. Why are you looking for me?"

"They're your partners, too, aren't they? They've been with you every step of the way, helping with Jason Truhler in Thunder Bay and all the rest."

"Junior partners. You said Jason?"

"Truhler asked me to find you. He's tired of paying your blackmail. I'm sure all of your victims are."

"That just breaks my heart."

"I thought it might."

"Just out of curiosity, what is Jason paying you?"

"Why? Are you going to bid higher?"

"I just want to know."

"He's not paying me anything."

"Why help him, then? You're not his friend. Jason doesn't have any friends."

"I'm a friend of Erica's."

"Erica, Jason's daughter? Yeah. I know her. I like her. She's a sweetheart."

"Yes, she is."

I kept glancing from one of Vicki's bodyguards to the other. They both now seemed more interested in their frilly coffee drinks than they were in what was going on around them. Amateurs, I thought.

"Does Erica know her old man is a pedophile?" Vicki asked.

"I don't think it's come up in conversation."

"I actually thought about recruiting her, you know, recruiting her for Roberta. God knows she's pretty enough, although I'm not sure how important that is to our clients. I decided against it, partly because I didn't think she'd go for it, but mostly because Erica doesn't look like someone you can take advantage of, and in our little market niche, that look is essential."

"Who's taking advantage of whom?"

I would have heard Vicki's laugh even without the phone.

"I still can't get over how easy it was," she said. "The johns all wanted underage girls, expected underage girls. Yet they were all so very surprised when they learned that the girls really were underage."

"How did you convince them of that?"

"I sent them copies of counterfeit student IDs. Naturally, Roberta told them it wasn't true, but whom would you believe in a situation like that, Roberta or the IDs? Besides, I had photos. A picture is worth a thousand words. Lots of money, too."

"What about Truhler?"

"Jason? Jason was my masterpiece. Jason knew me from fencing. Do you know he actually hit on me at a high school fencing meet? In front of his daughter? I knew the underage girl scam wouldn't have worked with him, so I had to try something a bit more theatrical. If he had caught me, or called the police, something like that, I would have told him it was just a practical joke. Turned out it wasn't a problem. He never even felt for a pulse, just ran as fast as he could. I had a good long laugh over that."

"I'm sure you're very proud of yourself."

"My, don't you look fierce when you're being all self-righteous. Go 'head, tell me how much you pity all those poor family men who hire young girls for prostitutes. Tell me how your heart bleeds for each and every one."

"I have no sympathy for them, Vicki. But what you're doing . . ."

"I'm not losing any sleep over what I'm doing."

"Why are you doing it?"

"For the money. Call it my college fund. Do you know how much it costs to go to a top-flight school these days? Cornell gets over fifty thousand a year after you add room and board. I couldn't afford it when they accepted me. Now I can."

"So quit. According to my calculations, you already have more than enough to go to Cornell."

"Yeah, but not in style. Besides, money is only part of it."

"Given who you're dealing with, I'd say you're playing an awfully dangerous game."

"I have it under control."

"Tell that to Denny Marcus."

Vicki looked away again. I heard her gasp over the cell even as I saw her body cringe on the other side of the room, and for a moment, I thought she might actually start weeping. She didn't. She closed her eyes, then opened them abruptly. When she spoke, it was again through gritted teeth.

"Do you know why most gamblers lose, McKenzie? It's because they stay too long at the table, because they don't know when to quit. I'm not greedy. One more round of collections and I'm through."

"You might be through with your victims, but they won't be through with you. They won't forgive and they won't forget. No matter where you go or what you do, they'll still believe that you're a threat to them."

"They wouldn't pay me if I weren't a threat, now would they?"

"Vicki, I'm trying to help you."

The way she laughed, I knew she didn't believe me. I didn't take it personally, though. I doubt she would have believed the pope when he did the benediction.

"Caitlin said that you said you could help me," Vicki said. "I don't need help. I know exactly what I'm doing."

"I don't think you do."

"Because you offered and because you're a friend of Erica's, I'll let Jason off the hook. Poof. See how easy that was? Now you can leave me alone."

"It's not enough, Vicki. Roberta and the Joes are still after you. They killed Denny Marcus, remember? They might go after other people who are close to you. Your mother. Caitlin. Your victims, they're still after you. Some of them are scarier than the Joes. Then there's a man named Muehlenhaus who's scarier than all of them put together. Do you know who he is? He's the prince of darkness, Vicki. He wants you, too, but I made a deal with him. If you give up the files you downloaded off of Roberta's computer and whatever other incriminating material you have, he'll let you keep your money, he'll let you disappear, and he'll see to it that you're left alone."

"Oh, please, McKenzie. We both know better than that. My files are the only things protecting me. Not knowing where they are or what'll happen to them if they lay hands on me is what's keeping my enemies at bay. If I give them up, it'll be open season. I might as well paint a target on my forehead."

"It might be your only chance."

"We'll see."

"I'm not kidding."

"Good-bye, McKenzie."

Vicki deactivated her cell phone and dropped it into her bag. I stood and called to her across the coffeehouse. Her pals stood at the same time.

"You can trust Muehlenhaus," I said.

The white kid slid between us. I might have done something about it except I couldn't think of any reason why I should. Jason Truhler was off the hook, Vicki said so. That's what I came for. As for Muehlenhaus, I delivered his message. That's all I said I would do. I remained by the table. Vicki didn't even bother giving me a backward glance. She stepped outside; the door of the coffeehouse closed slowly behind her. The black kid soon followed. A moment later, the white kid joined them. I watched the trio through the window. They stood in a tight circle and talked it over, a foolish thing for someone on the lookout to do. The two kids were looking at Vicki, oblivious to what was going on around them, another error in judgment. The lights of the parking lot were bright enough to play ball under, yet there were still plenty of shadows between parked vehicles where someone could be lurking. They should have been watching the shadows.

If Vicki's bodyguards had been any good, their vehicle would have been close at hand, their route carefully mapped out, their itinerary already planned. One guard would have stayed with Vicki—inside the coffee shop—while the other inspected the vehicle and then brought it up. Transferring her to the vehicle would have been done swiftly and efficiently, and then the vehicle would have moved out. Instead, the three of them sauntered through the parking lot as if they didn't have a care in the world, taking a circuitous path to their SUV parked nose-in in the third row—I recognized it as the vehicle that had ambushed me on Highway 61. It was yet another mistake. The SUV should have been parked to allow for a fast exit.

I didn't hear the gunshot through the thick pane of glass.

The white kid took the round low in his shoulder, and the way the back of his green jacket exploded with blood made me think the bullet went straight through. He fell against a parked car and slowly slid down into a sitting position on the asphalt.

The black kid didn't turn to face the threat or move to cover Vicki as he should have. Instead, he bent to help his friend. He took two rounds in his back that lifted him off his feet and threw him on top of the white kid.

By then I was out the door and moving up on the scene. I was shouting, "Get down, get down." I found Vicki crouching between two parked cars and screaming. Her clothes were splattered with blood. The fact that she was still alive proved that she had been right—her enemies wanted her files as much as they wanted her. I didn't see the killer, but I knew he was close at hand.

I automatically moved into a Weaver stance just as I had been trained to do at the police academy, the Beretta in my right hand, my left hand supporting it, my left arm close to my body, my head slightly bent to align the gun sights on the target. Only there was no target. Whoever had fired on Vicki and her bodyguards must have seen or heard me coming and backed off. I swung the gun slowly to my right and then to my left. Bystanders were gathering, attracted by Vicki's screams like moths to a flame, yet I saw no one with a gun.

"Get up," I said.

Vicki's screams had become howls of anguish.

"Get up," I repeated.

I reached down with my left hand, clutched her elbow, and pulled upward.

"Get up, dammit."

She rose reluctantly. I had parked my Jeep Cherokee close to the door of the coffeehouse, where Vicki should have parked her SUV. I spun her toward it and gave her a push. She staggered but kept her feet.

"Go, go, go," I said.

I kept swinging my gun right, then left, in a short, controlled arc, searching for a target, trying hard not to be distracted by the bodies on the pavement in front of me. Vicki was moving at a snail's pace, her body racked with fear and sorrow. I turned, grabbed her arm above the elbow, and half pulled; half pushed her toward the car.

That's when they shot me.

The bullet smacked high into my back between the shoulder blades. The force of it propelled me forward until I fell to my knees, yet it did not penetrate the Kevlar vest. Which isn't to say that it didn't hurt. I felt as if I had been hit by a fastball delivered by a pitcher with major league potential. Yet knowing that the vest worked, that it had stopped the bullet, made me feel wonderful.

I pivoted on my knees and looked behind me. A shadow was ducking down behind what appeared to be a Toyota Tercel, a subcompact I didn't think they even made anymore. I threw four shots at it. The bullets smashed into the rear quarter panel where the shadow had fled. I was point shooting with one hand from the shoulder, a not particularly accurate firing position, yet if I missed it wasn't by much.

Vicki had resumed screaming.

"You're shot," she said.

I thought it was nice that she noticed.

I scrambled to my feet and pulled her to the Cherokee. I opened the passenger door with my key and stuffed her inside, all while gazing behind me and sweeping the lot with the sight of my gun. I circled the SUV, keeping it between Vicki's assailants and me until the last possible moment, then dashed to the driver's door, opened it, and climbed inside.

I started up the vehicle and drove off. There was a maze of unmarked thoroughfares throughout the massive parking lot. I chose to ignore them. I threaded the vehicle through the spaces between parked cars until I found an opening. I hit the accelerator and aimed for the lot's high curb. A curb can be easily jumped as long as you remember to hit it at about a forty-five-degree angle at a speed under forty-five miles per hour. The Cherokee made the jump and began skidding down a grassy hill toward the boulevard bordering France Avenue. Vicki bounced in her seat and her head banged against the roof of the Cherokee as we jumped another curb and landed on France heading in the wrong direction.

"Put on your seat belt," I said.

Vicki started adding actual words to her cries.

"Oh my God, we're going to be killed," she said.

I wove around two vehicles coming straight at me and a third driven by a man who was smart enough to turn hard to his right while I cranked the wheel to mine, missing him, and pushing the Cherokee across the median into the proper lane. I accelerated hard even as I glanced through my side and rear-view mirrors, searching for a trailing vehicle. Vicki fastened her safety harness.

"What is happening?" she asked.

"Who knew you were going to be at the coffeehouse?"

"No one."

"Think."

"No one."

"Then you were followed."

"We weren't followed. We were extra careful. Sean and Tony—oh, God, Sean and Tony." Up until then I didn't know the kids had names. "They shot them. They shot them. Do you think they're dead?"

I didn't answer. By then I could see a high-performance

German sedan coming up fast on my left in my sideview mirror, and I was starting to worry about me becoming dead. I was outmatched. My Jeep Cherokee was unstable. There was a very real chance that it could tip over when cornering at high speeds, unlike a vehicle with a low center of gravity and a powerful engine like, say, my Audi or whatever the hell the shooters were driving. Also, the Cherokee had four-wheel drive, which was swell for off-road excursions yet greatly reduced its acceleration. On the other hand, I didn't just learn how to shoot at the police academy. I also learned how to drive.

The shooters were about two car lengths behind me when I swung the steering wheel of the Cherokee hard to the right, jumped another curb, careened across the lawn of a small office building, and ended up on a side street heading west. The shooters followed, yet by the time they made the turn I was already a full block in front of them. I was relieved to see that they weren't leaning out the windows of their vehicle and spraying the street with bullets the way they do in the movies.

Not the Joes, my inner voice said. *Professionals. They're the guys who followed you last night.*

The most important thing to remember in a high-speed pursuit—especially if you're the one being pursued—is not to crash, because even if you survive the accident you're going to be a sitting duck. That's why high speeds are not recommended. By keeping your speedometer under sixty miles per hour, you'll have greater control of your vehicle, and evasive maneuvers will be easier to accomplish. At least that's what I was taught. 'Course, if I had a superior car, I would have been able to flat outrun the sonsabitches.

"I can't believe you killed my Audi," I said.

"What?" Vicki asked.

She was turned in her seat and staring out at our pursuers.

"Never mind," I said.

"What are we going to do?"

"I'm working on it."

I let the Cherokee drift to the far side of the narrow street as I approached the corner. I started braking the car, gradually at first, then more heavily, as I downshifted. I swung the steering wheel hard to my right again, making sure my tires were as close as possible to the inside edge of the corner as I turned, then stomped on the accelerator. It is a commonly held belief, sustained by most Hollywood action movies, that the best way to handle a corner is to blast through it. Not so. Any NASCAR fan will tell you that the speed at which you exit a corner is far more important than the speed at which you take the corner. If you don't believe me, just ask the guys chasing us. Even though my taillights warned them in ample time to prepare for the turn, they still lost ground.

Unfortunately, they gained half of it back when a woman in a Subaru backed out of her driveway in front of the Cherokee, forcing me to brake nearly to a stop. Vicki screamed into my ear as I accelerated around the woman.

"I wish you would stop doing that," I said.

The area of Edina located between France Avenue and Highway 100 on the east and west and Highway 62 and Interstate 494 on the north and south was mostly residential. There were plenty of high-priced houses, parks, and at least three lakes that I knew of. Most of the time it was a fairly quiet neighborhood. However, at six thirty on a Saturday night, it was alive with traffic. The Subaru wasn't the only car I encountered. I had to ease around several others as well as avoid a handful of pedestrians. I turned on my high beams, but they didn't help much. What I should have done was replace my sealed-beam headlights with quartz-iodine headlights that throw off twice the light and would have allowed me to see better at night. I should have bought the best radial tires money could buy and filled them with run-flat puncture repair foam in case they were shot. I should have invested in better shocks and springs. I should have paid the extra twenty thousand dollars to armor the Cherokee against a .30 caliber rifle round. My psychiatrist ex-girlfriend called such thinking hindsight bias, which was one of the reasons we broke up. She had an answer for everything.

Yet even without the extras, I continued to gain ground. I took a left, then a right, two more lefts, circled a lake, took another right and then a left again. Each time I felt the Cherokee listing precariously against the turn, yet it always remained on all four wheels.

Somewhere along the line, I lost the shooters. To make sure, I blasted through a stop sign and drove two blocks going the wrong way on a one-way street before I found a quiet avenue without streetlamps, parked, and shut down the Cherokee.

"What are we doing?" Vicki asked.

"Waiting."

"Why?"

"Because I have no idea where I am, and I'm afraid that if I start wandering around looking for a familiar landmark, they're going to find us again. We'll sit for a while."

Despite the chill in the air, I rolled down the window. I could hear the sound of traffic like surf in the distance, yet I had no idea where it was coming from. Vicki leaned back in her seat. She closed her eyes and rested her hands in her lap. She inhaled, held her breath for a beat, then slowly exhaled, and I thought she was doing some kind of Zen breathing exercises to control her emotions. It didn't do any good. After a few moments her shoulders began shaking, followed closely by the rest of her body. She wrapped her arms around herself, leaned forward, and rested her head against the dashboard. Long, painful sobs drowned out the traffic noise.

"It's my fault," she said. "It's all my fault."

I didn't say a word. What was I going to do? Argue with her?

We sat there for what seemed like a long time, yet was only a few minutes, until I saw the car. It had its high beams on and was coming fast.

"Nuts," I said.

Vicki's head came off the dash. She swung around and looked out the rear window.

"Are they back?" she asked.

"Get down," I said.

Vicki did what I asked without hesitation.

I slid down in my seat as well.

The German car flew past, and for a moment I thought it had missed us.

It got half a block before it slammed on its brakes. Its squealing tires sounded like an alarm.

I immediately fired up the Cherokee and threw it into reverse. I accelerated until I was traveling backward at about thirty miles an hour. I got off the gas, cranked the steering wheel all the way to the left until the car spun ninety degrees, jumped back on the accelerator, and straightened out the steering wheel until I was driving nearly fifty miles an hour in a straight line.

"Yes," I shouted. "Yes, yes, yes. Did you see that?" I patted the dash of the Cherokee. "Good car."

I glanced at Vicki. She didn't seem nearly as thrilled by the maneuver as I was.

I made a few turns, yet it didn't take long before the shooters were back on my bumper. The Cherokee just didn't have enough giddy-up.

The shooters feinted right and then left, causing me to swerve to block them. It was obvious that they were trying to pull up alongside, either to shoot us or run us off the road. It was just as obvious that they preferred to come up on my left. I decided to let them. I didn't know what else to do. I was running out of options.

"Hang on," I said.

It was a simple act of pure desperation.

When the shooters feinted to the right, I purposely moved too far to block them, giving them the opening they wanted. They accelerated hard, coming up on my left side. When their front bumper was even with my passenger door, I pulled up hard on the emergency brake. The Cherokee skidded across the pavement, making a sickening high-pitched screeching sound. The shooters flew past. I released the brake, downshifted, and stomped on the gas. The Cherokee lunged forward. The shooters tried to escape, but it was already too late. I rammed their bumper on the left-hand side with the right-hand side of my bumper as though I were trying to pass but didn't give myself enough room. At impact, the rear of the German car started sliding sideways toward the right. The driver tried to compensate. He spun his wheels in the direction the car was skidding—like any good Minnesota driver who hits a patch of ice—but instead of slowing, he stepped on the gas. His tires gained traction. The car shot off in the direction it was pointed, off the road, up a boulevard, and into a tree.

Vicki looked back, but I didn't.

I worked my way west, using the bridge at Edina Industrial Boulevard to cross Highway 100. I drove along Normandale Boulevard until I entered the City of Bloomington, then hung a right at West Seventy-eighth Street. From there I drove to the back of the parking lot of the elegant Hotel Sofitel.

"What are we doing now?" Vicki asked.

"We have to get rid of the car." I opened my door and slid out.

Vicki followed me. "Why?"

I circled the Cherokee and examined the damage to my front end. The right-side headlight was broken. Beyond that, the damage wasn't nearly as bad as I thought it would be; I was guessing not more than a thousand dollars' worth of body work, including paint.

"Because it's possible you weren't followed to the coffeehouse," I said. "It's possible that I was followed. I didn't see a tail, but someone could have tagged my car with a bumper beeper or something. That would explain how the shooters found us after we parked."

"What's a bumper beeper?"

"It's an electronic bug with a two-mile range that attaches to the underside of your car with a magnet. It's usually kept in a small metal box with two skinny antennas sticking out. Unfortunately, we haven't got enough time or light to do a sweep. Nuts."

"What?" Vicki asked.

"Your clothes. They're covered with blood." I looked at the hotel behind me. "You can't go anywhere looking like that."

Vicki looked down at her violet sweater and white tank top. The red splotches were clearly visible in the lot's harsh lights. She picked at the stains as if they were pieces of lint she hoped to pull off her clothes, starting slowly and delicately at first, then increasing in speed and fury until she was grabbing and slapping herself in a frenzy. She moaned loudly, and I quickly searched the lot for witnesses.

"Vicki," I said.

She covered her face with both of her hands and wept into the palms. I wrapped my arms around her and pulled her close.

"It's okay, it's okay," I said.

I waited. Slowly her shallow, rapid breathing became more regular. I wondered if her cupped hands had formed a pocket that allowed her to breathe her own air, not unlike someone who breathes into a paper bag when suffering an anxiety attack—it allowed her to inhale the carbon dioxide she was expelling, thus producing a calming effect. I released her and stepped back. Eventually she dropped her hands to her sides and looked at me.

"Are you okay?" I asked.

"What should we do?"

I had already taken off my brown leather jacket and was removing my sweater. I gave the sweater to Vicki.

"Put this on over your blouse," I said.

She did what I asked. The sweater was big and bulky on her. She had to push the cuffs up; the hem fell against her thighs.

Still, putting it on over her bloodstained clothes seemed to cheer her somewhat.

"I look ridiculous," Vicki said.

"Didn't that used to be the height of fashion a while back?" I asked. "Oversized sweaters?"

"Not in my lifetime."

The Kevlar vest was clearly visible beneath my blue dress shirt, and I had to button the shirt all the way to my throat to keep the top of it from peeking out.

"I thought you were shot," Vicki said. "The vest—that's why you weren't hurt."

"That's why," I said.

"I want a bulletproof vest. Can I have it?"

"I can protect you. Can you protect me?"

She shook her head.

"Then I'll keep the vest." I checked the Beretta, holstered it on my belt, and put my jacket on over it. "C'mon."

Hotel Sofitel boasted a fine French restaurant called Chez Colette that had its own street entrance. There was an unoccupied maître d' stand just inside the door near a sign that read PLEASE WAIT TO BE SEATED. It was still early for a Saturday night, and there were plenty of empty tables. I ignored the sign and the tables and led Vicki across the restaurant to a second entrance just off the hotel's lobby. We crossed the lobby to the front of the hotel.

The doorman said, "Good evening, sir." He touched the brim of his hat with two fingers when he looked at Vicki. "Miss."

"Good evening," I said. "I'd like a taxicab."

I reached into my pocket and produced a handful of folded bills to prove I meant business. The doorman hailed the first taxi in line at the cabstand. The taxi drove up, and the doorman opened the back door for us. Vicki slipped into the seat. I gave the doorman a five-dollar bill for his trouble and slid in after her.

The driver put the taxi in gear and started driving off even before he said, "Where to?"

"Airport," I said.

"Which terminal?"

Not long ago, the two terminals that made up the Minneapolis–St. Paul International Airport were named after Charles A. Lindbergh, the Minnesota-born pilot who was the first man to fly solo across the Atlantic, and Hubert H. Humphrey, the state's longtime senator and U.S. vice president. However, it was decided by the powers that be that those names were far too confusing for travelers, who occasionally mixed them up. So now they're designated Terminal One and Terminal Two. That, of course, cleared up everything.

"One," I said.

"That would be the old Lindbergh Terminal," the driver said. See?

To pass the time, the driver waxed poetic about the ineptitude of the Minnesota Vikings and how their season had pretty much ended before it had even begun. He then segued into a dissertation on the continuing futility of both the Wild and the Timberwolves, his general thesis being that professional sports in Minnesota sucked and don't get him started on the Gophers. For the most part I agreed with him.

"Except for the Twins," I said.

"Baseball?" He spoke the word as if it were an obscenity. "Baseball?"

"My good man," I said, "baseball is the only sport God approves of."

"He tell you that Himself, did He?"

I held up my crossed fingers so he could get a good look at them in his rearview.

"We're like this," I said.

The cabbie thought it was pretty funny.

"Do you believe that, Miss?" he asked. "Him and God?"

Vicki didn't answer. Vicki didn't say a word throughout the drive. Instead, she kept glancing at me as if she were hoping to get a glimpse of my plans in my face, in my gestures, and in my words. Yeah, like I had a plan. Well, actually, I did.

After we arrived, I paid off the driver and escorted Vicki into the terminal. From there we went one level down and followed the signs to the Red and Blue parking ramps. Vicki still refused to speak. She let me lead her around like a visitor from abroad who didn't know the language.

On the second level between the ramps, there were seven car rental companies. I chose the one with the shortest line. Twenty minutes later we drove off in a black Altima two-door coupe. A few minutes after that, we were on Highway 5 heading into St. Paul.

"McKenzie?"

"How are you holding up, sweetie?" I asked.

"Where are we going?"

I gave my standard smart-ass reply to the question—"Straight to hell unless we change our ways."

She nodded as if it were the answer she was expecting.

SIXTEEN

Highway 61 ran through the City of Hastings as Vermillion Street. When Hastings was founded in 1857 and for many years afterward, it was considered important. The city was located at the junction of the St. Croix and Mississippi rivers and proved to be a good deep-draft riverboat port. Plus, it was close to the hydropower of the waterfalls on the nearby Vermillion River. 'Course, those days were far behind it and celebrated now once a year during Rivertown Days. Like a great many other small towns scattered across America, Hastings no longer had a reason to exist. If its population had increased in the past decade, it was solely because it was located eighteen miles south of St. Paul and twenty-six miles from Minneapolis—close to the Cities, yet not part of them, which, I was sure, came as a great comfort to commuters.

Hastings had a couple of nice hotels, including the Afton House and the Rosewood Inn, yet we registered at a cheap dive on this side of the river. To say the motor lodge was located in a strip mall would have been an insult to strip malls. The motel took up one end. It was surrounded by a hard-packed sand and gravel parking lot; you could park directly in front of your motel room door. A self-service gas station that also acted as a miniature grocery store and bait shop was on the other end. Between them there was a café that proudly served "American Cuisine," including all-you-can-eat hotdish between 4:00 and 8:00 P.M., an office for State Farm Insurance, and a video rental store that looked as if it had been closed since the invention of the DVD. Across the street there was a fried chicken joint popular among customers who have never had really good fried chicken and a bingo parlor. The windows of the parlor had all been painted over with colorful promotional messages—"Thursday and Saturday late night sessions," "Max Pack $10 Off," "Thanksgiving Weekend Specials," "Concessions! Everything from popcorn and pizza to burgers and Coke products. Mmmmm," and "Viking Sundays! If Bret Favre plays all side packs are $4 (paper only)."

The motel manager smirked when I paid in cash and told him I didn't know how long I was staying. The smirk gave me a creepy feeling that quickly turned to anger. I would have liked to correct his lewd impression of me with a quick spear hand to his throat, since demanding two double beds obviously had no effect, except Vicki's golden hair if not her face was clearly visible in my car through the manager's office window. If I were him, I probably would have smirked, too.

The city also had a couple of decent restaurants—the Mississippi Belle and Levee Café were well regarded—yet we ordered burgers at a drive-through and ate them in the Altima. Afterward, we stopped at a Target store, and I bought new clothes for Vicki, including a lightweight robe, as well as a few things for myself while she waited in the car. It was just after

10:00 P.M. by the time we were safely ensconced in the motel room.

The first thing I did after we entered the room was turn on the light. There was a low-wattage bulb hidden behind a glass cover in the center of the ceiling that gave the room a sickly orange tint. I carefully locked the door behind me and went to the window. After making reasonably sure that no one was lurking outside, I closed the tattered drapes.

The first thing Vicki did was turn on the TV. She didn't tune it to a specific channel or search for a program. In fact, she turned her back to it once it was on and went into the bathroom. It was strictly white noise. And I thought *I* was a member of the TV generation.

I heard running water. Vicki said something, but I couldn't hear. I turned down the volume on the TV.

"What was that?" I asked.

Vicki stepped out of the bathroom. She had removed the sweater and was drying her hands with a small white towel.

"I look terrible," she said. "I need to take a shower. Can I take a shower?"

"Sure," I said.

Her eyes became wide, and her mouth hung open for a moment. A hand slipped out from under the towel, and she slowly pointed at the TV. I turned to see what she was looking at. A female news reporter standing in front of a coffeehouse filled half of the screen. Vicki's face filled the other half. The photo had been taken before she switched her hair color from roses and wheat to startling blond; it was much shorter then, too. At least we had that going for us, I told myself. I quickly turned up the volume.

"Police are looking for Vicki Walsh, age nineteen, in connection with the shooting," the reporter said.

A female news anchor started quizzing the reporter.

"Do we know that she's a suspect in the shooting?" the anchor asked.

"Not at this time," said the reporter. "It's still very confused here. Vicki Walsh could be a suspect or she could be a witness. All we know for certain is that police want to question her as soon as possible and are asking our viewers for help in locating her."

"Thank you, Karen." The scene shifted to the news anchor sitting alone at her desk. "Once again, two unidentified men were shot and killed in a parking lot near Southdale Shopping Center in Edina tonight. Police continue to investigate. We'll be right back."

I turned off the TV just as the commercial began.

"Muehlenhaus," I said.

"Who?"

"I think I might have mentioned him earlier."

"The guy you said was the prince of darkness?"

"It's been less than three hours since the shooting, and they haven't identified your friends Sean and Tony, yet they've not only identified you, they've distributed your photo to the local TV stations. On top of that, they're not actually accusing you of the shooting. They're only saying they want to question you about it. It's their way of letting you know that all this can be made to go away if you give them what they want. They're using the news media to offer you a deal. Pure Muehlenhaus. That sonuvabitch."

"You said I could trust Muehlenhaus," Vicki said.

"Did I? I can't imagine what possessed me."

Vicki sat on the edge of the bed farthest from the door, holding the hand towel in her lap.

"I still have the high card," she said.

I sat on the edge of the bed closest to the door.

"The flash drive with Roberta's files?" I asked.

She smiled at my naiveté.

"No," Vicki said. "Flash drive? Do you think anyone is going to be afraid enough to pay blackmail because their name appears in a ledger? I have photos, I have taped phone conversations, I have video of my johns in the act, I have audio *and* video. I have corroborating evidence like credit card receipts and hotel room invoices. And I have a friend, an accomplice if you will, who is prepared to upload all of it onto the Internet, put it on YouTube, send it to newspapers and TV, e-mail it to all those citizen journalists like the Drudge Report. I don't even have to talk to him directly. The way we have it worked out, we have a code, a code word. He hears the code, he sees the code—it could be on his cell, could be something I upload on Facebook, could be a text, an e-mail, a postcard, someone whispering in his ear on the street—he hears the code and everything happens automatically. I've already paid him. Don't bother to ask his name or what the code is. I'm not telling. I still have the high card, McKenzie. I'm keeping it."

"I don't think you understand, Vicki. These people are playing for keeps. They're prepared to have you arrested for murder. Or worse. What good will your high card do you then?"

"Do you have any suggestions?"

"I have friends with the cops. We can arrange to have you turn yourself in, give up your files, and turn state's evidence.

You could bring Roberta down. You could bring them all down."

"Do you really think they'd let me? Who am I? I'm a nineteen-year-old prostitute. Who are they? Pillars of the community. C'mon, McKenzie. You know how it works." Vicki pointed at the TV. "Besides, this guy Muehlenhaus—you said he already has the police. I bet he has judges and prosecutors, too."

"Not all of them."

"Yeah, well, I don't have to take that chance. Fortunately, there's an alternative."

"What alternative?"

"The one I intended to take all along—get my money and disappear. No more collections. I am officially retired. All I ask is that you give me a ride down to Rochester and put me on a bus."

"When?"

"Monday. After the banks open and I can get to my safe deposit box."

"You placed all that money in a safe deposit box?"

"Some of it. Traveling money. The rest is in money market funds."

"Where would you go? Ithaca, New York?"

Vicki smiled at that. "No, not Cornell," she said. "Somewhere else. Somewhere no one can find me."

"I don't know where that is."

Vicki smiled again. "I do," she said.

"You think you do. Vicki, I know how to find people, and so do they—and they will find you. Maybe not next week or next month or even next year, but they will find you and they will hurt you. What happened tonight at the coffeehouse was only the beginning. They'll find you and it'll be the same thing all over again. Think of your friends Sean and Tony."

"They were not my friends. I don't have any male friends."

"Not even Denny Marcus?"

Vicki rose from the bed.

"I'm going to take my shower now," she said.

Before she went into the bathroom, Vicki fished a purple BlackBerry smartphone out of her bag.

"No calls," I said.

She carelessly tossed the phone to me.

"Take a look," she said. "I'm a bitch. What are they?"

I surfed the files on the phone, watched videos, listened to conversations. It was all incredibly lewd. Vicki usually played the innocent. The men were always less than kind. Yet as evidence of a crime, I thought Vicki had overestimated the files. There wasn't a single shot of money actually changing hands. The johns all had adhered to Roberta's system of payment. There were ledger entries that listed names and amounts, yet nothing that actually linked the payments to the services provided. If it all got out, certainly careers would be damaged, marriages ruined, reputations irretrievably lost—but criminal charges? The johns, and I recognized a couple of them, could all argue they were having voluntary relations with a woman that they knew to be over eighteen. It would be their word against Vicki's, and Vicki, after all, was a blackmailing whore, or so a jury would be instructed in no uncertain terms. It was all about ego. As long as the johns were afraid of publicity, Vicki did, in fact, hold the high card. If the johns decided to risk public exposure or if it was forced upon them, she would be defenseless.

I set the BlackBerry on the credenza next to Vicki's bag. Watching her have sex with all those middle-aged men, listening to her pretend to enjoy it even when they hurt her, left me feeling a thousand years old. I spent a lot of time staring at the cheap motel room door, wondering why I didn't just walk out it, jump in the Altima, and drive home. I had done my bit for God and country; I had gotten Jason Truhler off the hook. He could go on being an asshole, and I could go on pretending to Erica that he wasn't. If I felt a need to make the world a better place, I could simply call Bobby, give him the names of Roberta Weltzin and Caitlin Brooks, and then watch while major crimes did its thing.

I lay back in bed and stared up at the light fixture in the center of the ceiling. The glass cover was square and undulated with a tiny sailboat painted on each corner. It looked like it hadn't been dusted in a decade.

Why don't you go home? my inner voice asked.

Vicki needs help, I answered.

Vicki is not a nice person.

Neither are all the others.

Denny Marcus. Tony and Sean. They're all dead because of her.

She didn't kill them.

That doesn't make her any less responsible.

She didn't kill them.

Are you choosing sides in this?

For all her faults, Vicki never killed anyone.

You are choosing sides.

The lesser of two evils.

Oh, please.

What was it Bobby Dunston said—johns pay a fine and the girls do the time? Wouldn't it be a kick to change that equation just this once? Besides, if I leave now, Vicki might be killed, too.

That's not your problem. You saved her once. You're under no obligation to do it again.

Would it be such an imposition to take her to Rochester? It's a lousy sixty-minute drive from here.

What would that get you?

Peace of mind.

Bullshit.

Yeah, I know—but tomorrow's Sunday. It's not like I have anything better to do.

You could stay home and watch the Vikings.

Exactly my point.

I continued to argue with myself, with neither side giving way, until Vicki opened the bathroom door. A cloud of steam followed her into the room. She was wearing the faint scent of strawberry shampoo and a smile. Her face might have looked fourteen, but her healthy young body seemed to have been carved out of marble five thousand years ago by a particularly gifted Greek sculptor.

"Did I keep you waiting long?" she asked.

"Don't do that, Vicki," I said.

"What?"

I left the bed and went to the credenza. I pulled the light-weight robe out of the shopping bag and tossed it to her.

"I don't know what you're trying to accomplish, but I wish you'd stop," I said.

A petulant smile spread across her small mouth.

"You did save my life," she said.

"There's no charge for that."

"I want to thank you."

I admit she unsettled me. I had watched all the pretty young girls, as I'm sure most males my age had, with wistful imagining. Yet I had never ventured beyond the paternal smile and head nod, never really considered the possibility of bedding a child. Her eyes, her smile, the timbre of her voice—she had deliberately taken me beyond possibility and was now offering herself in no uncertain terms. The question demanded a simple yes or no.

"No," I said.

I have never made any claims to virtue. Truth be told, there was a time, and not so very long ago, that I might have succumbed to the young lady's charms. Why not? She was over eighteen. Yet the sordid images on her cell phone were still fresh in my mind, and instead of arousing me—which might have been the reason Vicki wanted me to see them—they had the opposite effect. Besides, it was just plain wrong.

"No?" Vicki asked.

"No."

"I'll be damned."

Probably, my inner voice said.

"Maybe not," I said aloud.

Vicki carefully put on the robe and cinched it at the waist.

"I've been told no by men before," she said, "but only after they carefully weighed the chances of getting caught by their wives or someone else. You're not afraid of that."

"I'm too old for you, Vicki. Too involved with someone I care about. Too—I hate to use the word—too mature for you."

"I knew a mature man once. My stepfather. Being too old didn't bother him. He loved me. He loved me every way he could think of, and when he couldn't think of any more ways he got me high on drugs and loaned me out to his friends and they loved me, too. He had a lot of friends, and they had friends. One of them strangled me while he was ramming it in, called it erotic asphyxiation, said I'd enjoy it. He did such a thorough job they had to take me to the emergency room. To cover their crimes, they said I did it to myself; they said I attempted to strangle myself while masturbating. So, after I got out of the emergency room, they sent me to the psychiatric ward. I was fifteen. Don't worry, I'm better now. While I was away, my mother divorced my stepfather. Last I heard he was married to another middle-aged woman with daughters. I've often thought of paying him a visit. I just never got around to it. Don't look at me that way, McKenzie. I don't want your pity. I don't even want your understanding."

"What do you want?"

"Acknowledgment. I exist."

"Yes, you do."

"Okay, then."

"So to prove that you exist you've decided to get revenge against all men."

"Not all men. Just those who try to take advantage of me."

"I saw some of your videos, Vicki. There are those who would accuse you of entrapment."

"You can't cheat an honest man."

"If you say so."

"Are you telling me that I'm wrong?" Vicki pulled her robe tighter. "Are you saying I have no right to revenge?"

"No. I've sought revenge once or twice myself—and got it."

"How did it make you feel?"

"Better."

"Exactly."

"There was always an endgame, though. A point that I reached where I could say, 'I'm satisfied.' What's your endgame? When is enough enough?"

"I'll know it when I see it."

"Will you? Let's say for argument's sake that you pull it off. That you collect your money and you disappear and your enemies never find you. Are you going to rebuild your life? Find happiness? Or are you just going to do the same damn thing all over again?"

"Decisions, decisions."

"Do you think it's funny, Vicki? I've known prostitutes, I've known strippers; I met them on the job. They all had a plan. Every damn one. Go to school, start a business, get married. The same shit that Roberta preached to you. You remember Roberta? The woman who recruited you?"

"I remember."

"Only a very few ever went through with it. They let the lives they were living destroy the lives they wanted to live."

"Stop it, McKenzie. You're breaking my heart."

"Yeah, I get it. I'm just an old man talking."

Vicki thought that was an amusing bit of self-deprecation.

"You're not old, McKenzie," she said. "Just old-fashioned."

"I'm going to take a shower," I said.

I went to the door of the motel room, made sure it was locked, then braced a chair against the doorknob. I looked down at Vicki as she slipped under the covers of her bed. I held up three fingers one at a time for her to see.

"Do not answer the door," I said. "Do not answer the phone. Do not make any calls. Okay?"

"Okay," she said.

I went inside the bathroom, carefully locking the door behind me. Five minutes later I was under the shower. I stood there for a very long time. For reasons I had a hard time explaining to myself, thinking of Vicki made me want to weep. I didn't, though.

SEVENTEEN

The sound of two men shouting at each other woke me. I had been sitting in a chair behind the small table next to the motel room window. My Beretta was set on top of the table. My hand covered the butt of the gun, but I released it when I realized the voices were coming from the TV. Vicki was sitting on the edge of her bed and watching a Sunday morning interview program. The two men were pretending to discuss immigration reform. I say pretending because they were talking over each other, neither listening to the other, arguing vehemently about their own solutions, both of which seemed vague to me.

The sudden movement caught Vicki's eye, and she turned to look at me.

"You slept in a chair all night when you had a perfectly good bed?" she asked. "I didn't scare you that much, did I?"

"I wasn't sleeping," I said. "I was just resting my eyes."

"Your eyes snore, then."

"What time is it?"

"A little after nine. Do you want to get some breakfast? I'm starving."

I glanced at the motel room door. The chair that I had braced against the handle had been removed.

"Did you go out?" I asked.

"I went for a run. I've been up for hours, McKenzie."

Some sentry you are, my inner voice said.

"You're supposed to be in hiding," I said aloud.

Vicki put on a pair of sunglasses and pulled the end of her long blond hair across her mouth.

"Don't worry," she said. "I was in disguise."

Vicki was wearing her new jeans, her new white shirt, and her new light blue cardigan sweater; her hair had been tied behind her head. Nothing in her appearance suggested what she did for a living. Nothing in her smile indicated how she had spent the past eighteen hours. If you had told me that she was the lead singer in a church youth choir, I would have believed you.

"You shouldn't take chances," I said.

"McKenzie, it's Hastings."

I took the chair I was sitting on and braced it against the door.

"I need a minute to get cleaned up," I said.

Vicki's smile followed me into the bathroom.

She was still smiling when I returned. I had reclaimed my sweater. The Kevlar vest was secured beneath it.

"Where should we eat?" Vicki asked.

"Prescott."

"Prescott? Isn't that in Wisconsin?"

"Just down the road and across the St. Croix River."

"Why there?"

"I want to keep moving. We'll cross into Wisconsin, drive

to Madison, maybe Milwaukee. Stay the night. Come back tomorrow. Go to your bank. Stop at your place—"

"There's nothing there that I can't live without."

"Then get you on the first stagecoach out of Dodge."

"And that will be that."

"Unless you decide to go back to Thunder Bay. There's a detective constable up there who wants to chat with you."

"I think I'll avoid Thunder Bay, although Canada is awfully big. A girl could easily get lost in Canada."

"Send me a postcard."

I crossed the motel room. I seized the chair and pulled it away from the door. That was as far as I got before my prepaid cell phone rang. I read the name off of the screen before I answered.

"Who is it?" Vicki asked.

"Jason Truhler."

I did not want to leave Vicki Walsh alone in a run-down motor lodge that was about as secure as a box of corn flakes, especially since I knew she'd probably break her promise to me before I reached the city limits. Despite protests to the contrary, I was pretty sure she'd leave the room to get something to eat or go to the movies at the multiplex down the road or shop for clothes or play bingo at the parlor across the highway or all of the above. Despite everything, she just didn't seem to appreciate the danger she was in. I kept telling her.

"Remember what happened last night," I said.

"It's Hastings," she said. "Nothing bad happens in Hastings."

I couldn't imagine what made her think so.

Unfortunately, Jason Truhler's situation seemed much more dire.

"It's the Joes," he said. "The Joes."

I knew I'd have to deal with them sooner or later, and now seemed as good a time as any. I contacted Dailey and Moulton. I told them that the Joes were putting the arm on Truhler today and I would give them the time and place as soon as I knew it.

"You can charge them with felony coercion," I said.

"Yeah, that's exactly what we're going to do," Dailey said. "Arrest the pricks for felony coercion."

I drove Highway 61 north to west Interstate 494 and worked my way to Truhler's town house in Eden Prairie. It took about an hour, and I found myself becoming more nervous as the minutes and miles sped past. Even with Dailey and Moulton backing me up, the Joes were not people you wanted to trifle with. I checked the magazine in my Beretta before I left the car. I made sure there was no one watching when I went up the walk to Truhler's place—God knew where the Joes might be hiding. I rang the doorbell and then rapped heavily on the door when Truhler didn't respond quickly enough.

"Hey, McKenzie," he said. He spoke as if I were a guest he was expecting for an afternoon of beer, barbecue, and football.

"Are you all right?" I asked.

"Well, sure," he said.

Truhler looked it, too. He was wearing a black chef's apron with the name and logo of *Iron Chef America* embossed in red on the front and holding a red stir spoon. The apron was identical to the one Erica had given me for Christmas the year before. It had been one of my favorite gifts of the season, and seeing Truhler wearing it made me feel a twinge of jealousy.

"I'm glad to see that you've recovered from your concussion," I said.

"My what?" Truhler asked.

"Didn't the doctors diagnose you with a Grade Two concussion?"

Truhler waved the remark away. "That was so long ago," he said.

Three whole days, my inner voice said. *What a fast healer.*

"C'mon in," Truhler said. "I'm making jambalaya. It's not exactly a Sunday brunch item, but I like it."

He turned and casually walked into his kitchen. I followed after carefully locking the front door.

"Rickie said you make a pretty good jambalaya," he said over his shoulder. "I bet mine's better. You put in shrimp and crab, am I right? I use a classic chicken recipe straight from the bayou. Plenty of andouille sausage."

Apparently a love for cooking was another thing besides music that Truhler and I had in common. I was beginning to seriously question Nina's judgment in men, only I didn't linger over it.

"Am I missing something?" I asked.

"What?"

"You don't look frightened."

"Should I be?"

"You said the Joes called. You said they wanted their money today. You said they would call later and tell you where to deliver it." I tapped my own chest. "I'm frightened. Why aren't you?"

"Did you bring the money?"

"I'm not going to give those bastards fifty thousand dollars."

Truhler's face clouded over for a moment, but it was an expression of disappointment, not alarm.

"Okay," he said.

"Okay?"

"The jambalaya needs to simmer for at least another hour. Do you want a beer?"

"Are you kidding me, Truhler? The last time we spoke about this you were damn near paralyzed with fear. What's changed?"

"You're not going to let anything bad happen, are you, Mc-Kenzie?"

There was a mocking quality in Truhler's voice that I had a hard time getting my head around.

"Whatever happens, I promise it's going to be bad," I said.

Truhler went to his refrigerator and pulled out two bottles of Summit Extra Pale Ale, my favorite, brewed in St. Paul, my hometown. He twisted the cap off one bottle and handed it to me.

"The football pregame shows are on," he said. "Do you want to watch?"

He is mocking you, my inner voice said.

"Talk to me, Truhler," I said.

"Talk about what?"

"Have it your own way. I'm outta here. You can confront the Joes on your own."

"Okay."

"Okay, what?"

"Okay, I'll confront the Joes on my own."

He smiled when he said it, actually smiled. Then I knew.

"You made a deal," I said.

Truhler's smile became broader.

"What deal?" I asked. "What deal did you make?"

"Relax, McKenzie. It's all working out."

"What are you talking about?"

"I got us both off the hook."

I carefully set my bottle of ale on the kitchen counter, reached out, grabbed a fistful of his apron, and pulled him close.

"What deal?" I asked.

"Don't do that." Truhler pushed against me, yet I held firm. "I did you a favor, man."

"What favor?"

"I got you out of the motel room before the Joes showed up. Okay? Nobody gets hurt. You don't get hurt, and we don't owe the Joes anything. You should be happy."

It took a couple of beats for it all to sink in.

"The Joes know where Vicki is?" I asked.

"Yeah, they know where she is. They know you were watching over her. I did you a favor, McKenzie. Now you're out of it. They'll get Vicki, and then they'll forget about the thirty-five thousand we owe."

"What about Vicki?"

"She's a blackmailer. She's a whore. What do you care about Vicki?"

"What have you done?"

"I've saved your ass, that's what I've done."

"Give me a second," I said. I was talking more to myself than I was to Truhler. I released the apron and took a step backward.

Think it through . . .

"How did the Joes know Vicki and I were in Hastings?" I asked. "How did you know?"

"What difference does it make?"

"Why would the Joes make a deal with you?"

"That's where it gets a little complicated."

I grabbed Truhler by the apron again and pushed him backward until he bounced off the door of his refrigerator.

"Tell me," I said.

"What do you care?" he asked. "It all worked out. That's the important thing."

"Tell me."

"The Joes knew you were looking for Vicki."

"How did they know?"

"I told them. Okay? I told them."

"When did you tell them?"

"The night they came to my place. The Joes wanted their drugs or their money. I knew Roberta had hired them to find Vicki because they had asked me about her before; they talked to everyone who was involved with Vicki. I told them that you were looking for her, too, and that you were pretty smart about that sort of thing and that when you found her I would tell them if they would forget about the money. The money they would make with Vicki's files was so much more than the thirty-five thousand we owed they figured it was a good investment."

"I told you that night that I wasn't going to look for her anymore."

"That's why I had to—they didn't really hit me that hard. Just hard enough, you know? Look, I know you're upset, but it all worked out for the best. Now everyone's happy."

"What about Vicki?"

"Christ, McKenzie, why are you worrying about that slut? She's getting what she deserves."

"You sonuvabitch."

I released Truhler's apron and made for the front door.

"Where are you going?" Truhler asked. "Are you going back to Hastings? Are you crazy?"

I stopped only long enough to look into his mystified eyes.

"I'm not going to forget this, Truhler," I said. "I'm not going to forget that you used me. I'm not going to forget that the Joes wanted thirty-five thousand for their shit and you tacked on an extra fifteen for yourself."

I heard him calling to me out of the open door as I rushed to the Altima.

"Don't be like that," he said. "C'mon. It all worked out. C'mon."

I threw a plume of dust and dirt into the air when I pulled too fast into the motel parking lot and hit the brakes. I had tried to call Vicki several times while speeding there from Eden Prairie, but her cell phone was not answered. Seeing that the door to the motel room had been left open made me believe the worst. I called Vicki's name as I rushed inside just the same, shutting the door behind me. The drapes were still closed over the window, and I turned on the overhead light to see more clearly. I was half expecting to find Vicki's body. I was relieved to see that it wasn't there. The room had been torn apart—the drawers had been taken out of the credenza, the mattresses had been overturned and ripped open, the carpet had been taken up in some places, and Vicki's green leather handbag had been turned practically inside out, its contents strewn everywhere. I searched carefully, but I couldn't find her BlackBerry, either.

I slumped into the chair where I'd spent the previous evening, feeling completely and utterly defeated. I covered my face with my hands.

They had her, those sonsuvbitches, I told myself. They had Vicki—and her files.

My entire body began to tremble at the thought of it.

The Joes had Vicki. A beautiful young woman. I tried not to imagine what they were doing to her, laughing while they did it, but I kept seeing the photograph of Denny Marcus in my mind's eye, and I couldn't make it go away.

"Dammit. How did they know she was here?"

This is your fault, my inner voice told me. *You should never have left the coffeehouse. You should have stayed there, protecting Vicki until the cops came. You should have turned her over to the police after you saw the news last night. You should have called Bobby Dunston. You should never, ever, ever have left her alone. What else should you have done?*

Bobby's words came back to me. *Are you still a good guy, McKenzie? Are you on the right side of the line? Do you even know where the line is anymore?*

"Oh God, what am I going to do?"

The walls of the motel room wouldn't give me an answer, so I looked up at the ceiling. There was a crack that I hadn't noticed the previous night. My eyes followed it. It ran from the center of the wall just above the TV all the way to the light fixture, disappearing under one of the sailboats painted on the cover.

I could see a rectangular shape outlined against the glass that had not been there before.

I stood and snapped off the light, and the rectangle disappeared.

"Vicki," I said.

I hopped on the bed, reached over the glass cover, and pulled the shape out.

It was Vicki's purple BlackBerry.

She knew how important it was to her survival. That's why she hid it. She was buying time.

"Clever girl," I said.

It made sense. The Joes had searched for Vicki's files and didn't find them; otherwise she would have been killed on the spot. They took her, and I guessed they would keep her until she gave them what they wanted. I did not find much solace in the thought, knowing what those bastards had done to Denny Marcus. Still, it meant Vicki was alive and would stay alive until the Joes had the BlackBerry. It gave me precious time.

Time to do what? my inner voice asked. *How are you going to find her? Where are you going to look?*

"I'm not," I said aloud.

By my watch the Joes had been holding Vicki for as long as two and a half hours. Given what I knew about them, if they hadn't broken her yet, they soon would. Then they would be coming back here.

I put the BlackBerry in my jacket pocket and stepped outside. The harsh sunlight caused me to shield my eyes with the flat of my hand. I did a quick scan of the parking lot. Most of the cars were parked nose-in facing motel rooms. Others were parked along the perimeter.

That's where you should be, my inner voice told me.

The Joes didn't know I was driving an Altima. I could park across the lot, slump against the door, and wait. They would never know I was there. Sooner or later they would come for the BlackBerry. Most likely they would bring the girl with them. One would go into the room. The other would stay in their Buick with Vicki. I would come up from behind, using the Buick's blind spot. When the Joe left the motel room, I'd shoot him. Then I'd shoot the Joe driving the Buick.

I glanced at my watch.

"Don't wait too long, Vicki," I said. "Tell them everything."

I left the door to the motel room the way I had found it and moved toward the Altima. Again I scanned the parking lot. There was no traffic on this end of the strip mall. It was all up by the gas station and café. I put my hand on the door handle—and stopped.

There, at the door of the gas station, dressed in a white shirt, light blue cardigan sweater, and blue jeans, with golden hair tied behind her head, sipping a slush drink through a straw—"Vicki," I shouted.

I ran toward her, calling her name. She looked up, smiled, and waved. When I was close enough to hear, she said, "That didn't take long."

I grabbed her by the arms, nearly knocking the drink from her hand.

"Where were you?" I asked.

"McKenzie, you're hurting me."

"Where were you?"

"Stop hurting me."

Vicki twisted in my grasp. "What's wrong?"

I hugged her close, surprising myself by the gesture.

"I thought they had you," I said. "I thought—but you're all right. You're all right."

"We could have done this last night if you had wanted," she said.

I took her arms again and pushed backward so that I could look into her eyes. She was smiling broadly.

"The Joes know you're here," I said.

The smile went away.

"What?"

"They lured me away so they could take you. They broke into the room, but you weren't there."

"I went across the street to play bingo," Vicki said. "I lost every game. Oh, no, my BlackBerry."

"I found it. I have it. Why didn't you take it with you?"

"What if I lost it? McKenzie, it's my get-out-of-jail-free card."

"You didn't take your bag, either."

"Just my wallet." Vicki showed it to me and put it back into her sweater pocket. "Did they wreck my stuff?"

I pulled the Beretta from its holster and held it low with both hands, the muzzle pointed toward the ground. I spun to face the parking lot. Vicki set her drink on the ground.

"What is it?" she asked.

"I just realized, the Joes didn't get what they came for."

"Do you think they're still here?"

"Get behind me."

"They are here."

"I would be."

Together Vicki and I worked our way back toward the motel room, moving cautiously, yet also quickly. I scanned the parking lot and the rest of the strip mall as we went, searching for a battered Buick, yet didn't find one. I was surprised that nobody in the gas station or café seemed to notice us. When we were close to the Altima, I slipped the keys from my pocket and gave them to Vicki.

"I need you to drive until we get out of here," I said. "You can drive, right?"

If she was insulted by the question, she didn't show it.

"Right," she said.

We had ten yards to go when they appeared.

Only they weren't the Joes and they weren't driving a Buick.

A black German sedan, its front end now in desperate need of repair, came to a screeching halt in front of us. It was stopped at an angle so the driver and the passenger could use the car doors for cover. Two men dressed in suits—suits!—hopped out with guns in their hands. I fired first, forcing them to duck. That gave me enough time to push Vicki down between two parked cars.

The suits came back up firing. Bullets tore through the Chrysler Sebring I was hiding behind; someone's going to be pissed, I thought. Vicki sat on the gravel next to me, her back against the car, holding her hands over her ears.

"What are we going to do?" she shouted above the gunfire.

Before I could answer, another vehicle arrived, a Buick. This one stopped on the far side of the Altima. Big Joe and Little Joe parked at an angle just like the suits, using the Buick for cover. I threw a single shot at them. They threw a lot more back at me. Some of them whizzed past the suits, who promptly returned fire. I stayed down. Without Vicki and me as targets, the suits and the Joes seemed perfectly content shooting at each other. The air became thick with the pungent odor of nitroglycerin and graphite.

"This is crazy," Vicki shouted.

I agreed.

"Stop it," I said. "Stop it, stop it, cease fire."

Amazingly, both the suits and the Joes stopped shooting at each other. I slowly rose from cover. Probably I wouldn't have done it if I hadn't been wearing Kevlar. I held the Beretta by the trigger guard so they could see it wasn't an immediate danger to anyone.

"What do you want, McKenzie?" Big Joe asked.

"What do I want? What do you want?"

Big Joe drew a bead on me. I waved my hands.

"No, no," I said. "Listen to me, please listen."

"Go 'head," Little Joe said.

"We're listening," said one of the suits.

"You guys are making a terrible mistake shooting up the place," I said. From their expressions, neither group wanted to hear that. "Now listen to me. You guys"—I was speaking to the suits—"you were hired to take Vicki's files so you can protect the men she's blackmailing, and you guys"—now I was talking to the Joes—"want her files so you can do the blackmailing yourselves. Am I right?"

At least they didn't say I was wrong.

While I was speaking, Vicki crawled on elbows and knees away from the Sebring and edged her way toward the motel room. I thought she was looking for a better place to hide until, out of the corner of my eye, I saw her change course and move toward the Altima.

"So?" asked Big Joe.

"You guys know what a dead man's switch is? Of course you do. Well, Vicki has one in place. An accomplice that you don't know anything about, that I don't even know. If Vicki is hurt or killed, the accomplice will automatically upload all of Vicki's files onto the Internet and everyone is screwed. You guys"—I was talking to the suits again—"will be screwed because the johns you were hired to protect won't be protected. Who's going to pay you for that? And you Joes"—I gestured toward the brothers—"you'll be screwed because the johns won't have any incentive to pay you off. You guys will lose your big payday."

"What are we going to do about it?" a suit asked.

Good question, my inner voice said.

"We can make a deal," I said.

I had no idea what that deal would be. I was playing for time. After all, I was standing in a strip mall in Hastings. You would think the cops would show up sooner or later.

"It don't matter," said Big Joe. "Whatever you come up with, you can't make a deal with both of us."

He had me there.

"We're tired of waiting," a suit said. "Give us the girl and the files or we'll kill you all."

"Fuck you," said Little Joe.

"Don't be stupid."

"Who are you calling stupid, asshole?"

It was then that Vicki started the Altima, threw it into reverse, quickly backed as far away from the motel as she could get, shoved the transmission into forward, and gunned the engine. The Altima spit gravel and sand as it fishtailed out of the parking lot onto Highway 61 heading north. The four assailants raised their guns to shoot, and I yelled, "No, no, no, think of the money," and they all lowered them.

"Shit," said Big Joe.

"You dumb-asses," a suit said. "Now look at what you did."

"What we did?" Little Joe repeated. "If you assholes would mind your own business . . ."

The suits had holstered their guns and were settling back in their German sedan. The driver called to Little Joe out of his window.

"You guys are so fucking stupid you made that dumb blonde look smart," he said.

Little Joe raised his gun and killed them both.

He probably would have shot me, too, except I was running as fast as I could past the motel rooms toward the gas station at the far end of the strip mall. They did not pursue. Instead, the Joes climbed aboard their Buick and drove off.

By then a sizable crowd was gathering. The question "What is happening?" was asked.

"I think a couple of guys just got shot over there," I said and pointed at the German sedan.

No one seemed much interested in me after that. The crowd moved cautiously toward the car. The sound of police sirens seemed to come from everywhere. I extradited myself from the group and made my way into Hastings. No one stopped me when I walked past or pointed or asked where I was going. Eventually I found a chain restaurant that had an open booth. The Vikings football game was being broadcast on each of about a dozen TVs scattered throughout the restaurant. Despite what the taxi driver had to say the night before, they were actually playing pretty well. A waitress the same age as Vicki set a menu in front of me. I ordered a beer to start, and she went off to fetch it. It was then that I noticed my hands had stopped shaking.

Now what? my inner voice asked.

I didn't have an answer. I didn't have a plan. I didn't even have a car. Although . . .

Although what?

I did have Vicki's BlackBerry.

EIGHTEEN

Margot suggested that I make a fancy candlelight dinner for two as payment for her driving all the way into Hastings to pick me up and then driving me to Eden Prairie.

"With wine," she said. "Plenty of very expensive wine."

She also said something about keeping her in bed for at least two days, but I thought she was joking about that.

My plan was to have Margot drop me off and then wait at the Eden Prairie Center until I called. I changed it when I saw the Altima parked in the lot adjacent to Caitlin's apartment building.

"Are you sure?" Margot asked.

"I'm sure. Go home."

"Okay, but if I have to come out here again, that's going to cost you another day in bed."

I made my way to the lobby as Margot drove off. Back in the good old days, it was fairly easy to gain entry to a secure apartment building without permission. Just hit all of the buzzers for each apartment. Sooner or later someone was bound to let you in without bothering to call down and ask who it was. Caitlin's building was somewhat more sophisticated. It demanded that I call the tenant directly from the lobby, using her phone number and not an apartment number, identify myself, and ask for a code that changed daily that I would then punch into a keypad next to the locked door. The problem was, I had no idea if Caitlin would let me in or not. If there had been only a thin piece of wood between us I could cajole, plead, bribe, even pound on the door and shout her name like Stanley in *A Streetcar Named Desire* until fear of annoying her neighbors caused her to open up. Only how hard would it be to hang up a phone and then take it off the hook? Which is exactly what I thought she did during the long pause after I identified myself.

"What do you want, McKenzie?" she asked.

"I want to talk about Vicki."

"What about her?"

"May I come up?"

There was another long pause before she gave me the six-digit code.

Her apartment was on the top floor, and I took a slow-moving elevator to get there. The first time I had visited Caitlin, she had been waiting for me when I got off the elevator, standing in the corridor while holding her apartment door open. This time I had to press her doorbell. Even so, she kept me waiting a full fifteen seconds.

Finally, "Come in," she said.

I stepped across the threshold, and she closed the door behind me.

"I don't know what I can tell you that I haven't told you already," Caitlin said.

She moved to her expensive sofa and sat down, curling her

bare feet beneath her as she had before. Instead of a running outfit, Caitlin was wearing a black sleeveless dress with a plunging neckline and a wide white belt. There were two strands of saltwater pearls around her pretty throat. She looked like a little girl playing dress-up.

"Where is she?" I asked.

"Who?"

"No games, Cait, c'mon. Tell me where Vicki is."

"I have no idea."

"The rental car she stole is in your parking lot."

Caitlin had to think about that for a moment.

"I don't know what you're talking about," she said.

I made a big production out of pulling the Beretta from its holster. Caitlin gasped loudly and rose up onto her knees. She held the back of the sofa to keep her balance.

"McKenzie, what—what are you doing?" she asked. Not once did she take her eyes from the gun.

"One last time, Cait . . ."

"McKenzie."

The voice came from behind me. It belonged to Vicki Walsh. She stepped out of the corridor and slowly walked into the living room. She was wearing the same outfit as earlier. She pointed at the Beretta.

"McKenzie, are you going to shoot Caitlin?" she asked.

"I'm glad to see you," I said. I put the gun away. "It saves me the trouble of forcing Caitlin here to tell me where you live."

"Were you going to shoot her? Caitlin doesn't know where I live. We both figured it would be safer if she didn't know."

"Certainly it worked out that way. Otherwise, you'd probably be dead by now."

"McKenzie, what are you talking about?" Vicki asked. "Why did you come?"

"To save your life, of course. How long have you been here?"

"About an hour. I drove around for a long time to make sure I wasn't being followed after I left the motel. I'm sorry, McKenzie. I'm sorry I left you like that. I was so scared."

"You have every reason to be scared, doesn't she, Caitlin?"

"What do you mean?" Vicki asked.

"Vicki, has Caitlin used the phone since you've been here? Has she sent a text or an e-mail?"

Vicki stared at Caitlin as if she weren't sure whether she should be suspicious of her or not.

"A little while ago, fifteen minutes ago—she said she was canceling a date with a client."

"Come with me. It's time to go. Now."

Vicki backed away.

"No, McKenzie," she said. "I'm not going with you. I went with you before and I was nearly killed. I'm safe here. I'll be safe until I leave, tomorrow."

"No, Vicki, you're not safe. You won't be safe."

"I'm staying."

"You don't understand. Caitlin's the one who sold you out. She's the one who sent the thugs to the motel."

"No," Caitlin said. She brought her hand over her mouth. "No, McKenzie, please don't say that."

"I don't believe it," Vicki said. "Caitlin's my friend."

"She was. Not anymore."

Caitlin revolved on her knees on the cushion of the sofa until she was facing Vicki.

"You know me," she said. "You know I'm your friend. Vic?

When you started all this, did I tell? I'm the one who said, 'You go, girl,' remember? I never told Roberta what you were planning to do or anyone else. I even watched out for you, told you what Roberta was up to, what she was telling the clients. Remember? I never told anybody that we hung out. Instead, I told everyone that you retired, that you moved away. Vicki? I told them that. You know I did."

"That's true, McKenzie," Vicki said. "Caitlin has been my friend. She's kept all my secrets."

"It used to be true," I said. "Something changed, though. What changed, Caitlin?"

"I don't know what you're talking about," she said.

I held up the purple BlackBerry. Vicki reached for it, but I pulled it away.

"Like all good cell phones, yours has a call log," I said. "Incoming and outgoing. According to the log, eighty percent of your calls in the past month were to Caitlin."

"I told you she was my friend," Vicki said.

"Caitlin called you late Saturday afternoon just after I spoke to her, after I told her what happened to Denny Marcus. You called me a short time later. According to the log, you didn't speak to or text anyone else that night."

Vicki lunged for the cell again, but I kept it out of reach.

"Yet a couple of assassins knew exactly which coffeehouse we were meeting at and when," I said. "Who could have told them if not Caitlin?"

"The bug," Vicki said. "What did you call it, the bumper beeper? That's how they found out."

"This morning, while I was sleeping"—I could kick myself for that—"you called Caitlin again. Right after you got off the phone, I got a message that lured me from the motel. The Joes arrived soon after and tore the place apart looking for you, followed by a couple of guys in suits who were looking for you, too. How did they know what city we were in, much less the exact room number of the exact motel? How did they know I was protecting you, unless Caitlin told them?"

"I didn't." Caitlin was sobbing now.

Vicki stood perfectly still, her arms at her sides, her face blank, as if she were waiting for the details to fill it in.

"Vicki," I said, "did you tell Caitlin that you were meeting me at the coffeehouse?"

She didn't answer.

"Vicki?"

She spoke so softly I could barely hear her.

"Yes," she said.

"Did you tell her this morning that we were hiding at the motel?"

"Yes."

"What changed, Caitlin?" I asked.

She didn't reply.

Vicki moved toward her slowly.

"Vic?" Caitlin said.

Vicki slapped her so hard the force of the blow nearly knocked her over the back of the expensive sofa.

"Why?" Vicki asked. "Why? Why? Was it the money? Tell me why."

Caitlin spoke in between sobs.

"I was afraid," she said. "They kept threatening me. Roberta. The men she hired, these guys who were always wearing suits. The Joes, too. They told me what they would do to me if I lied to them, horrible things. Rape me. Burn me. But I kept telling them that I didn't know where you were or how to contact you. I told them I hadn't seen you since July. I protected you. And then, and then . . . McKenzie told me what happened to Denny Marcus. I was so afraid. I knew Denny. He was my friend, too, remember? I didn't want—I didn't want what happened to him to happen to me. Vicki, you were always smarter. You were always stronger and braver. You had friends. Sean and Tony. McKenzie here. McKenzie was your friend and he didn't even know you. But I was alone. Look at me. I'm a four-hundred-dollar-an-hour whore and I was alone. Do you know what that means, to be all alone? I'm sorry, I'm so sorry, but I tried to help. I really did. I called Roberta first. I told her about the coffeehouse because I knew she would send the guys in the suits. I knew they weren't going to hurt you, just take your files. Not like the Joes. When I heard that you got away—I saw it on the news and I was glad. I really was. I thought you would run, then. Vicki, why didn't you run?"

"I was going to," Vicki said.

"After you got away Roberta called. She wanted me to tell her more. I didn't have any more to say, only she wouldn't believe me. Then the guys in the suits called and they wouldn't believe me, either. Then the Joes—the things they said they would do to me, oh, God, they said they'd do to me what they did to Denny. Then you called and I panicked. What would happen to me if the Joes found out that we spoke, that I knew where you were and I didn't tell them? Oh, Vic, why didn't you just run away?"

"Why did you call Truhler?" I asked.

"I knew Jason was working with the Joes," Caitlin said.

Of course she did. It's the only way it made sense. The night the Joes showed up at Truhler's town house, Caitlin was hiding in the corridor. She told me so. She must have overheard Truhler arranging with the Joes to use me to find Vicki. She must have called Truhler and told him where we were hiding. That's how Truhler was able to make his deal with the Joes. They didn't contact him; he called them. I could almost hear him now making his offer to the Joes, the girl for the money he owed, take it or leave it. What I didn't fully understand was why he got me out of the motel.

Erica, my inner voice said. *If I got hurt, Erica would never forgive him.*

"I thought if I told Jason and he told the Joes it wouldn't be so bad for me," Caitlin said. "No one would know that I was involved. It was a terrible thing to do, but . . . Afterward, after I calmed down, I tried to make it good. I called Roberta because I figured she would send the suits and the suits were better than the Joes."

"Why didn't you tell me about Truhler and the Joes at the hospital or when we met the following day?" I asked.

"I was lying to help Vicki."

"But after, you could have told us after."

Caitlin hung her head, and her hair fell over her eyes. Vicki reached out and gently brushed the hair off Caitlin's forehead.

"She didn't know how to tell us," Vicki said. "Everyone lies because everyone has secrets. Some of us lie so often for so long it becomes almost an addiction. We lose our ability to tell the lies from the truth. We can't help ourselves."

"I'm so sorry," Catlin said.

"I'm sorry, too," Vicki said. "This was my fault."

The two young women hugged.

Heartwarming, my inner voice said. *If only this were the end of it.*

"Vicki, we don't have time for this," I said. She wasn't listening. I pulled her by the arm. "We have to go. Now."

"Yes, yes, Vicki," Caitlin said. "You have to go. After you escaped from the motel, the Joes called. They said if I knew what was good for me, I'd better contact them if you came by. They said if I didn't . . . Vicki, I called them. I called the Joes. They'll be here any minute now. You have to run. Run."

I positioned Vicki so that she could keep the inside security door open in case we needed to retreat and moved cautiously across the apartment building's lobby and out the front door. I searched carefully and didn't see the Joes or their Buick. However, the parking lot curved around the back of the building, and there was a part of it I couldn't see from the doorway. I moved at an angle across the pavement, hoping to get a clear view of the rest of the lot, only there were a couple of pickups and an SUV parked in such a way that the cars behind them were hidden. I motioned for Vicki. She scurried out of the lobby and moved to join me. I directed her toward the Altima, following ten paces behind, my head on a swivel, my eyes scanning the lot from one end to the other.

I didn't see Big Joe until Vicki screamed my name.

I spun and there he was, holding Vicki tight with one hand as she twisted and turned, trying to escape. The other hand held a .357 Magnum Colt King Cobra wheel gun, a twin to the one I took off of him at Rickie's. He brought the gun up and pressed the muzzle against the back of Vicki's head. At the same time, the Buick appeared. It had been concealed behind a GMC Yukon, one of the largest SUVs. It came to a halt at the corner where the parking lot turned to face the street. Little Joe got out. He was carrying an M-1911 Colt .45, the standard-issue sidearm of the armed forces until 1985—another cannon.

By then I had my own Beretta in both hands. I was in a Weaver stance and moving the sights from one Joe to the other. We stood about twenty feet apart.

"Drop your gun, McKenzie," Big Joe said.

He had wrapped an arm under Vicki's shoulder and was holding her against his chest. He continued to press the muzzle of the Colt against her head, but that didn't seem to bother her. She kept struggling. Big Joe lifted her off her feet, then dropped her down again. She flailed her arms, and he whacked the back of her skull with the side of the Colt. Vicki slowed down but didn't stop. Big Joe moved his hand up and viciously squeezed her breast. He smiled. "You like that, don'tcha," he said.

Little Joe took two steps toward my right, hoping to flank me. I didn't want to shoot him. That would cause Big Joe to open up on Vicki or me, neither a good thing. Yet I could not allow myself to be flanked. Having Little Joe on one side of me where I couldn't see him while I was watching his brother and vice versa—I knew I'd never get out of the parking lot alive. I sighted on his chest.

"Don't move. Don't even think about it."

Little Joe stopped. He cast his eyes on Big Joe. I followed his eyes. If there was traffic in the street, pedestrians walking by, I didn't see them. If there were birds singing or sirens from approaching police cars, I didn't hear them. The entire world was directly in front of me.

"Drop your fucking gun, McKenzie," Big Joe said. "Drop it. Drop it."

Like that was going to happen. I hadn't been retired from the cops for so long that I had forgotten the First Commandment: Thou shalt not give up thy weapon. Never! If you give up your weapon, chances are that both you and the hostage will be executed.

"I'll kill the whore," Big Joe said. "Drop your gun or I'll kill the fucking whore."

"No," I said. Possibly I might not have been so resolute if I hadn't been wearing Kevlar, but there you are.

I turned just enough to sight on Big Joe's head. He could see it, too. He slid farther behind Vicki, using her as a shield.

"Drop your fucking gun," he said.

"I'm not dropping my gun," I said.

"I'll kill the girl."

"Then I'll kill you."

The unpredictable Minnesota weather seemed to shift again while I was standing there. Despite the November chill, I felt very, very warm. Perspiration beaded up on my forehead. My hands became sweaty.

Little Joe made another effort to flank me. I turned and sighted on him again.

"If you take another step, Joe, I'll shoot you."

He stopped.

I sighted on Big Joe again. He was still shouting.

"Drop it, drop it, drop the fucking gun. I'll kill the fucking girl, the fuck I won't."

"Shoot and I will kill you, Big Joe," I said. "You'll be dead before she hits the ground."

He turned the muzzle from Vicki's head and pointed it at me. "We'll all die," he said.

"Shoot 'im, shoot 'im," Little Joe shouted. His .45 was up and pointed at me, too, yet he didn't take the shot. I don't know why.

"What's the point of that?" I asked.

Little Joe took another step to my flank. I swung the Beretta and pointed it at him again.

"Don't fucking move, Little Joe," I said. "It's the last time I'm telling you."

"Kill 'im, kill 'im," he chanted again—but he stopped moving.

Vicki continued to struggle. Big Joe squeezed and twisted her breast some more.

"I like it when they fight back," he said.

I was standing twenty yards away and pointing a gun at his head, yet he was copping a feel.

What is wrong with this picture? my inner voice said.

"Let her go," I said aloud.

He pressed the Colt against Vicki's head some more.

"Drop your fucking gun, goddamn you," he said.

Everyone was shouting. I deliberately lowered my voice, hoping to calm the situation.

"You don't need to do this, Joe," I said. "You don't need to hurt the girl."

"Fuck you, McKenzie," Little Joe said.

"Listen to me," I said. "Are you listening? We can make a deal."

"Like in Hastings," Big Joe said. "That kind of deal?"

"You don't need the girl. You need her files, am I right? It's the files you want. She doesn't have them."

"Kill 'im," Little Joe said.

"Shuddup," Big Joe said. "Keep talkin', McKenzie."

"The files have names, addresses, they have video; audio and video," I said. "Everything you need to take those dumb jerks to the market."

"Where are they?"

"I got them."

"Where?" Little Joe asked.

"In my pocket," I said.

"No, McKenzie, no," Vicki said.

"Shut the fuck up, bitch," Big Joe said. He slammed his gun against Vicki's head. She slumped in his arms yet did not fall.

Little Joe held out his hand.

"Give 'em to me," he said.

"Let the girl go, first," I said.

"Fuck that," Big Joe said.

"Give 'em to me," Little Joe said.

I pointed the Beretta at Little Joe with one hand and reached into my jacket pocket with the other. I was moving slowly, not wanting to startle them. I pulled out the purple BlackBerry and held it up for everyone to see.

"Give it to me," Little Joe said.

He took a step toward me.

"Don't move, Joe," I said.

"Give it to him," Big Joe said.

I kept holding the BlackBerry aloft.

"Release the girl," I said.

Big Joe responded by pulling Vicki closer.

"It has everything you need," I said. "Everything to get yourself a real nice payday. Isn't that right, Vicki?"

Big Joe squeezed her breast again.

"Is it?" he asked.

Vicki nodded. There were tears in her eyes, yet I was convinced they had been caused by the repeated blows she had taken to the head and not by fear. Despite everything, she did not seem frightened.

"Tell me," Big Joe said.

"Yes," Vicki said. "It has everything."

"Give the phone to my brother," he said.

"If your brother takes one step I will kill him," I said.

"I'll kill the girl," Big Joe said.

"Then I'll kill you."

Big Joe took the muzzle from Vicki's head and pointed it at me again.

"I'll shoot you first."

"Maybe so, but you'll be dead before I fall. Look, we've been through this before."

Like I said, the Kevlar was making me feel more confident than I would have been otherwise.

"What do you want to do?" Big Joe asked.

I squatted slowly, careful to keep the Beretta trained on Little Joe's chest, and set the BlackBerry on the pavement. I stood up and gripped the Beretta with both hands.

"Release the girl," I said. "She backs away. Once she's safe, I'll back away. Your brother takes the BlackBerry and you both leave and everyone's happy. No one gets hurt."

Big Joe shifted the muzzle of the Colt from Vicki's head to her throat.

"How do I know I can trust you?" he asked.

"You don't," I said.

"What the fuck, then?"

"I don't need the files," I said. "I don't want the files. I sure as hell am not going to die for the files. Why would I? To protect a bunch of shitheads? You can have the damn files. Do your worst. What do I care? How 'bout you, Vicki? Do you care?"

She smiled, actually smiled.

"He can have them," she said.

"Oh, can I?" Big Joe asked. He licked the side of Vicki's face, and she cringed. "You gonna give 'em to me, huh? What else you gonna give me?"

"Is that why you came here, Joe?" I asked.

Vicki smiled some more. She said, "It's like my Facebook friend Drew Hernick likes to say—Situation normal, all fouled up."

"I think that's the sanitized version," I said.

"SNAFU by any other name will be just as sweet."

One way or the other, she will get her revenge, my inner voice said. *Let's hope she's alive to see it.*

"What do you say, Big Joe?" I asked.

"Give me the phone."

"Give me the girl."

"Fuck, Joe," Little Joe said. "Kill 'em both."

"Kill the girl and I'll kill you, Joe," I said. "Even if you kill me, you'll be dead. Where's the profit in that?"

"I still owe you from the other time," he said. "My fucking knee hurts like hell."

"We can come to terms about that later," I said. "Right now, let the girl go."

"Or what?" Little Joe asked.

"Or nobody gets rich."

I was looking to see how Big Joe took it. He was grinning

as if he'd just drawn three cherries on a pulltab. He kept pointing his gun at Vicki's throat, yet his arm came out from under
her shoulder. His empty hand rested on the back of Vicki's
neck.

"Okay," he said.

"Oh, fuck that shit," Little Joe said.

He took three long strides toward me, his .45 automatic leading the way.

I shot him in the center of his chest. The bullet went right
through him.

I pivoted to face Big Joe. There was a stunned expression
on his face. He should have been firing. Instead, he was shouting his brother's name.

Vicki dove to her left, hit the pavement, and rolled away.

I fired twice. The first round missed. The second caught
Big Joe high in the shoulder. He spun around and fell. The gun
left his hand and skittered across the pavement. Vicki climbed
to her feet and ran full speed toward the Altima. I moved just
as quickly to Big Joe's side. The Colt was near his hand, but he
paid it no mind. He was crawling toward his brother's body. I
kicked the big gun away just the same.

"Joe, Joe," Big Joe said. "Ah, Joey."

Vicki started the Altima and drove it around the Buick.
The car's tires squealed as she made the corner that led to the
main drag.

Again? my inner voice asked. *You're leaving me again?
Really?*

I hovered above Big Joe. The wound to his shoulder didn't
seem that bad to me.

"Is he dead?" Big Joe asked. "Did you kill my brother?"

I went to check. I reached Little Joe just in time to see his eyes close and hear his last breath.

"He's gone," I said.

"You're dead, McKenzie," Big Joe said. His hand was pressed against his wound; blood seeped around his fingers. "Do you hear me? This doesn't end here. I'm gonna get you. I'm gonna kill you real fucking slow. You're gonna beg me to kill you before I'm done cuz you killed my brother. Think I'm goin' to prison, asshole? On what charge? I didn't shoot anyone. That was all you. Call it self-defense, I'll call it felony assault with intent. Your word against mine. Who the fuck you think they gonna believe, huh? I'm the one who's shot. My brother's the one who's dead. Think that little whore's gonna back you up? Think she's gonna testify? Not goin' t' happen. I know the law, man. Think I don't? I know the law, and I ain't goin' to prison. You might, though. Yeah, yeah, you're the one who's goin' to prison. I'm gonna fuck you up, man. I'm gonna tell 'em my story and they gonna put you in fuckin' Stillwater, not me. And while you're gone, man, while you're gone I'm goin' to find everyone you love. Your mama, your wife, girlfriend, sisters—whatever, asshole. I'm goin' t' find 'em, every one of 'em and I'm gonna take 'em and I'm gonna hurt 'em. I'm gonna hurt 'em bad. I'm gonna nail their hands and feet to the floor and rape 'em, rape their pussies, their mouths, their assholes. I'm gonna stick cattle prods up their cunts. I'm gonna burn them with an acetylene torch. I'm gonna git 'em all, and there ain't nothin' you can do about it. And then when you git outta prison, I'm gonna git you, too."

While Big Joe ranted, I looked deep into his eyes. They held all the humanity of a plastic doll.

"I believe you, Big Joe," I said. "I believe every word you say."

NINETEEN

It was night by the time I parked the Buick on the North Side of Minneapolis. I walked one block down and two blocks over to Bug's house. I found Bug there, sitting on his stoop in the dark and playing with his lighter just as he had before. I stood outside his gate.

"Mr. Ritzer?" I said.

"Come ahead."

I pushed the gate open and moved up the crumbling sidewalk to where he sat. Bug's clothing, his hair, his face, his breath, those terrible bloodshot eyes were all the same as they had been the first time we met. You couldn't prove to me that he had moved so much as an inch since then.

"Where did you park the car?" he asked.

"Exactly where you told me to," I said.

"They in the trunk?"

"Yes, sir."

"They alive?"

"One is."

"You gonna get the pigs off me?"

"Just like I promised."

Bug reached out his hand. The prepaid cell phone I gave him was resting in his palm.

"You should get rid of this," he said.

I took the phone, replacing it with Big Joe's car keys.

"I will," I said.

"I'll be going to prison next week," Bug said. "Probably die there. You won't see me again."

Fine with me, my inner voice said.

"Good luck, Mr. Ritzer," I said aloud.

I turned and left Bug's yard without even a backward glance. Officers Dailey and Moulton were parked up the street, as I knew they would be. I walked slowly toward their unmarked car. When I reached it, I rested my hands against the sill of the driver's side window and looked in.

"What was all that about?" Dailey asked.

"What do you mean?"

"What do you think we mean?" Moulton asked. "That little conversation with Bug."

"Did I have a conversation with Bug? I don't remember."

"Don't mess with us, McKenzie," Dailey said. "What did he give you? What did you give him?"

"Nothing."

"Nothing?" Moulton asked. "Sure looked like something to me."

"Can you guys do me a favor?"

"What favor, McKenzie?" Dailey asked.

"Give me a lift to the Hotel Sofitel in Bloomington. I left my car in the parking lot."

"Then how did you get here?" Moulton asked.

"I'm not here," I said. "You never saw me."

Dailey and Moulton looked at each other, then at me, then at each other again.

"What happened about the Joes?" Dailey asked.

"We've been waiting for your call all day," Moulton said. "You never called."

"So what happened?" Dailey asked.

"It's being taken care of," I said.

Both Dailey and Moulton looked away from me and studied Bug. He was still on his front steps, still playing with his lighter. I could almost hear the two officers thinking.

"We've wasted enough time watching this guy," Dailey said.

"He's going to prison for ten years," Moulton said.

"Sentencing is Tuesday," Dailey said. "In the morning."

"How much trouble can he get in?" Moulton asked.

"Screw it," Dailey said.

"Yeah, screw it," said Moulton. "We're not even getting overtime for this."

"Where did you say you were parked, McKenzie?" Dailey asked.

I gave him directions as I hopped into the backseat. The car was started, and we drove off, passing Bug's house as we did. Bug was smiling. It was a terrible smile.

Dailey and Moulton dropped me next to my Jeep Cherokee. The lights in the parking lot showed them the damage to the front end.

"You'll want to get that headlight fixed," Moulton said.

"We'd hate to give you a ticket," Dailey said.

"I'll take care of it first thing tomorrow," I said.

"You do that," Dailey said.

We lingered there for a moment as if we had more to say to each other, yet couldn't think of the words.

Finally Dailey said, "See you around, McKenzie."

"Yeah," Moulton said. "See you around."

"Later," I said. By then their vehicle was already heading to the driveway, and I doubt they heard me.

I turned back to the Cherokee and fished in my pocket for the key. I was inserting the key into the lock when a voice spoke to me from behind.

"McKenzie," the voice said. "Turn around slowly. Make sure I can see your hands."

I did what the voice told me.

John Brehmer stepped out of the shadows. He held his service weapon in his hand, yet he wasn't threatening me with it.

"Detective Brehmer," I said.

"I'm sorry about this, McKenzie," he said. "I really am."

"Sorry about what?"

"Rushmore McKenzie, you are under arrest."

Brehmer installed me in the interrogation room of the Eden Prairie Police Department. While he handcuffed me to the stainless steel table bolted to the floor in the center of the room, I asked what it was all about.

"Suspicion of murder," he said.

"Who did I kill?"

"Tony Rothman and Sean Koepke."

"Do you believe that?"

"Witnesses place you at the scene with a gun in your hand.

Your vehicle was photographed fleeing the scene by traffic cameras."

"Did the witnesses see anyone else in the parking lot?" I asked. "Did they see me being shot? Did the cameras show another car chasing me? And the two men in it? Was there a report filed by a homeowner somewhere between France Avenue and Highway 100 claiming that a German sedan jumped the curb and crashed into a tree in his front yard?"

Brehmer didn't answer.

"I didn't think so," I said. "Tell me something, John. Just between you and me—what is an Eden Prairie detective doing arresting a man in Bloomington for a crime that was committed in Edina?"

He didn't have anything to say to that, either.

I told him that I had nothing more to say; that I refused to answer any questions without my attorney present, and that if I was forced to drag her down there, I would still refuse to answer any questions. Answering the questions police and prosecutors asked, whether you were guilty or not, would only get you into trouble. Anyone who watched *Law & Order* or *The Closer* on TV could tell you that.

Brehmer said he didn't have any questions to ask. That was someone else's call.

"You were a cop," he said. "You know how it works."

Brehmer left me alone in the interrogation room. Enough time passed for me to become alarmed if I hadn't already known what was coming. Finally Brehmer reappeared. He was carrying a cell phone. He handed it to me without a word. I spoke into the microphone.

"This is McKenzie," I said.

"Where are the files?" a voice asked. "Where is the girl?"

"Hello, Mr. Muehlenhaus."

"No names, please."

"Of course, Mr. Muehlenhaus."

"Dammit, Mr. McKenzie."

"Dammit, Mr. Muehlenhaus."

Brehmer moved against the wall of the room and pretended that he wasn't listening.

"I repeat," Muehlenhaus said. "Where are—"

"The files are with Vicki," I said. "I don't know where she is."

"I don't believe you."

"I don't care."

"Mr. McKenzie, there is no need for this rancor."

"Says the man who isn't sitting in jail," I said. "You know, the black kids have a saying—don't start nothing, won't be nothing."

"That sounds like a threat."

"I would never be so foolish as to threaten you."

"Mr. McKenzie, I was under the impression that we were on the same side in this affair."

"Mr. Muehlenhaus—oh, wait, I used your name again. Mr. Muehlenhaus, I found the girl as promised. I delivered your message as promised. As for being on the same side, that ended when your thugs shot me in the back. Luckily, I was wearing body armor at the time. Still, you can imagine my—what was the word you used? Rancor?"

"I did not know. In any case, they were not my thugs, as you say. They were not in my employ."

"Of course they were. They followed me from the party

where we met. After that you supplied them to your good friend Roberta. You said something could be arranged for her, and the suits were that something. She didn't have access to that kind of talent on her own or she would never have hired the Joes."

"I am dreadfully sorry for your trouble, Mr. McKenzie. You must believe that. Yet whether you do or do not has no effect on our current impasse. I need Ms. Walsh's files, if not Ms. Walsh herself. If you promise to deliver them into my hands—"

"No."

"Mr. McKenzie, this affair might yet come to an amicable conclusion."

"I don't think it will."

"Mr. McKenzie, it is true that the evidence against you will not bear up under close scrutiny. However, you and I both know that people have been convicted and sent to prison with far less. No doubt you are putting your trust in your extremely competent and resourceful criminal defense attorney. That would be a mistake, as I am sure she will inform you. If you wish to see yourself clear of this situation, I would strongly encourage you to cooperate."

I thought about it for a good ten seconds, I really did. It would have been so much easier for me if I had simply gone along with the old man, but I had had enough. Too many people had been killed to protect the interests of Mr. Muehlenhaus's acquaintances. As rotten as Vicki Walsh's behavior had been— and it had been very rotten indeed as far as I was concerned— theirs was far worse.

"Don't start nothing, won't be nothing," I said.

"Mr. McKenzie—"

I deactivated the phone. Brehmer came off the wall of the interrogation room and walked toward me. He reached out his hand for the cell. I cradled it against my chest.

"C'mon, McKenzie," he said.

"John, I get the impression that you don't want to be involved in any of this."

"You know I don't. But what am I going to do? You used to be a cop. You know . . ."

"Yeah, yeah, yeah. I haven't actually been charged yet, have I?"

"There's an assistant county attorney on the way that's going to do the honors. He's probably like me. He had his instructions, too."

"I understand that you're being squeezed, John. Both you and the ACA. I understand that there's nothing you can do about it unless someone comes along who can squeeze harder."

"What are you telling me, McKenzie?"

I handed the cell back to Brehmer.

"I need my iPhone," I said. "Can you get it for me?"

Brehmer gave me a hard look for about five long seconds.

"Yeah, I can," he said. Brehmer left the interrogation room. He returned about two minutes later. He handed the iPhone to me. "Is this what you want?"

I activated the device and searched for a number in the cell's memory.

"Are you calling your attorney?" Brehmer asked.

I didn't answer. Instead, I listened intently as the phone rang one, two, three, four, five times. For a moment I was frightened that it would go unanswered. Finally, in the middle of the sixth ring, a woman's voice said, "Hello."

"Hello," I said. "Lindsey? This is McKenzie."

"Hey, McKenzie. What's going on?"

"Same old, same old. Say, Zee, may I speak to the governor? I need a favor."

One of the things about pulling strings is that the pullers usually don't want anyone to see them doing it. Which is why it took several hours before I was released from the Eden Prairie cop shop with no paper or electronic record left behind to prove that I was ever there. I collected my belongings, and John Brehmer was kind enough to drive me back to my vehicle.

"You have a lot of friends in high places," he said.

"Unfortunately, I now owe them all favors, and nothing good can come of that," I said.

"If it makes you feel any better, I figure we're square."

"You're a good man, John."

"I try to be."

So do you, my inner voice told me, *and yet you fail so often.*

I waited until I was safely ensconced in the Jeep Cherokee and Brehmer was nowhere in sight before I used my iPhone to access Vicki Walsh's Facebook page again. I found Drew Hernick's name and contact information. I called him.

He answered on the third ring. "Yes?"

"Drew Hernick?"

He hesitated before answering. "Yes."

"A mutual friend asked me to deliver a message. SNAFU."

"Could you repeat that, please?"

"Situation normal, all fucked up."

"Is this McKenzie?"

I was surprised he knew my name.

"Yes," I said.

"Our mutual friend called earlier. She also used the code word. She said that if you called, I should tell you that the information concerning Jason Truhler could be removed from the files if you wish. Do you want the information removed?"

"No."

"Are you sure?"

"I'm sure."

Bobby Dunston asked me to come up to his office on the second floor of the James S. Griffin Building, headquarters of the St. Paul Police Department, located in a neighborhood of the city old-timers used to call the Badlands. I declined. I didn't want to run into anyone I knew. I didn't want to answer any more questions than necessary. Instead, we gathered at a coffeehouse not far from the state capitol building. It seemed as if I had been spending a lot of time in coffeehouses lately. Coffeehouses and parking lots.

I was sipping a simple dry-roasted brew when Bobby entered. He was smiling when he walked to my table.

"Your voice," he said. "The tone of your voice on the phone. I've heard it before. Something interesting is about to happen, isn't it?"

I set the purple BlackBerry on the table in front of him.

"Everything you've ever wanted to know about the My Very First Time prostitution ring," I said. "The owners, the girls, the clients, the money, the whole shebang."

"Who does the phone belong to?"

"A young woman named Vicki Walsh."

"Where can I find her?"

"I have no idea. How long have the banks been open?"

"A couple of hours, why?"

"If you're going to look for her, you better start now, because I suspect she'll soon be long gone."

"You found her."

"She wasn't hiding that hard when I was looking. Now she is."

He held the phone up and waved it at me.

"People will want to talk to you," Bobby said.

"I have nothing to say, and I don't care who asks. If you guys can't make a case with the files on the phone, there's nothing I can do to help anyway. Oh, by the way—I'm led to believe that everything you find on the phone will be soon uploaded on the Internet if it hasn't been already."

"Oh, that's great, just great. Are you responsible for that, McKenzie?"

"C'mon, Bobby. I'm lucky I can program TiVo."

"I'll be in touch."

"I'll be around."

Bobby called to me over his shoulder as he walked through the coffeehouse door.

"You should get some sleep," he said. "You look like hell."

"It's always a pleasure to see you, too," I said.

Marvelous Margot was standing on her side of the pond, her hands on her hips, a determined expression on her face, when I returned home. I assumed she was wondering about the ducks until I realized that there were no ducks. Apparently they had decided to take flight while I was away. The problem was, I didn't know if they decided to fly south on their own volition or if they were driven out. That's because there were now thirteen—count 'em—thirteen wild turkeys gathered around the pond, each big enough to feed a family of twelve.

"Where the hell did they come from?" I asked.

"I don't know," Margot said. "I came back to see the ducks and there they were. What do you call a bunch of turkeys, anyway?"

"A flock, I think."

"They don't seem to be particularly fearful."

They certainly weren't. I was able to walk right up to them, and while they shied slightly, they neither ran away nor attacked me.

"I heard that they're becoming like deer," Margot said. "As they lose their natural habitat, more and more turkeys are migrating to the suburbs."

"I thought that was all that lived in the suburbs."

"You should know, McKenzie. You're a resident. What should we do with them?"

"Feed them, I guess."

So we did, tossing to them the dried corn that we had previously fed the ducks. Afterward, I called my pal Doug Clausen with the Minnesota DNR.

"You didn't feed them, did you?" he asked.

"Well, I had all this dried corn left over . . ."

"Oh, McKenzie. You look at these birds and you think, how cool, I have wild turkeys living in my backyard. So you feed them, encourage them to stay. It's all swell until the turkeys claim your home for their own; until they start roosting on your roof or your deck or in your trees, until they start damaging your property, until their droppings start to accumulate,

until they become aggressive and chase you and your neighbors and your neighbors' kids. Then it's not so much fun."

"What should I do?"

"Leave them the hell alone. People want to be helpful, I appreciate that, but more often than not they just make matters
worse. Sometimes, the best thing you can do to help is nothing
at all."

"If only I could learn to do that," I said. "If only I could
learn to do that one thing."

Just So You Know

Not all homicides are solved. Hell, not all homicides are even investigated. Cops look at a murder and determine what the chances are of clearing that specific crime versus all the other crimes they have on their desks, then allocate their limited resources accordingly. Case in point—the Joes. They were found dead in the trunk of a smoldering Buick in a vacant lot on the North Side of Minneapolis. The only way the cops were able to identify their badly burned bodies was by tracing the ownership of the car. It was believed that a pyromaniac known as Bug, who held a grudge against the Joes, might have had something to do with it. Unfortunately, he died of a heart attack two weeks after he was incarcerated at the Minnesota Correctional Facility in Stillwater, and the Minneapolis cops didn't have a chance to interview him, so they lost interest. Eventually a forensic pathologist at the Minnesota Bureau of Criminal Apprehension managed to connect the murders of two young men outside a coffeehouse in Edina to two suits who were found dead at a motel in Hastings, using ballistic evidence taken from guns and bullets found at the scenes. He then matched the bullets found inside the suits to a gun found inside the burned Buick. That allowed all the law enforcement personnel involved to close their various investigations—such as they were—with a clear conscience.

This information was relayed to me while I was having drinks with Officers Dailey and Moulton. None of us laughed over it or chuckled or even smiled. We didn't make a toast to justice. We didn't talk about the ends justifying the means. Come to think of it, we didn't talk much at all.

A few days later, Bobby and I were sitting on the brick patio that we built together in his backyard a few years ago, having one last beer before Bobby stored his furniture in the garage for the winter. The myveryfirsttime.com case was still in the news. That was pretty much how the news media referred to it, by the Web address. As far as they were concerned, the fact that the case so closely utilized the Internet was what made it news; otherwise it would be just johns and whores, and we've all heard that before.

"I tried to do the right thing," I said. "I really did."

"Stop beating yourself up," Bobby said. "You did fine."

"Prosecution has been a mess."

"Oh, I don't know. Better a messy prosecution than no prosecution at all. All that Internet exposure didn't help. On the other hand, it made sure that a lot of johns are being held accountable that probably would have skated otherwise. I know some divorce lawyers that are very happy."

"All they got was fines and probation."

"You didn't think anyone was really going to jail, did you?"

"Roberta did."

"A three-year jolt in Shakopee; she'll be out in eighteen

months with a nice payday. She was a good little soldier. Kept her mouth shut, refused to name names even when the names and pictures were set in front of her. You know the big boys will take care of her. My favorite was Caitlin Brooks. I like how she gave the media a lecture on the courthouse steps about the place of call girls in history."

"She got nine months."

"That's only because the judge ruled she demonstrated a clear lack of remorse for her crimes. I wish we could have found Vicki Walsh. I would have loved to hear what she had to say. I wonder where she is."

"God knows," I said.

The cops found my rented Altima in the parking lot of the American Bank on the corner of Snelling and University in St. Paul five days after Vicki stole it. She could have taken the bus from there to Cleveland Avenue and jumped on the Amtrak. I shared that possibility with Bobby. There were a few others that I kept to myself. I didn't want Vicki found.

Bobby pushed his chair back and put his feet on the patio table.

"It's funny," he said before taking a long sip of beer.

"What's funny?" I asked.

"How in all the photos and videos on her cell phone Vicki's face was out of focus or turned away from the camera or in shadow or just plain pixelated."

"You'll notice Vicki had different hair colors and styles, too," I said. "She was trying disguises on for size."

"Interesting girl."

"She was that."

"Too bad about Jason Truhler, though."

"Yeah, too bad."

There were many more prominent names revealed during the prosecution of the case than Jason Truhler's, yet he seemed to get most of the attention. That's because while we might all snicker at the johns, drug dealers are no laughing matter, and that's how Truhler was portrayed, as a major drug dealer. It wasn't entirely true, of course, and for a long time I thought hanging Truhler out to dry was Muehlenhaus's way of getting back at me. If it was, though, it worked against him—or, I should say, it worked against Muehlenhaus's many acquaintances, because unlike Roberta, Truhler had no intention of taking one for the team. He was happy to name names, thrilled even. He cut a deal with the prosecutor, giving up every single one of his friends and customers in exchange for a token sentence at the Level 1 minimum-security prison in Lino Lakes, about a half-hour drive north of the Cities.

Erica was desperate to help her father, of course. She kept asking me if there was anything I could do. I kept telling her it was out of my hands, at the same time I was terrified that she would somehow learn that I had the chance to cover up her father's many sins and chose not to.

"He'll need a lawyer," she said. "I have money saved."

"That's for college," Nina said.

Erica didn't care. She offered the money to her father, and he took it, even though his case never actually came to trial. As a condition of his plea agreement, Truhler was forced to allocute fully in open court. Erica sat in the back row and listened intently to every word while her father explained his involvement with drugs and prostitution. She did not react to what she heard, at least not physically. Emotionally—she never spoke of it, not to her mother and not to me except to ask once, "What happens to people?"

"They change," I said. "Sometimes for the better, sometimes for the worse."

"Why?"

"I don't know."

After Truhler was sentenced, he asked Erica to visit. She said she would, but it would be difficult since she was going to Tulane University in New Orleans in the fall. All nine colleges that she applied to had accepted Erica. I'm sure it was just a coincidence that Tulane was the one farthest away from Lino Lakes.

I finished my Summit Ale and set the empty bottle on the patio table.

"It just wasn't worth it," I said. "Erica asked me to do a favor for her father, and I agreed because I wanted to help her, but what help did I give? It all turned out to be just one monstrous SNAFU."

"A what?" Bobby asked.

"Never mind."